Also by Olivia Glazebrook

The Trouble with Alice
Never Mind Miss Fox

The Frank Business

Olivia Glazebrook

JOHN MURRAY

First published in Great Britain in 2019 by John Murray (Publishers)
An Hachette UK company

This paperback edition published in 2020

1

A CIP catalogue record for this title is available from the British Library

Paperback ISBN 9781473691841

Typeset in Sabon MT by Hewer Text UK Ltd, Edinburgh
Printed and bound in Great Britain by Clays Ltd, Elcograf S.p.A.

John Murray policy is to use papers that are natural, renewable and
recyclable products and made from wood grown in sustainable forests.
The logging and manufacturing processes are expected to conform
to the environmental regulations of the country of origin.

John Murray (Publishers)
Carmelite House
50 Victoria Embankment
London EC4Y 0DZ

www.johnmurraypress.co.uk

Frank dropped down dead on Christmas Eve at four minutes past midday. He died alone – alone in a crowded mass of travelling humans – and underneath a big yellow sign: *Bus Train Underground Taxi Cashpoint Toilets Tickets Information Help*. He fell to the ground in the grip of a dreadful agony; his heart, to all intents and purposes, was splitting in two.

This is London Heathrow airport and everyone passing has somewhere to be, but somebody stopped (because somebody always stops) to kneel beside Frank, hold his head and call for help:

'Help! This man's—'

People came quickly, bringing equipment. A circle of onlookers gathered; stood back; pressed forward. Instructions were issued and followed, calm voices murmured, efforts were made to save him but then—

Silence fell like a velvet curtain.

Once the body had been removed the nearest spectators breathed out and looked at each other. Some were half-smiling with nerves and some shook their heads saying 'Well I never' and 'Isn't that sad' and 'It makes you think'. Then everyone picked up their bags and went on with Christmas Eve just as before.

I

of Hamlet

Frank had flown to London from Marseille. He had driven
to Marseille from his home in the Luberon where he lived
alone on a forested ridge, close to the village of Saint-
Victor. He had got up early in the morning to catch his
flight.

To fly at all had been a last-minute decision – he had only
booked his ticket the previous evening, on an impulse, because
of something he heard on the radio. He liked to listen to Radio
4 online, on his laptop, while he worked in his studio. To live
in the south of France and hear the burble of British voices on
Radio 4 was reassuring, as if he were shipwrecked alone on
Mars and tuning in to voices on Earth. He did not want to go
back to London but he liked to know it existed.

It was eight-fifteen in France and seven-fifteen in England.
The Archers had just finished. Because of Christmas, the
announcer said, there would be no *Front Row* tonight.
Instead, a performance of *Hamlet* would be transmitted
live from The Playhouse in London.

Frank did not call the eve before Christmas Eve
'Christmas' – not yet – but it seemed that any excuse to
muck about with the regular schedule was good enough for
the BBC. There was no telling what might happen at this

3

time of year and one just had to go with the flow. He was working on a Christmas card for his friends Pierre and Agnes, who were coming to dinner on Christmas Day, and since he was already working he might as well listen to a bit of *Hamlet*.

Frank was an illustrator and he was often commissioned to draw pictures personalised with messages in his beautiful, old-fashioned handwriting, but he made this particular effort for his friends Pierre and Agnes because, every year, they took care of him at Christmas: dining with their lonely friend on the loneliest day of the year. The card was a way of showing his appreciation.

'But it's not pity,' they protested. 'We want to come.'

He did not believe them. It was the same every year.

After the announcement about the change of schedule came an introduction to the play by a radio presenter who was at the theatre waiting for the play to start. She spoke into her microphone in a low voice as the last members of the audience took their seats.

'. . . Veteran star of stage and screen, Kathleen Griffin, will play Gertrude and her son Scott Griffin will play Hamlet, a relatively young Hamlet at only twenty-four, in tonight's final performance of this acclaimed production, which has sold out every night of its three month run . . .'

When Frank heard 'Kathleen Griffin' his pen nib stopped what it was doing. He broke off inking holly leaves a rich green and sat motionless, listening to the rest of the introduction. He marvelled at the skill of the radio presenter, who kept talking until the auditorium lights were dimmed and the audience was hushed by the authoritative magic of the darkness.

'. . . and,' she whispered finally, 'the light of one star shines on the battlements. The scene is set; the play begins.'

Then Francisco and Barnardo began their conversation on the battlements:

– *Who's there?*

– *Nay, answer me: stand, and unfold yourself.*

Frank listened. As he listened he dipped his pen nib into a jar of water and swirled it about to wash off the ink, then he dried it on a rag he kept beside him for that purpose. His hands, he noticed, were shaking. He put the pen down. He was waiting, listening and calculating: *Scott Griffin, twenty-four years old.*

Now here was Horatio and here was the ghost. This first scene seemed interminable. Frank waited. At last he heard Hamlet:

– *A little more than kin, and less than kind.*

Frank tilted his head, listening, but he could not tell from a voice what he wanted to know.

Then Gertrude:

– *Good Hamlet, cast thy nighted colour off . . .*

It was Kathleen. Frank shivered and his eyes pricked with tears as if she had walked into the room. He had not heard her voice for twenty-five years.

He did not move until first Gertrude and then Hamlet were dead. Then he blinked and looked around and realised that it was dark and he was alone. Generally speaking he did not notice solitude because it was his usual state, but he noticed it now. He muted the laptop and sat in silence for a minute or two. He looked at his reflection in the black window and let untidy, dark ideas settle on his mind like rooks on a stubble field.

Pulling the laptop towards him he typed 'Scott Griffin actor' into Google. He peered at the biography and then, clicking on 'Images', he peered at those. It seemed very quiet in the room, as if it had just been emptied of a lively group of guests. Along with solitude Frank did not usually notice silence, but he did tonight.

He got off the stool on which he sat to work and went through a connecting door into the kitchen. Here he poured into a tumbler two inches of the quite good cognac he had bought to drink with Pierre and Agnes. The glass shook in his hand. He took a gulp of the drink and then carried it from the kitchen into the sitting room, across the hall and into the study where he sat down on a wheeled chair in front of the desk. He switched on the anglepoise light, opened the third desk drawer down on the left-hand side and pulled out an envelope containing a handful of photographs.

All these pictures had been taken before the death of his wife, more than sixteen years ago. He did not like to look at them often, but nor did he want to throw them away. He shuffled through them quickly, pausing only to glance briefly at one or two: himself and Romy on their wedding day; the car they had driven from London, filled with all their belongings; Romy in front of the finished house, pregnant; their baby Jem, who would now be twenty-five.

He was looking for a photograph of himself as a young man. When he found one, an old passport picture, he took it back to the studio. He threw a log into the woodburner, sat back down on his stool and leant the little portrait against the screen of his laptop in order to compare his own face with that of 'Scott Griffin actor'.

There was no need to look for a likeness because it was perfectly obvious. He examined the images for a minute or more. He was transfixed. He scrolled down through the rows of little pictures offered up by Google until they became more loosely attached, and then entirely unattached, to the intended subject – pictures of other Hamlets, other Scotts and other Griffins. Pictures of no interest.

He finished his drink and got up. He had a curious urge to dash the glass against the wall. Instead he went back into the kitchen and poured more cognac. He felt anger tighten the bolts in his chest and skull. He put a hand to his face, blinking fiercely – he feared that hot tears might burst from his eyes even if he expressly barred them from doing so. The house had never felt more silent or more empty; tonight it was a container in which he existed like a spider fallen into a bucket.

In the study again he pulled open another drawer of the desk and got out a bundle of old address books and diaries tied up with string. In an address book he had not opened for more than two decades he looked up the name 'Kathleen'. He knew it would be written under K for Kathleen rather than G for Griffin. He remembered deliberately not writing down her surname in case Romy had turned to the page and seen it. She would have been surprised. 'But you didn't know Kathleen. You never met her. Did you?' And there would have been no reasonable answer he could have given her.

Kathleen had given him her number by accident: he had found her passport in her handbag and read in her

7

enormous and bright blue handwriting on the inside back cover under the heading EMERGENCIES –

Walter Griffin
36 Beech Road NW3
01-794-2826

Frank had copied everything down, first secretly onto a scrap of paper in his pocket and then later into the address book. He had never dialled the number – he had never dared risk it. To break cover would be to break the unspoken pact.

But 'Scott Griffin actor' changed everything. Tilting the shade of the lamp on the desk so that the light did not glare at him Frank took a gulp of his drink and lifted the receiver of the telephone on the desk. He adjusted the number from '01' to '0207' and pressed each button on the keypad carefully.

A gruff male voice answered after five rings. 'Hello?'

Frank's mouth was dry. 'I'm looking for Kathleen Griffin.'

'She's out. Who is this?'

Could it be Walter? Could it *still* be Walter? For a moment Frank was paralysed with nerves. When he was able to speak again he asked, 'And Scott Griffin?'

'Sonny's out too. Who is this?'

'I edit the arts pages here at the *Sunday Times*,' Frank lied smoothly. 'I was hoping to set up an interview with Kathleen and Scott. You can tell Kathleen I remember her from *Yellow Afternoon*.'

'I'll tell her nothing of the kind.' Walter sounded suspicious as well as irritated. 'Unfortunately for you I happen to know the arts editor of the *Sunday Times*, and you are not she.'

'Oh . . .' Frank stuttered. 'I—'

But Walter had hung up.

Frank replaced the receiver. He was embarrassed but also resentful. He got up and moved through the house to the kitchen. *You'll see*, he thought. *You'll find out who's in charge*. He realised he was sweating under his arms and that his grip on the empty glass was tight and strained.

After drinking another two inches of cognac and spending another few minutes staring mutely into the black window, past his reflection and into the night, Frank sat down again in front of the laptop and looked up flights from Marseille to London the next day. It would be Christmas Eve and therefore expensive but he did not care. When he found an available seat he clicked on 'Buy Now' and filled in his name, address and credit card details. Because his hands were shaking he made several mistakes that needed correcting, and when he had finished buying the ticket he tried to calm himself. *Twenty-five years have already passed*, he thought. *There's no rush. Scott Griffin isn't going anywhere.*

He poured another drink, which took him quite close to the end of the bottle, and imagined how the next day would play itself out: he would get to London in the early afternoon, he would travel by Underground to Belsize Park, he would fortify himself with a drink at a nearby pub and then he would walk up to Kathleen's front door and knock on it with his knuckles. And after that? Here his imagination failed him.

II

1

A long time ago Frank had told Jem that when he shot a rabbit dead its relatives around it would not notice. Brothers and sisters might look up, startled by a sound they could not identify, but then they would forget about it and carry on eating or scratching behind their ears with their hind feet or chasing each other around a dandelion while their sibling, alive a moment before, lay dead on the ground beside them.

This was a horrible thought and somehow more horrible because Jem had just been given a pet rabbit for her eighth birthday.

'Which rabbits?' she asked.

'Wild ones. I used to shoot them with my air rifle when I was a boy.'

'Why don't the other ones notice? The brothers and sisters?'

'Because rabbits don't understand about death.'

'Why not?'

'Because they're too stupid.'

Frank did not believe in making things sound nicer than they were. If something was brutal, vicious, merciless or just 'too stupid' he would tell you. This made things more interesting but often also more unpleasant.

On this occasion Jem wanted to know more but there was a rule about not asking too many questions and she did not want her father to lose his temper, which was mighty and colossal. She resolved to ask her mother, but later when they were alone.

On Christmas Eve in the afternoon Jem took two Underground trains and a bus to the hospital near the airport. Inside the hospital she followed signs to the mortuary where she was asked to show her passport to identify herself: Jocelyn Eloise Martell, twenty-five years old, daughter of the deceased.

She had been informed of her father's death by her guardian, Marian Frost, who had rung her up an hour ago from her retirement home in Norfolk. Marian was elderly: 'eighty-odd'. She had always been something-odd. When she had first taken on the guardianship of Jem she had been 'sixty-odd' and Jem had been eight and three quarters.

Today Marian had been summoned to the telephone from a screening of *The Spy Who Loved Me* in the Community Room. On the other end of the line was an official-sounding young man whose name she did not catch. He wanted to know how to get hold of Jocelyn Martell. When she asked why he informed her that Jocelyn's father, Frank Martell, was dead and that his remains were in a hospital morgue near Heathrow. He said that a formal identification was needed and that Miss Martell was next-of-kin.

A person's next-of-kinship was not, it seemed, altered by an estrangement, however long or bitter. Jem had known this day would come. She agreed to identify Frank's body.

She *wanted* to do it: he was harmless. If she did not see him today she would never see him again.

'I want to see what he looks like.'

'You may not recognise him,' Marian said. 'And it may not *be* him.'

'Of course it is. They've got his wallet, his passport and his driving licence.'

'They'll pull back a sheet,' Marian said. 'I've seen it on the telly a hundred times.'

At sixty-two Frank did not look old, but older than he had when Jem last saw him. His thick hair had turned grey – dark like a badger's – and he seemed smaller, as if he had lost some of his stuffing. She remembered his face full of rage, but here it looked empty. Was it really her father? It seemed unfair that he should look so benign.

But when she saw the many different coloured ink stains on his fingers she was reminded as forcefully of his presence as if he had been alive.

'Yes, that's him.'

Now that she was here she had nothing to say to him. It would have been ridiculous to say anything: there was no point complaining to a corpse.

She took away his belongings in a plastic bag she found stuffed in her jacket pocket. She could not remember where it had come from or what it had once contained. It bore no brand name but only a printed instruction: *Please Use Me Again.*

Frank had not been carrying any luggage and so only the contents of his pockets needed to be collected: house key, car key, wallet, passport, the stub of a boarding pass and the parking ticket that would allow his car to exit the car park at Marseille airport. He had been wearing a watch but it was not an expensive one, only a black Swatch with a rubber strap and a white face. Jem tried it on and did it up. Her wrist was smaller than her father's by three holes.

– *What big arms you have!*

– *All the better to GRAB you with.*

She took off the watch and dropped it into the plastic bag, which she shoved into her handbag to join all the other rubbish she kept in there and forgot about.

She retraced her steps: out of the hospital and back to the bus stop where, she noticed, one bus might take her back to the railway station but another might take her to the airport. She looked at the timetables posted on the rear panel of the bus shelter and it occurred to her that she had in her possession Frank's wallet, his car key and the key to his house. She did not have the money to fly to France but he did. She looked inside the wallet and found a credit card, a wodge of euros, another of sterling and a driving licence. She counted the cash: two hundred euros plus change, and seventy-five pounds sterling. To take his money would not be stealing because it was rightfully hers – the money, the wallet, the car key, the car and even the house were all rightfully hers.

It was cold, waiting here. A bus was approaching and the banner above its windscreen read 'Heathrow Airport'. Jem looked at it, considering. *If I wanted to*, she thought, *I could fly to Marseille, drive to the house and let myself in.*

The bus stopped and its doors opened with a hiss. No one got off, but three people boarded: two off-duty nurses wearing NHS lanyards round their necks and, at the last moment, Jem. The doors bleeped and closed and off they went.

As they rattled along, heaving and lurching over speed bumps and around corners, she looked on her telephone for a flight to Marseille. *There won't be a seat*, she thought, but there was: the last one on the latest British Airways flight leaving Terminal 5 this evening. It was expensive – Marian would have called it criminally expensive – but Jem wasn't paying: she bought it here and now, using her telephone and her father's credit card. She checked herself in online and downloaded the boarding pass to her telephone. She would make it by the skin of her teeth.

At Terminal 5 she hurried towards Departures and scrabbled through her handbag trying to find her passport. Not looking where she was going she bumped into a young man heading the other way—

'Sorry—'

'My fault.'

She met his apologetic smile with an apologetic glance and then passed through the cattle crush of departures and security. Once she was through she breathed a sigh of relief. What an interesting day this was turning out to be.

At the gate she sat with the other passengers, waiting to board. It was the very last moment that anyone could fly home in time for Christmas and most of the other travellers were tired-looking businessmen no doubt looking forward to seeing their wives, sons and daughters. Jem wondered if her father had ever missed his only child at Christmas.

She looked at his passport photograph and compared it with her own. She peered to see a likeness. Perhaps the shape of her eyes? Perhaps the tilt of her upper lip? She hoped not. It used to keep her awake when she was younger, worrying that she might be like him. 'God isn't interested in what's on the outside,' Marian had told her. 'It's what's on the inside that gets you to heaven.' But God was not the consolation He should have been.

Inside the back cover of the passport there were spaces for the details of 'two relatives or friends who may be contacted in the event of accident'. The spaces were blank. Jem wondered if there were any circumstances under which her father might have tried to reach her, other than the occasion of his sudden and unexpected death. She decided not.

2

Elsewhere in the same terminal of the same airport Scott Griffin, known to those who loved him as Sonny, had just waved goodbye to his American girlfriend Nina. He watched her wind her way through the departures channels and into security and out of sight. He waited until she had definitely gone and could not come back. Then he turned away, relieved.

As a matter of course he took his telephone out of his pocket and checked the screen. No messages. Not looking where he was going he was bumped into by a young woman hurrying the other way, towards Departures—

'Sorry—'

'My fault.'

He gave her an apologetic smile and then went back to his phone. As he walked towards the Heathrow Express train station where he could catch a train for London he tapped out a message to his best friend Becka: *Pub later?* He felt that the Christmas holiday was now truly able to begin. Last night had been the last performance of *Hamlet* and today he had got Nina off the continent. There was nothing else to be done besides enthusiastic festive drinking.

When his phone rang he knew it could only be either his

sister or his mother – no one else he knew still used a telephone for speaking to other people. But his sister Lauren
was eight years older than him and antique in her ideas: she
used her telephone to ring people up, she smoked straights,
she took sugar in her tea and she played chess.

'Larry?'

'Don't call me that. Where are you?'

Lauren always sounded as if she were right at the end of
her tether.

'Heathrow. Just dropped Nina off. Why?'

'Because you're not here. I need you here.' (Sonny heard
the draw and exhale of cigarette smoke.) 'I just arrived. I
hate Christmas. Mum is already being a massive pain.'
Lauren had abandoned her flat a mile away for a two-night
stay with her mother, father and brother at Christmas.
Every year she complained about it.

Sonny laughed. 'She's got a massive hangover.' There
had been a party and then an after-party to mark the end of
Hamlet. 'I've got one too.'

'I don't care about your hangover. I care about my
sanity.'

'I'll be there in an hour.'

'Hurry *up.*'

The line went dead.

'Rude woman,' Sonny murmured to himself. He checked
his telephone screen. A reply had arrived from Becka: *Nina
too?* Sonny smiled – Becka had not liked his girlfriend. *No,*
he typed back, stopping dead in the middle of the concourse
and forcing the crowd to flow around him. *Just dropped her
off at Heathrow.* He sent the message, pocketed his telephone and walked on.

Arriving at the subterranean station he looked up at the screens for the next train to Paddington and then shuffled onto the already crowded platform. Everyone seemed to be walking incredibly slowly and dragging a suitcase for him to trip over. These obstructions reminded him how ill he was feeling – better than he had first thing this morning but still dreadful, as if he weighed twice as much as usual and his head were full of cold gravy.

The train arrived with a long, deathly squeal and he squeezed on board to stand just inside the doors with someone else's rucksack pressed against his face. This really was intolerable. He turned around so that he was at least facing the glass door and could manoeuvre his telephone out of his pocket to look at photographs taken last night. Ugh, he had been drunk. Here was Nina, still wearing Ophelia's make-up and therefore looking mad as well as beautiful, and here God help us all was a picture of his mother looking trashed and much older than she looked when sober. Knowing how much she would hate the photograph he deleted it. He also removed Nina from his screensaver and replaced her with a photograph of the family dog, Mike.

He was pleased to have got rid of Nina without actually having to break up with her. Putting 5,000 miles between them (and he wondered briefly if it was further) would do the job for him. He hated arguments and scenes. He hated breaking up with girls because they always got cross and asked why and there was never much of a reason beyond 'I just don't like you any more', which never sounded good enough. He would be accused of having led them on – of having told them he loved them and made them think he was serious before changing his mind and ghosting them shortly after. But what was he supposed to do differently? When he said 'I love you' he always meant it at the time but then the feeling vanished and he didn't. He never understood their right to fury and tears – it was just as disappointing for him as it was for them.

He had loved Nina for almost the whole three months that *Hamlet* had been on stage, and then suddenly he had stopped loving her and found her annoying. He had gone off her last week when she asked him to go all the way to Tunbridge Wells on a crappy Sunday train to meet some obscure English relative whom she had met once, years ago, at a family wedding in Santa Barbara. He did not go, of course, but it was selfish and demanding and presumptuous of her to have asked. He had not broken up with her because he knew she was leaving five days later. Thank God for the Atlantic Ocean.

Now it was Christmas and he had nothing to do but enjoy himself. He wanted everything at home to be the same as it was every year. He wanted to walk in and find his mother and sister arguing in the kitchen, his father sitting in the winged armchair, the dog upside-down on the rug begging to be tickled, the fire in the grate and the too-small and only half-decorated Christmas tree winking like an alcoholic uncle in the window. He wanted to go to the pub and drink beer and then zigzag home and fall into bed only to be disturbed five minutes later by his mother delivering his stocking. He wanted to sleep late tomorrow morning and wake up to the familiar yet never tiresome comforts of Christmas at home.

*

In that very home at that very moment his mother and his sister were indeed arguing in the kitchen as Sonny had predicted.

'Do you want me to cook or not?'

'I'm trying to *help*, Lauren. Sonny doesn't like potatoes too *big*, that's all. He likes them cut up small.'

'Dear God in heaven.'

'He lives here so I know these things. You do not.'

'I can't quite believe—'

'There's no need to get in a huff about it.'

'– I'm listening to this. Shall I go home and let you cook dinner?'

'Home to your bedsit? Don't be ridiculous.'

Kathleen insisted that Lauren's minuscule home on the other side of the Heath was a bedsit. Everyone else called it a studio. 'It's big enough for two,' Kathleen liked to joke, 'as long as one person sleeps in the washing machine.'

From the sitting room next door Walter listened. In the old days he would have got up, gone into the kitchen and told them both to put a sock in it, but he did not do that sort of thing these days – it required quick, decisive movement and a confident bark, neither of which were his strengths any more. He was not certain he could do anything to shut anyone up: with the diminishment of physical capability came the surrender of domestic authority. He was more retiring now among loud voices and competing characters. That was the truth of 'retirement': a quiet life. He switched on Radio 4 and turned up the volume.

Walter was going blind. He had finished with doctors – they had nothing new to say. Macular degeneration, it was called, and it would march its relentless course. He had been told it was 'common', which did not make him feel better, and 'more common in women', which made him feel worse.

'And are you still working?' This from the youngest of several ophthalmologists he had consulted.

'I am a photographer.' Walter, still gulping the prognosis like a fish gulping air, wanted to throw a chair through the window of the doctor's office, leap after it and gallop away through W1.

Opposite him the doctor's expression said *Not for long you're not*. Walter could feel it in the silence.

'I have been a photographer for over fifty years.' He spoke as if he were pleading his case for clemency. 'I bought my first camera when I was seventeen.' He had saved up for it by working in an abattoir, but he could not say this because his mouth had dried out.

The doctor was looking at his panic-stricken face. 'It takes time for these things to sink in,' he said, 'but remember: it's not a death sentence.'

No, it was worse. It was death in life.

One day he would be more blind than not. One day he would be a passenger, no longer consulted about the direction of travel or allowed to take charge of the vessel. Even now, he had a right of passage but no authority. His future was one of dependency.

But he must not allow these thoughts to run away with him. It did him no good.

Having lost her argument with Lauren Kathleen came in from the kitchen to complain, turning the radio down and relating the latest injustices.

'I was listening to that,' Walter protested mildly.

'She's only just got here and she's completely taken over.'

'Do you want to cook dinner?'

'No.'

'Then don't interfere.'

'Honestly, Walter – you *always* take her side.'

'Nonsense.' He held a hand out to his wife and she took it. 'Don't be cross,' he said. 'Sonny will be here in a minute.'

'I suppose.' Kathleen cheered up. 'Want a drink?'

'If you're making one.'

Kathleen sloshed whisky and water into a glass and handed it to him.

'Here you are.'

Then she made a drink for herself: ice cubes, a generous slug of gin and a dabble of tonic.

'What about Lauren?' he asked.

'I don't know what she likes.' Kathleen kicked off her shoes and flumped down on the sofa. Noticing Mike the dog on the cushion beside her she said, 'Get *off*, dog,' and pushed him to the floor where he stood for a moment, rudely awoken, before giving Kathleen a cold look and going to lie at Walter's feet.

Mike was a medium-sized, black, woolly-looking dog who looked much like a medium-sized, black, woolly-looking rug when lying flat on his side. When he got up off the floor it sometimes startled visitors, as if a sheepskin had turned back into a sheep.

Everyone loved Mike but for Kathleen, who regarded him with suspicion because he did not like her. He preferred Walter. It troubled her to be so plainly disliked – she felt as she did when she smiled at a baby and it started to cry. What did it see?

It was true that Mike preferred Walter. He always had, but now that Walter's sight had begun to fail him Mike's presence was reassuring as well as companionable. Not only this: Mike could also sense Walter's need for physical contact – that he liked the dog to be near enough to touch – and so the dog would often sit on his feet, or lean against his shins, or press a wet nose into his palm when they were out walking.

Walter feared that if he went blind – and he still refused to admit to 'when' – he would no longer be woven into the fabric of human endeavour. His little thread would unravel and trail behind, out of reach and unnoticed. 'What's happening? Who's that? Where are we?' He could not bear to keep asking for illumination.

But Mike attached him securely to the living world. Every morning Mike stepped out of the house with confidence and certainty; every morning he was curious, optimistic and fearless. Anything Walter might miss, Mike would see: he knew the way to the shop, the cafe, the Heath and the Mixed Pond; he knew about traffic lights and pedestrian crossings; he never got bored or cross or impatient and, most vitally, he never had anything better to do than coexist. He did not need to make telephone calls or go to work but only to dedicate himself to Walter's safety and well-being.

This duty was rightfully Kathleen's own and although she did not want to fulfil it she did not like Mike to show her up. It made her resentful. Mike had become the epitome of responsible companionship. She was not.

'That dog makes me look like a bad wife,' she complained once to Walter.

Walter laughed and kissed her. 'I love my bad wife,' he said.

'I forgot to tell you,' Walter remembered now, 'that a man telephoned here last night. Someone odd.'

'Oh yes?' Kathleen was massaging her toes inside their Wolford tights.

'You were at your party. He said he was ringing from the *Sunday Times*. He pretended he was Linda – I mean that he was arts editor. I told him he wasn't.'

'How odd.'

'He wanted to speak to Sonny as well.'

'Did you find out why?'

'Some nonsense about an interview with you both. Said he remembered you from *Yellow Afternoon*, but I thought no one saw that film. Wasn't it the one—'

'Yes, that one,' Kathleen interrupted him. 'No one saw it. It was never finished.' She had stopped rearranging the foot of her tights neatly over her toes and now she shivered as if someone had blown cold air at the nape of her neck. For a moment she was far away. Then she said absently, 'What did this man sound like?'

Walter considered. 'A bit of a creep.'

Kathleen said again, 'How odd,' and then resumed the arrangement of her Wolfords.

At that moment the front door was opened from outside with a clatter and Sonny's voice – 'Hello, everyone?' – was heard in the hall. Mike leapt to his feet, barked and rushed out of the room, sneezing and chuntering in welcome.

Kathleen brightened. She breathed his name, 'Sonny,' and then she put on her shoes and stood up. 'Come on, husband,' she said to Walter, reaching out her hands to help him up. 'Now it's really Christmas.'

3

On the plane to Marseille Jem thought about the dead
bodies she had seen in her life. First her mother's, although
she remembered it only sometimes and unexpectedly, as if
lit by lightning in the darkness. Second that woman who
had jumped in front of a train. Now her father's made
three.

'Thoracic aneurysm and dissection,' the doctor had
called it. Something had burst and ripped Frank's heart
open. 'It looks like a normal heart attack but it's not.' The
doctor's name was Dr Pandya. He was good-looking and
wore a wedding ring to protect him, Jem supposed, from
bare-knuckled females like herself. 'Familial, it's sometimes
called.'

'Familial? My father? That's a joke.'

Dr Pandya did not smile. 'It means that it runs in families.
You might be predisposed.'

He was looking directly at her and he would not look
away – she supposed it was a way to hold her attention –
but Jem did not want to meet his gaze and so she looked
over his shoulder, with some envy, at the running green man
who signalled an emergency exit. 'We can screen you to
find out. Give you an ECG.'

'Screen me? My heart?' Jem frowned. 'But I haven't had anything to do with my father for years and years.' Afterwards she wondered what had made her say something so illogical.

'You're still related even if he's dead. Miss Martell, I recommend you take this seriously.'

'I will. Just not right now.'

He did not give up. 'There's not a lot we can do for you if you suffer an event like your father's out of the blue. If, however, we find something in advance . . .' and he spoke on, continuing to explain the workings or non-workings of this valve or that chamber and the comings and goings of blood. He mentioned the odds of a continuing basic risk to her life and she watched him speculate: eyeing her as if he could see through her clothes to her ribcage and the beating blood-fist within. He was trying to communicate a sense of urgency and she appreciated the effort but she would not believe for one moment that there was anything wrong with her. She felt fine. It did not surprise her that Frank had been killed by a defective heart – she had needed no further evidence of that particular deficiency – but she knew she was nothing like him.

Listening, drifting, she wondered whether Frank had been afraid, felled like a tree onto the glossy floor of the airport terminal. Had he known he was dying? Had he struggled to live? Had his life flashed before his eyes?

'Did anyone talk to him? Did he say anything?'

She had interrupted. With some irritation Dr Pandya broke off what he was saying and answered her.

'I don't know. I imagine he would have been preoccupied by the pain. It's a fairly comprehensive internal rupture' –

a brief pause for effect – 'which is why we'd like to screen you. Do you smoke? Do you have any brothers or sisters? Any children?'

'No, no and no.' Jem shook her head. 'Just me.'

From her seat at the back of the aeroplane Jem looked out of the window and down at orange lights on the ground below: suburbs, towns, villages and roads.

Just me.

The plane flew out over water and tilted in the darkness, turning a slow corner. For a minute there was nothing beyond the window but black: black above and black beneath. Then it straightened its course in line with the runway and Jem felt the wheels come down. Rows of lights galloped up to meet them and finally they touched the tarmac: the squeak, bounce and rattle of landing. Jem felt a brief and unexpected elation. *Just me.* She was free.

Outside it was colder than she had expected. She walked the aisles of the car park pressing the unlock button on Frank's car key. She had no idea of the type, size or colour of car she was looking for. Then she heard a *thunk* and saw a BMW flash its lights a few yards away: an old black saloon with French number plates. The car was the last in its row, parked at an acute angle. Jem imagined her father turning off the engine, getting out and going into the airport. It had only been this morning, and now he was dead.

She got into the driver's seat on the left-hand side and slung her handbag into the back. Then she put the key into the ignition and took a deep breath, inhaling the smell of leather and engine fumes. She felt a momentary unsteadiness, as if a halted escalator had started moving, but told herself not to be foolish. She started the engine and buzzed all the windows down. She needed to be alert.

Driving north she left the sea behind her and gained altitude, noticing the air becoming cleaner the further she travelled until each breath was like a draught of cold water. She passed towns with names she recognised – Salon, Lamanon, Sénas, Orgon and Cavaillon – before she began to see signs for places she remembered well: Oppède, Ménerbes, Gordes and Goult.

Here was the sign for Saint-Victor and a right turn, off the main road and onto a smaller road that curled like smoke from the floor of the valley, into a deeper cold and a velvet darkness. She chugged through the silent village, shutters shut and streets empty, before she twisted out at the top of the hill to sit on top of the ridge and pause for breath. The sparkling valley was spread out beneath her; the dark woods closed in beside her. It was only a few hundred yards from here to the house.

She had travelled this road as a child, leaning her head on her arm, looking out of the window and up at the sky, a hot sun dabbing at her face through a blur of black branches. Since those days she had peered at a map or squinted at Google Earth countless times, but she had never been back.

Houses and humans were rare up here on the ridge. Jem drove on, her headlights lighting the trees and the silver road. She felt a prickle under her collar. If the dead man she had seen this morning had stepped out of the woods and in front of the car she would not have been surprised.

She slowed down, looking out for two stone gateposts that marked the track leading to the house. Here they were, just the same. She felt a flicker of nerves as she passed between them and bumped up the track through the woods. It was further than she remembered. Her headlights lit up the garden: huddled shrubs, colourless grass, ghost-white tree trunks and a canopy of evergreen oaks. Here was a wheelbarrow half-filled with leaves; there was the well, enclosed by its stone collar; here was the house. Nothing had changed.

She parked on a bare circle of dirt, switched off the engine and sat watching the house through the windscreen as if she had arrived at a hospital bedside and found the patient asleep. She looked for signs of change or marks of neglect but there were none. The wooden shutters were painted green and pinned neatly open against the stone walls, just as before. The apricot tiles on the roof were mottled and slipped in exactly the way she remembered. Beside the kitchen door a heap of logs lay tumbled under a sloping piece of corrugated tin. She could have sworn those logs had been arranged that way on the day she left.

She switched off the headlights and got out of the car. The silence was total. She tilted her head back and looked up at the tinselled arc of the night sky, a glittering roof-scape; the stars a shivering mass without their moon.

It was simpler than she had ever imagined to walk up to the kitchen door and unlock it; to turn the handle and push it open. It was simpler still to cross the threshold and walk in. Now she was here. She stood in the dark, listening. She heard the tick of a clock and the hum of a fridge that had ticked and hummed every day since the day she had left.

4

In London dinner was over and Lauren was filling the dishwasher while Sonny, standing on one side of the table or the other, got in her way. He was defending himself on the subject of Nina.

'It was a fling. That's all.'

Mildly Lauren said, 'You're an arrogant little shit, aren't you?'

'Why do you care?'

'Because' – Lauren dumped a handful of forks in the cutlery basket – '*she* might not have known it was a fling. Because *you* didn't tell her. Because *I've* heard this too many times. Because . . .' she stopped. 'Never mind. One day you'll fall in love with a woman and she won't give a shit about you. Then you'll know.'

Sonny grinned. 'That will never happen.'

'Ugh.' Lauren straightened up from the dishwasher and itched the end of her nose with one yellow-gloved finger. 'Men.'

'Do you ever take those things off?'

'Do you ever offer to help?'

'No.' Sonny turned away to open the fridge and stare into it with deep and total concentration as if he were memorising the contents for an exam. 'I'm still hungry,' he said. 'What else is there to eat?'

The doorbell rang and Mike gave a sleepy growl from his basket under the table.

'Who on earth?' Lauren gave up trying to fit more glasses on the already full top rack. She put them into the sink.

'Becka, probably.' Sonny shut the fridge door. 'We're going to the pub.'

Lauren lowered her voice. 'You're leaving me here? On my own?'

'Can't you spend one evening in with your parents?'

'I don't mind Dad,' Lauren said. 'It's Mum. She drives me bananas.'

'What's happened to your Christmas spirit?' Sonny taunted her. 'Peace, love and understanding?'

'You're a rat, Scott Griffin.'

But Sonny had grinned and gone.

On the front step Sonny found Becka. The collar of her overcoat was turned up and on her head she wore a black furry hat. She looked exceptionally pretty, as she usually did, but Sonny had known her too long to remark on her prettiness.

'Who died to make that hat?'

'Your teddy bear. Shall I come in and say hi to your parents?'

'Fuck no.' Sonny quietly closed the front door behind him. 'I don't want them to know I've gone out.' He took Becka's arm and led her away from the house, down the steps to the street. 'Mum will freak.'

'Really? Annie couldn't care less.' Becka called her mother by her Christian name, a habit which Sonny thought quirky and Kathleen pretentious. 'Here . . .' she pulled a joint from behind one ear and waved it in front of his nose. 'Want some?'

'Of course.'

Sonny lit the joint and they walked in the direction of Haverstock Hill, smoking.

'We listened to *Hamlet* on the radio last night,' Becka said. 'Annie blubbed.'

'She did? Aw, she's cute your mum.' Sonny inhaled and held the smoke in his lungs. When he exhaled he said, 'And didn't you? Blub?'

'No.' Becka blushed. 'Definitely not. I cheered. "The rest is silence"! At bloody last!'

They had reached the end of their street and now they turned the corner to walk down Haverstock Hill. Sonny took a last couple of little puffs on the spliff and then flicked the stub into the road. Quickened by the hash, humming with it, he looked about himself at these surroundings, familiar and beloved: the tree that had caused the wall to bow outwards over the pavement; the lost cat notice which had been Sellotaped to a lamp post for a year; the bus stop with its rotating advertisement board and surgical lighting; the overflowing bin with a tide of litter at its foot. Here was the pub, glossy red and cheerful, and a blackboard reading '1 More Sleep 'til Christmas', and here were three smokers, standing outside, who parted to let him approach the door, tugging Becka behind him, pressing his palm against the fingerprinted brass plate, pushing the door open, finding his way through the close, noisy crowd inside – everyone laughing or cheering or singing – and noticing the Christmas tree wobbling in the corner. Holding

Becka's gloved hand Sonny led her towards the bar as if he were pulling her onto a life raft and when he got there the barman turned from handing out change and asked him, 'What'll it be?' And Sonny wanted to kiss him on both cheeks and buy a drink for everyone in the pub, so happy was he to be himself.

5

Jem could tell at once her father had not intended to stay
away long. The shutters had been left open. The Bialetti was
still half-full of coffee, left on the kitchen counter, and a
dirty mug sat beside it. On a calendar pinned to the kitchen
wall Frank had written 'Pierre & Agnes' beside 'Decembre
25'. When she opened the larder door she found a fat,
featherless duck on the cold slate slab, dressed for the oven.

These small discoveries – the duck, the calendar and the
coffee pot – were puzzling in a small way, but the bigger
puzzle was confounding her: on the one hand Frank had
expected to be hosting dinner tomorrow here in this kitchen;
on the other hand he had left France this morning with no
luggage and no return ticket. It was inexplicable.

She imagined these strangers, Pierre and Agnes, walking
into the house tomorrow and finding her here. It would be
awkward. She would have to tell them that Frank was dead
and they might not believe her – they might think she was
an imposter, breaking into his house and into his larder like
Goldilocks.

The sort of responsibilities that might come with being
here had not occurred to her before, but now she considered the prickling bother of explaining who she was and

why she was here to Frank's sorrowful friends and neighbours. They would ask questions. They might have heard rumours. She would have to identify herself: his long-lost daughter.

When she came out of this reverie it seemed even quieter than before, as if whispering voices had abruptly stopped. She felt again that stirring under her collar.

She needed signs of life: heat and light. She walked through the house switching on lights and closing shutters. In the hall she flicked a switch and an opaque glass globe, hanging above the stairs, sprang to life like the sun coming out. This was better.

Upstairs she stopped on the threshold of what had once been her parents' room. She could not bring herself to go in. A bedside light had been left on and she could see the rumpled duvet and scattered pillows on the mattress. The bed looked as if Frank had just a moment ago climbed out of it. In the bathroom she found his toothbrush, toothpaste and razor. Had he expected to come back from London this evening, brush his teeth and get into bed? It was a mystery she might never solve. When she lifted her eyes to the mirror she suffered a moment's terror – that she would see him standing behind her. She knew he was dead and yet his breath still hung in the bones of the place. She looked at the closed door of her old bedroom for a moment, deciding, and then quickly turned the door handle and went in. She found the room unaltered: the blue bedspread; her father's drawings framed on the walls; a red velvet armchair; that mobile swinging above the bed, made by Frank of seagulls carved from balsa wood.

She turned away. Coming to the house she had feared she

would find things changed, but to find nothing changed was stranger still.

In the spare bedroom stood a tall cupboard. When opened it released from its dark interior a trace of her mother's scent, fluttering out to freedom like a butterfly held captive all these years. It was a shock – Jem flinched – and then she closed her eyes and inhaled deeply, desperately, as if with the scent alone she could make her mother whole again, but when she opened her eyes even that faint smudge of coloured air had gone. A coat still hung in the cupboard – it had been a favourite – and Jem slid it from its wooden hanger and tried it on. In one pocket she found a scrap of paper:

> *coffee*
> *soap*
> *crayons*

Her mother's handwriting had been unruly, generous and haphazard. Jem traced the letters with her thumb. *Crayons*. They must have been for herself. Her mother seemed suddenly so near that Jem felt faint and breathless.

She pattered downstairs. Frank had left a light on in the study: an anglepoise casting a bright, gold disc on the desktop. Jem sat down in the wheeled chair. In front of her lay an address book, open at 'JKL'. The names were written out in Frank's neat script:

> *Joly*
> *Julien*
> *Kathleen*

38

Konstantin (framer)
Lefevre
Lucas

Beside the address book lay an open envelope containing photographs, some in black and white and others in the yellowed tones which betrayed their age. Jem examined these one by one, squinting in particular at the few of her mother. She craved these rare images like salt. When she finished she blinked up at the room. She had forgotten where she was.

In her father's studio she lit the stove, still warm when she put her palm on it. The flames crept up around the kindling and soon the stove was groaning as it warmed up. Jem left the door ajar. She looked at the matchbox in her hand and then around the room. The stove had been warm and so her father must have sat in here last night, working at his desk, his bottles of coloured ink laid neatly out in front of him, different pens in their jars of water and rags nearby for cleaning them.

On the desk she saw an unfinished Christmas card:

Pierre et Agnes
Joyeux Noël

The words were tangled among strands of holly and ivy and they framed a landscape haunted like one of Arthur Rackham's: a forest, a castle, a village. It was Saint-Victor made into a fairy tale. The colouring was unfinished – only half the ivy was green. He had been interrupted.

Jem opened the laptop nearby on the work table. Shut

between the screen and the keyboard was a little photograph, passport-sized, of Frank as a young man. Jem looked at it briefly and then set it aside and turned to the computer. She expected to be asked for a password which she had no hope of guessing, but instead the screen sprang to life and showed her the last page at which Frank had been looking, the message that confirmed his air ticket from Marseille to London:

You're ready to fly!

Jem frowned. Frank had bought his air ticket *last night*? He had been sitting here drawing, and then he had bought an air ticket to London? It did not make sense.

Thinking hard, she walked back into the study. She saw the telephone on the desk. She looked at the address book. She stared at the envelope of photographs. She was trying to understand something – trying so hard that her head felt under pressure, as if a storm was about to break. Then the lightning strike of a simple and perfect idea: she picked up the telephone receiver and pressed 'redial'.

6

Having cleared away dinner, Lauren joined her parents in the sitting room. Kathleen lay on the sofa, Walter sat in his armchair and Mike was spread out on the floor. Standing in front of the fire Lauren lit a cigarette.

'Who was that at the door?' Kathleen asked with a yawn.

'Becka.'

'What?' The yawn was snapped shut. 'She didn't come in?'

'No, Sonny went out.'

'Out?' Kathleen sat up. 'Out where?'

'Pub.'

'To the *pub*?' Kathleen was outraged. 'But it's Christmas Eve.'

'Don't shout at me, Mum. If you're angry with Sonny, shout at him.'

'I'm not *angry*,' Kathleen declared furiously, 'I'm *hurt*.'

'He's spent every night on stage with you for three months. Can't you do without him for one evening?'

'And what is that supposed to mean?' Now Kathleen turned her outrage on Lauren.

'It means, give him a break.'

'But it's Christmas. What's wrong with being here with us?'

41

'You've got me and Dad,' Lauren joked. 'Aren't we enough?'

'But it's *Christmas*.' She repeated the word with more emphasis, as if they had not heard the first time. 'Are we so repulsive and tedious that Sonny can't bear to sit in the same room with us for one evening?'

'Are Lauren and I so repulsive and tedious that you can't sit here with us?' Walter asked mildly.

Kathleen ignored him. 'Sonny is being rude and hurtful and downright . . .'

In the old days Lauren would have caught her father's eye, but these days he might not notice.

'. . . *selfish*. The minute that dreadful Nina is out of the picture then that dreadful Becka—'

'They can't all be dreadful, Mum.' Lauren, amused, flicked ash off her cigarette end into the fireplace. 'Becka and Nina and any of the other girls who've got a crush on Sonny.'

'They *are* all dreadful. Without exception.' Kathleen had got herself thoroughly worked up. 'Well I don't mind saying,' she said unnecessarily, 'that's completely ruined my evening.' She gave Mike a filthy look, as if including him by default in the ruination. 'I'm going to bed. Walter, are you coming?'

'Not quite. I might ask Lauren to play chess.'

This was annoying too. 'Don't you ever get bored of playing the same person over and over and *over*?'

'No.'

Kathleen deflated and then stood up. 'Well.' She huffed out of the room and into the kitchen just as the telephone began to ring. 'For heaven's sake. Who on earth would ring us on Christmas Eve at ten o'clock? Unless Sonny's

42

forgotten his keys.' She picked up the receiver. 'Sonny, darling? Is that you?'

But it was not Sonny. It was a woman and a stranger.

'Hello? Who is this?'

The voice spoke faintly, whether because of geography or nerves Kathleen did not stop to wonder.

'Who is *this*?'

'I'm . . .' And then the stranger stopped, as if she had thought better of the rest of her sentence.

After a silence Kathleen tried again, 'I said who *is* this?'

'No one. Sorry. A mistake.'

'What? Wait—'

But the line was cut.

Kathleen replaced the receiver. She stayed where she was for a moment, thinking. What had Walter said? *Someone odd*.

'Who was it?' Lauren called from the other room.

After a pause Kathleen said, 'No one.'

'What did no one want?'

'Nothing.'

'How mysterious.'

Kathleen could hear the *click-click-click* as Lauren set out the chess pieces. She had found a set of oversized pieces so that she and Walter could continue to play chess even as his eyesight failed and Walter, on opening the present, had been unusually touched. He had been so pleased, in fact, that Kathleen had felt jealous.

'I expect it was a wrong number,' she said. She hoped she sounded convincing; she had not convinced herself. 'Goodnight then, you two,' she said through the open doorway.

'Night, Mum.'

'Night, Kath.'

They were so alike. Too alike. Kathleen felt sometimes she had to push her way between them to stop them fusing like blobs of mercury.

She left the kitchen, crossed the hall and walked up the stairs very slowly. One hand drifted along the banister rail beside her and the other played with a gold chain at her throat. She frowned at the carpet as if she were trying to remember something important that had slipped her mind. The telephone call had unnerved her like the tremor of an Underground train, felt but not heard.

The pictures hanging alongside the stairs were often a little bit crooked because Walter trailed his fingers along the wall as he shuffled up and down, trying not to trip. Occasionally he would knock one frame or another an inch off the horizontal. Lauren straightened the picture frames when she visited, pausing on her way up and down the stairs, but Kathleen had stopped noticing the pictures years before.

Walter had bought the house forty years ago when it was still possible to do such a thing in NW3 without being richer than almost everyone else on the planet. Sonny liked to point out to his father that the entire house had, back then, cost half the amount that he would need today to buy himself a one-bedroom flat in the same area.

'Not adjusting for inflation,' Walter was compelled to add.

'Whatever. I'll still be living with you when I'm fifty.'

'I'll be dead when you're fifty,' Walter told him. 'You'll be living here alone with your mother.'

'You're right,' said Sonny, even more gloomily. 'Like Norman Bates.'

Tonight Sonny was saying goodnight to Becka at her front door – she, her mother Annie and her grandfather Lester lived two doors up from the Griffins.

'Happy Christmas, princess.' Taking her hands he pulled her towards him.

'You're drunk.'

Becka always accused him of being drunk when he came dangerously close to kissing her. It was how she excused him. She could not kiss him and never had because it would mean nothing to him and something to her, so she stopped him just in time, every time, when he was drunk.

'I am a bit. Not too much.' His breath and hers puffed between them into one cloud. He looked down at her. She stared at his coat lapels. It would be the work of a split second to look up at him – just to raise her eyes would be assent and then he would kiss her.

But Becka did not want a drunken kiss, she wanted the whole love story. She longed for love. She could feel tendrils reaching out from her heart for Sonny but she checked herself. *He's drunk. He doesn't want me when he's sober.*

'Go home.' She did not look up but smiled with her voice and pressed her palms on his lapels, one either side. 'Go to bed.' But somehow she seemed to be leaning on him instead of pushing him away.

Sonny could not move. She had come so close – had she ever come so close? He looked down at her hat, her lowered lashes, her lips and her throat – just a glimpse of that throat and he wanted to kiss it. He willed her to look up. One look would be enough, and then . . .

She stepped back before she looked up. Out of range, she smiled and tilted her head, closing one eye to look at him.

'You *are* drunk,' she said.

Sonny toppled forward momentarily and then regained his balance.

'Yes, I must be,' he said. Now he too stepped back. 'Goodnight.' He inclined his head like Jeeves. Then he turned around and hurried away along the pavement. 'Happy Christmas,' he called over his shoulder as he trotted for home. Becka watched him go.

At home Sonny let himself in and bent to pat a wriggling Mike who materialised at his feet, snickering with pleasure.

'Mikey-Mike. Who's a good boy then. Yes, you are.'

Mike, who was not put off by drunkenness, allowed himself to be kissed.

In the darkened kitchen Sonny drank some milk from a bottle in the fridge, ate two cold roast potatoes and dropped a bit of cold chicken into the dog's waiting jaws. Then he dragged himself up to his room where he undressed, crawled under the duvet and breathed deeply into the bedclothes. He shut his eyes and saw Becka. He still wanted to kiss her. He groaned.

When the bedroom door creaked open he rolled onto his back.

'Mum?'

'Ho ho ho.' Kathleen tiptoed in wearing her dressing gown and carrying a loaded Christmas stocking in her arms like a sleeping baby. 'Merry Christmas.'

'Very convincing,' Sonny said, laughing.

'Well if you must go out so late,' chuntered Kathleen. She laid the stocking – in fact a pillowcase – at the end of his bed. 'I can't stay up all night waiting. Goodnight, darling.'

'Have you done one for Lauren?'

Her voice changed. 'Lauren grew out of Christmas long ago.'

Sonny yawned. 'Goodnight, Mum.' He was asleep a moment later.

III

1

Waking in the dark Jem wondered where she was. She felt for a light switch; turned on the light; lay back on the pillow; tried not to panic. *That man. This house.* She looked at the time on her telephone, next to the bed: 05:05. Blinking at the ceiling she pieced fragments of memory into a whole, as if she were mending broken china. She remembered coming in here, finally, and getting into bed in all her clothes. She had thought, *How will I ever fall asleep?* It had been her last thought before falling asleep.

She looked up at the wooden seagulls, their wings outstretched, doomed to fly in circles over the bed. She blew at them as she used to do long ago, and watched them bob and sway on their threads. Frank had used fishing line to suspend them. He had made the mobile for her eighth birthday. He must have been in one of his good moods, less frequent and less memorable than the bad.

'Jem?'

'Mum?'

'Get up. Don't make a noise.'

That was the night her mother had tried to take her away: the worst night at the end of the worst day.

It was all because of Milou. Milou was Jem's pet rabbit, a present from her mother on her birthday. He had a wife, Mimi, but they could not live together because there were not enough hours in the day to drown so many fucking baby rabbits, pardon my French, said Frank in a voice that sounded as if he wished he could find the time. Instead Milou lived next door to Mimi. They kissed noses through the chicken wire every morning and when it was hot they lay stretched out in the dust, back to back with the wire between them, keeping cool in the shared shade of an ever-green oak, dozing.

Jem was eight and three quarters, which was old enough to know she should stay out of sight when her father was in a bad mood. On this day his mood rumbled around the house like a thunderstorm, coming and going, sometimes near enough to make her jump. In the afternoon he went to bed and it was quiet. Romy was watering her tomatoes and although Milou was not allowed in the house – 'I'll kill the pair of you so help me God' – Jem could not put him down outside because the neighbour's cat was sitting bolt upright at the edge of the garden, tail tip twitching, waiting for one of the animals to make a mistake. All the hens had retired to the shed to discuss it while the cockerel paced up and down outside, keeping watch.

So Jem carried Milou into the kitchen on her shoulder. This was the way he liked to travel: head and front paws over her shoulder and whiskers tickling her ear. She found a lettuce leaf in the basket and put Milou on the kitchen table to eat it. She sat on a chair opposite him. This way they were nose to nose. The lettuce disappeared into his mouth very fast, as if he were in a tearing hurry. She was so near she could hear the *crunch-crunch-crunch*. She could catch a glimpse of his teeth when he lifted his head a little: oddly huge. She knew they were sharp because once he had bitten her.

His lovely ears twitched forward and back even as he ate, listening out for danger. They did not twitch together but separately, one forward and one back and then an about turn. When he laid his ears back flat behind his head it meant he was scared, and when he was scratched between the ears he would close his eyes and go into a trance. He tucked his chin into his chest to concentrate on eating: *crunch-crunch-crunch*. Halfway through the lettuce leaf he stopped to scratch inside one ear. Then with a little shake, like getting crumbs off a napkin, he went back to his snack.

Jem put her arms on the table and her chin on her arms and watched him. She knew all about him. She knew that the bones in his feet were many and minuscule – she could feel them between her fingers when she gently picked up one of his feet. She knew that each of the pads underneath were smaller even than the print of her little finger. She knew that the pads were not rough like a dog's but smooth, cool and cushioned. She knew he was a Dutch rabbit which meant that he was black and white in patches and his ears pointed up like a wild rabbit's rather than flopping over to touch the ground. Lop-eared rabbits were toys but Milou was the real thing.

Jem liked to hold him but she also liked to lie on her stomach in the dirt beside his pen and watch him do rabbity things on his own: clean his face and whiskers with his front paws; yawn and stretch his back legs out one by one when he woke up; lie flat on his tummy with all four legs outstretched, and (best of all) give an occasional, sudden leap into the air out of sheer high spirits. The leaps were usually reserved for first thing in the morning or on a summer's evening as the sun set.

She watched the twitch of his independent ears, now forward and now back, but then he froze. Both ears went right back. There was a thundering noise as her father came down the stairs. Jem grabbed the rabbit and shoved him on her knee just as Frank came rolling into the kitchen like a hungry grizzly bear.

'What are you looking so scared about?' He eyed her. 'Have you got that rabbit in here?' He peered over the table at her lap and told her, 'Get up.'

Jem would not. She wrapped her legs around the legs of the chair and sat tight.

'I said, *get up*.'

She shook her head.

'Get *up*. Come round here where I can see you.'

Jem did not move a muscle. Milou did not move either. They were both scared.

Frank reached around the table and got hold of her by the elbow. He pulled her to her feet. 'Give me that!' He tried to grab Milou.

'Ow! Let go!'

Milou fell to the floor with a thud.

'I knew it.' Frank was triumphant. 'I warned you. I've told you a thousand fucking times—'

'Sorry-sorry-sorry!'

'– not to bring that animal into the house.'

He shook Jem and then let go of her and then he stooped to grab the rabbit from the floor by the scruff of his neck.

Milou's long back feet pedalled the air. His ears were pinned back and his eyes, round and rolling in terror, looked as if they might pop out of his head. He was carried to the door.

'Not. In. Here.' Frank opened the door with his free hand. 'Outside.'

Jem yelped at him, 'Dad! Stop it! You're scaring him!'

She jumped up to try to grab her father's arm but he elbowed her off and she fell on the floor. Before she could jump up again Frank had hurled the rabbit out of the door, overarm like a cricket ball, and Milou was turning untidy, star-shaped circles in the air. Then he landed hard – a flowerpot come off a windowsill – in a sprawl of legs and fur and now he was trying, puzzled, to scrabble to his feet.

For a moment Jem could not move or make a sound. She watched in horror. Milou paddled in the dust with his front paws, confused and struggling, getting nowhere. His back legs would not move. They were somehow knotted behind him, pointing the wrong way, useless as a pair of dropped socks.

When Jem found her feet she tried to push past her father and run out of the door but he caught her by the collar and held her fast. Blind with rage and tears she turned and punched him as hard as she could in the stomach with both fists. 'Let me go!'

'You little DEVIL!' Holding her with both hands, Frank shook her until she thought her head would fly off her shoulders and bounce on the kitchen floor. 'How dare you—'

'Stop it!'

'– lay a finger on me!'

He had lifted her off her feet and she tried to kick herself free – two kitchen chairs went flying – and then suddenly her mother was in the room.

'Frank! Put her down! Frank!'

She grabbed him but he shook her off.

'You. Stay. Out. Of. This.'

'Get off me!'

'Leave her! Stop it!' She had got hold of his arm and would not let go.

Now Frank did drop Jem. He turned on his wife. 'Get off me!'

'No – I won't – *Frank* . . .' Romy was clinging to his arm.

'Let go of me!'

With a bellow of rage Frank swung his forearm up and clouted the side of Romy's head with his fist. She dropped to the ground like a dishrag. Everything stopped.

Jem crouched beside her mother. 'Mum?' She patted her mother's shoulder over and over, quickly, fearful. 'Mum?'

When Romy stirred Frank bent and shouted in her face, 'I warned you!' Then he lurched out of the door.

'Jem—'

'Mum . . .' The tears came now.

Romy put out a reassuring hand. 'It's OK.'

'No it's not. What about Milou?' Jem ran out of the kitchen and across the dust.

The neighbour's cat had come to stand beside the rabbit, reaching out a curious paw to dab his bloody nose. 'Go away! Go away!' Jem shouted at the cat and it sauntered away to sit and watch at a distance. Jem turned to Milou. She knelt beside him. She did not know whether to pick him up. He was broken in the middle. Only his sides were moving in and out as he breathed too fast. Blood had come

54

out of his mouth and made little dark blobs in the dust. A bubble grew and shrank out of his nose. He was making a snuffling noise. He looked perplexed, as if he had been asked a question and could not for the life of him remember the answer.

'Milou.' Jem put out shaking fingers and touched him. Tears fell on his fur and muddled it.

From behind her Romy said, 'Go back inside.' She had pushed up her sleeves, right over her elbows. Half her face was red, the other half white. One of her eyes was smaller, the other bigger. She looked frightening.

'What are you going to do to him?' Jem, looking up, wiped her nose on her sleeve. 'Mum?'

'He's hurt.'

'What are you going to do?' She could hardly get the sentence out for crying. She knew what came next. It happened to the chickens. 'Please don't—'

'Go back inside.'

But Jem did not go inside: she ran away and did not come back until it was dark. There was a place in the woods where she always went until the coast was clear. When she did return she crept silently around the house to the front to make sure that the car was gone. Then she stood outside the kitchen window and waited to be noticed. Her mother was washing up on the other side of the glass. Not just her eyes but her whole face was bent out of shape.

When Romy looked up and saw Jem her expression changed with relief and she came quickly to the door. 'Where have you been?'

'In the woods. In my place.'

'I was worried,' Romy said.

Jem did not reply.

After a pause Romy said, 'He's not here. He's gone to the village.'

'Village' meant 'bar' at times like this. Jem stayed where she was, writing a secret message in the dust with one toe. *I hate him*.

Romy slung a cloth over her shoulder, folded her arms and leant on the door frame. 'I was worried,' she said again.

'What about Milou?'

'I buried him.'

Under the bare outdoor light bulb Jem could see her mother's cheek was the colour of blackberries and raspberries in the same bowl.

'Come in, will you? There's ice cream.'

'You killed him.'

'His back was broken.'

'You *killed* him.'

'I'm sorry.'

'You always say that.' Jem looked at her shoes and watched tears fall on them, splot, splot, splot. 'It doesn't mean anything.'

It was not a blow to the head but her mother flinched. 'Jem . . .'

But Jem pushed past her and went up the stairs to bed.

In the night she woke. Lying on her back she blinked at the dark room. Something had disturbed her, but the house was silent. For a minute she lay still – her eyes were closing again – and then the door opened a crack and she heard her mother's whisper:

'Jem?'

'Mum?'

'Get up. Don't make a noise.'

Holding her mother's hand she crept downstairs and out of the open front door. Her mother pushed her into the back seat of the car.

'Stay here. Don't move. Keep quiet.'

Romy went back inside. Jem watched through the car window. None of the lights were on and her mother seemed to be swallowed by the house as soon as she stepped over the threshold into the blackness.

Minutes passed. Jem's breath steamed up the window. She rubbed the glass to clear a circle with her pyjama sleeve. Her breathing and her heart seemed very loud, even though she was trying to make them quiet. Then her mother came out of the house carrying two suitcases. She did not pause to shut the door but tiptoed, hurrying, towards the car.

Then Jem realised: *We're leaving.* It was a shock, but not a horrible one. Her first thought was of Milou and then she remembered he was dead. What about Mimi? Perhaps her mother would fetch her now, from the hutch next to Milou's. She could travel on Jem's knee.

As she was wondering about all this a light was switched on in the house, upstairs above Romy's head. Jem froze. Romy froze. Inside her head Jem shouted, 'Mum! Hurry!' but she did not move or make a noise – she could not. She could not even breathe. She thought, *He'll kill us.* Her heart knocked in her chest.

Now the bulb outside the kitchen door was flicked on and the scene was lit by a ghoulish, metallic light: headlight white. Romy was facing Jem. She knew she was caught.

Jem watched her determined face collapse like a falling building.

When Frank appeared in the kitchen doorway his broad silhouette seemed to fill the whole space and more, as if the whole universe was suddenly Frank. Jem could see moths fluttering in crazed zigzags around his head, driven to distraction by the light. There was a moment while he took in the scene: wife, daughter, car and suitcases. The moment seemed very long.

Then he laughed. 'Where do you think you're going?'

'Frank—'

'I *said*,' he stopped laughing and spoke louder, 'where do you think you're going?'

'Frank—' Romy put down both suitcases and turned to face him.

'*Frank. Frank.*' He mimicked her in a baby voice. '*Frank. Frank.*'

Romy said nothing.

'I tell you what.' Now he moved: he stepped out of the doorway, down the step and strode towards her. 'I'll drive you.'

Romy held her ground but she shrank in front of him. She did not reply.

Jem was confused. She had thought he would try to stop them. Now he was going to drive them? Drive them where?

He strode towards Romy and picked up both suitcases. He leaned right into her face and said loudly, 'Get. In. The. Car.' He had got bigger. He was getting bigger and bigger. The suitcases were tiny little matchboxes in his hands. 'Get in the car,' he said again. 'I'll drive.'

Tell him NO, Jem thought. *Mum? Tell him* NO.

But Romy did not say no. She did not say anything. She shrank back from him and fumbled behind herself for the handle of the passenger door. When she opened the door Frank pushed her in and then slammed the door shut and walked around the car to throw the suitcases into the boot. After that he slammed the boot and lumbered round to the driver's door, pawing at it several times before he managed to wrench it open. In that moment Romy turned and whispered to Jem.

'Put on your seatbelt. Do it now.'

Jem put on her seatbelt. 'Mum,' she hissed. '*Mum*—'

But Romy hissed back, 'Keep quiet. Keep still.'

Frank clambered into the car which sank down on his side as if an elephant had got in. Jem could not think how such a big man could fold himself into such a small space. He had grown – he was both giant and beanstalk – and the car was a toy. He smelt of rotten apples and there seemed to be no room even for air to breathe with him inside. Jem could hear the *click-click-click* as her mother tried to snap her own seatbelt into its casing.

Frank started the car. He turned around and winked at Jem. 'We're going on an adventure.'

She saw his red eyes and felt his hot breath and she could not move a muscle, staring at him with her ears pinned back like Milou's. Then he faced forward again and the car was sliding away down the track, weaving between the trees, heading towards the road.

Her mother said, 'Frank *slow down* . . .'

And Jem remembered Mimi. She turned around in her seat. It was too late to see anything but the swirl of dust behind them, lit to scarlet by the tail lights. It was the last thing she remembered until after the crash.

And now Frank was gone for good.

Out of bed and downstairs Jem made coffee in the kitchen and watched dawn begin to lighten the trees outside the window. From a soft dark they took their shapes slowly as light stole into the sky. In the kitchen her movements stirred the silence; outside it was perfectly quiet and perfectly still.

Wearing her mother's coat she went out of the kitchen door. She watched the sun's first bright fingerprints touch the treetops, the branches and the leaves; at last she felt them on her upturned face, tilted to the sky. She closed her eyes to receive its delicate kiss; she felt its apricot warmth on her cheek. When she opened her eyes she saw the sky so pale and bright it gleamed like mother-of-pearl.

The dirt around her feet grew lighter and whiter. The air between her fingertips was as dry as diamond dust. She held her breath. She listened for earthly sounds – for sounds of life – but heard nothing. Nothing stirred. The silence was complete.

And then a blackbird shuffled its feet in the dry leaves – *tsk-tsk; tsk-tsk* – and the spell was broken: everything came to life.

2

In London one half of the Griffin family was still asleep while the other half – Lauren and Walter – had woken early, wished each other a happy Christmas over the coffee pot in the kitchen and then set out in Lauren's car for the Mixed Pond on Hampstead Heath. With them was Lester, Becka's grandfather, whom they had collected from two doors up. Mike came too, balancing on Walter's knee in the front passenger seat so that he could look out of the window and growl at other dogs.

To swim in an unheated pond in the middle of winter was, for those who did not feel it, a curious impulse. For Walter and Lester it no longer presented a challenge – more of a treat.

'Bracing,' said Walter, 'but not unpleasant.'

'Reminds us we're alive,' said Lester.

'You're both mad,' Lauren told them. 'What about pneumonia? What about heart attacks?'

'We've got to die of something,' said Lester from the back.

'We're going to die soon anyway,' said Walter in the front.

'Soon?' Lauren scoffed. 'Don't get your hopes up. You're

61

only seventy-four.' Lester and Walter indulged in competitive morbidity and Lauren liked to crush their hopes. 'Seventy-four's not old,' she continued. 'The oldest person ever was one hundred and twenty-two. You've got forty-eight years to go, Dad.'

'I'd rather kill myself,' Walter said cheerfully.

Lester was eating a Hobnob and coughed out crumbs. 'Ha!'

'*Not* funny,' said Lauren reprovingly. 'And why are you eating the Hobnobs? You haven't been swimming yet.'

'Fuel,' said Lester. 'No breakfast. Kitchen full of women.' He went on, 'I wish people would stop telling me I'm still young. I know what young feels like. This is not it. I feel old because I *am* old.'

'Hear hear,' said Walter. 'Can I have a Hobnob?'

Lester passed one forward, saying, 'I last felt young when I was fifty and still running up escalators.'

'You haven't felt young for thirty years? That's depressing,' said Lauren.

'Depressing? Try being me,' said Walter with his mouth full. 'I only feel alive when I'm up to my neck in freezing pond water.'

'That's it!' Lester leaned forward to thump Walter's shoulder. 'That's why we do it.'

Lester was eighty. He had moved in with Becka and her mother Annie ten years ago after his wife died of cancer, and it was then that he began swimming every day in the Mixed Pond. He was a small, barrel-chested man with frizzy white hair and a thick ginger beard that stuck out forwards from his chin. 'He's the right shape to live to a hundred,' Kathleen always said crossly, implying that

Walter – tall and bony as an old horse – would be dead much sooner and that Lester's continuing presence would be an affront.

At sixty-three Kathleen was not ready to worry about her own death so she worried about Walter's. In fact it was not worry so much as blame: Walter's extra years hung heavy on her mind. They indicated a thoughtlessness on his part. It was stressful and ageing to picture her own life without him in it. She left him in no doubt that if he died before he was ninety she would consider it a selfish act.

Walter had only begun swimming last year when he was forced, by the gathering dust cloud at the centre of his vision, to put his camera down. The end of useful work had been a kind of bereavement. He had despaired. He might as well be dead – there was no point to him now. A handicapped old age could only be meaningless. 'Handicap' was his word of choice: 'My handicap', he would excuse himself, 'forbids me.'

But Lester had knocked on the door one morning and said, 'Come on, old man, you're coming for a swim.' Now Walter, like Lester, did not like to miss a day for any reason – he did not want to go on holiday except by the sea and he had even sneaked out to swim on the morning of Kathleen's birthday.

Jealous by nature, Kathleen was irritated by the swimming and by the friendship. It excluded her, and what's more she wanted to go to Paris for the weekend and not to a cold beach in Devon or Normandy. But 'swimming is a better option than booze or other women,' as Lauren reminded her mother. 'You should be relieved. Those war junkies hate going cold turkey.'

She had privately not ruled out her father's suicide before swimming came along. On the way back from one eye appointment she had broken a grim silence to ask, 'You're not going to top yourself, are you, Dad?' To which Walter replied, 'I haven't decided.' Lauren suspected that these days he hoped swimming would do the job for him. She supposed it did not matter if it killed him as long as it gave him pleasure while he was alive.

She watched him descend the ladder slowly and deliberately like a spider down its web. Once the water came up to his armpits he struck out smoothly across the pond. His swimming style was quite different from Lester's: he submerged himself right up to the nostrils, never made a splash and left behind himself only the V-shaped ripple of a patient crocodile while Lester, like a fox and its brush, preferred to keep his beard out of the water and therefore swam with a high profile, his torso lifting and plunging with each stroke. He puffed air out of his cheeks – 'Phoo! Phoo!' – when he exhaled.

Lauren stood on the landing stage. She wore their towels draped over her shoulders like a boxing coach and folded her arms against the cold. A breath of vapour lifted from the water. Mike paced up and down, nervous as a ringside medic, and stopped every now and again to sit on his haunches and give Lauren a worried look: *Do something. Stop them.*

'I can't,' Lauren said to him with a shrug. 'I tried.'

3

Jem could not sit in Frank's study because it gave her a funny feeling to put her back to the door, as if someone might come and stand behind her and she would not know, but nor could she settle upstairs because there was something about those rumpled bedclothes on her father's bed that made the room seem not quite unoccupied; not quite vacant. She suspected the duvet of stirring when her back was turned, as if a rat lived underneath it, or something worse.

It was ridiculous: she knew he was dead; she had seen his dead body. What was she afraid of?

She did not feel as if she had a right to be here and she could not, therefore, be bold. Outside it was all right but inside she felt like an intruder – a burglar creeping from room to room without leaving fingerprints.

In the study she stood in front of her father's laptop. She picked up the little photograph he had left beside it. Idly she woke up the screen and clicked on 'history' and then 'show full history' in his browser. The results were arranged by date and time, the most recent listed first:

> – *you're ready to fly!*
> – *your payment*

– your search results
– skyscanner – Google Search
– scott griffin actor – Google Search
– kathleen griffin actor – Google Search
– BBC – Radio 4

K for Kathleen. It was something. She selected the page called 'kathleen griffin actor'. Sixty-three years old. A list of parts in films, television and theatre. Spouse: Walter Griffin, photographer. Two children named Scott and Lauren. Most recent role in *Hamlet* at The Playhouse with her son Scott.

Jem clicked on 'scott griffin actor'. Aged twenty-four. This play and that television show. Showed promise in a series on BBC2 called *Dark Art*. 'A standout performance from a new talent.' Next, *Hamlet* with his mother. A list of four-star reviews and a photograph.

A photograph.

When she saw it Jem paused. She looked at it carefully for a minute and then she clicked on 'images' at the top of the page. She looked at these even more closely. She picked up the little picture of Frank and held it next to the screen. She compared.

Something happened inside her: a door blew open and showed her a room she did not know existed. She got up, walked around, put her hands on her head, came back to the stool, sat down. She could not believe her eyes. Not yet.

Her hands were shaking as she typed 'kathleen griffin scott griffin' into Google. Here was a link to the BBC: a performance had been live-streamed on Radio 4, two nights ago.

Frank had been listening. She could see his digital footprints in front of her: he had sat here and listened to *Hamlet*. He had looked up Kathleen and Scott Griffin. He had telephoned K for Kathleen in London. He had bought himself an air ticket. Why? What for?

Son.

The word landed in her head like the first raindrop.

She shut the laptop, folded her arms and stared out of the window. She swivelled slightly on the stool from left to right and back again. She did not ask herself whether or not it was true, but only what to do next.

Brother.

4

Back at the house Kathleen had fumbled foggily downstairs to the kitchen in her dressing gown. She felt very tired. *Hamlet* had exhausted her and now it was over she allowed herself to feel exhausted.

While the kettle gasped and coughed into life beside her she stared out of the window and waited for the fog to lift. Was it booze-fog or old lady-fog? Neither was good but the first at least would be temporary. The two were linked: how old she felt in the morning depended directly on how much she had drunk the night before. This morning she felt every day of sixty-three. Yesterday, after the *Hamlet* party, she had felt a hundred all day.

Looking out of the window she noticed that the garden was oddly alive for a winter's morning. Lauren, who was the only one to notice they were empty, had filled all the bird feeders and now a shower of small birds flitted and twittered in argument and consternation beyond the glass.

The kettle finished boiling and Kathleen made a pot of strong tea. Just as she turned to the fridge for milk the telephone rang and made her jump. When she heard the voice at the other end she remembered that other call, last night.

'Hello?'

'Is this Kathleen?'

'Who is this?' Kathleen twisted the telephone cord in her free hand.

'My name is Jocelyn Martell.' This morning the voice was cool and calm. 'My father was Frank Martell. Do you know the name?'

Kathleen was neither cool nor calm. She said desperately, 'Stop calling this number.'

'Frank died yesterday. Yours is the last number he called. Did you speak to him?'

'Go away.' Kathleen hissed into the receiver. 'It's Christmas Day. You can't just—'

'Mum?'

Kathleen spun round. Sonny was standing behind her in his pyjamas.

'Just hang up,' he said. 'Cold callers? On Christmas Day? Just hang up.' He took the telephone out of her hand and placed it back in its cradle, ending the call. 'There's no point getting cross. It's probably a robot anyway. In fact . . .' He leaned down to the skirting board and pulled the telephone socket out of the wall. 'There. That'll shut them up.'

'Yes. Well done.' Kathleen stared at him stupidly. 'Good idea.' Now that she was empty-handed she did not know where to put herself. She turned back to the teapot and tried to pour a cup but her hands were trembling and she did not want Sonny to see and so she stopped. She was still processing the words 'Frank died yesterday'. At last she thought of something and said brightly, 'Happy Christmas, darling.'

'Same to you, Mum. Thanks for my stocking. I ate the

chocolate money.' Sonny grinned at her and then yawned, stretched and scratched behind his head in one movement like a dog climbing out of its basket. 'I haven't got you a present yet, sorry. No time to shop. Where's Dad? Where's Larry?'

'He's . . . They're . . .' Kathleen frowned. She had lost track of everything. Where *was* Walter? Where had Lauren gone? She must try to behave normally. To give herself away now would be absolutely . . . 'Oh yes,' she remembered, 'your father is swimming. Lauren took him and Lester and the dog.'

'Swimming today? In the pond?' Sonny looked out of the window. 'Foolish.'

'Silly old men. Just showing off to Lauren.' Kathleen squeezed the back of a chair with both hands as if she were wringing a dishcloth. She had not quite re-mastered the power of speech. 'Not bored of it like we are.' She had a feeling that if she let go of the chair she would float off into space like an untethered balloon. What was happening? *Frank. Dead.*

'You all right, Mum?'

'Fine. Tired. Sleepy. Going to go and run a bath.' She smiled blindly at him. 'Will you be all right having breakfast on your own?'

'I'll survive.' Sonny opened the door of the fridge and stared into its lit interior as if he had opened the Ark of the Covenant. It was a position he took up at least a dozen times a day. He never actually bought any food and put it in the fridge but he often checked inside to see whether passing fairies had restocked it.

Upstairs Kathleen shut herself in the bathroom. She

70

looked at her expression in the mirror, expecting the news *Frank is dead* to show on her face. *Frank died yesterday.* She mouthed the words at herself as if she were learning lines. She wanted to make a noise – she picked up a towel and pressed it against her mouth so that she could gasp into it.

She had never doubted that Frank would die before her and she had therefore often wondered what she would feel when this moment came. Now she knew the answer: relief. A relief so potent it almost disabled her. She put her hands on either side of the basin and leaned over the white porcelain, steadying herself.

Then she straightened up. *Yours is the last number he called.* She had known as soon as Walter said 'creep' that it must have been Frank. He might be dead but a daughter was calling her. What next?

Downstairs, the door opened and slammed. Voices spoke in the hall, Mike barked hello to Sonny and Lauren said, 'Go and have a bath before you freeze to death.' She heard Walter's careful tread on the stairs as he came up. Last week he had fallen and bumped his forehead, an accident more upsetting than it was painful, and now he travelled at half speed.

She looked briefly again at her face in the mirror. She must not give herself away. Everything was just as it had been. Nothing could be different.

Walter's bath: she turned on the bath taps and adjusted them to achieve the perfect degree of hotness.

5

Having been cut off Jem tried the number again. This time there was no answer and every time after that, nothing.

She gave up but she could not settle. *Brother.* She wandered from room to room, standing for a few minutes in one place and then another. She could not stay – not now. She locked the house and drove away.

After her mother's death, spoken of as 'the accident', Marian Frost became Jem's guardian.

Marian had been her mother's nanny. 'Much better than my actual parents,' Romy had told Jem. Romy had written in her will that Marian should look after Jem if anything happened, and 'anything' did happen: Romy died and Frank went to prison. So Marian drove to France from London in her Renault Clio, collected Jem and took her home. They lived together until Jem was eighteen.

Marian was not quite a stranger because of all the stories Jem had heard about her, but she still seemed strange. She was not at all like Romy, or indeed any mother that Jem had previously encountered. While Jem could be relieved that at least *someone* knew what to do with her, she could not quite be glad it was Marian.

For one thing, Marian was old. 'Sixty-odd' seemed very old to Jem – Romy had been only thirty. Marian was also quite *prickly*. Even though she softened her hands with special cream and stashed a Kleenex up her sleeve she was not cuddly. She called Jem 'Missy' in a reproving voice and when they held hands to cross the road Jem was jerked about like a mackerel on a line. Marian behaved as if looking after children had been a duty settled on her by a humourless God, not something she had wanted to do for her own sake or the child's.

By the time of 'the accident' Marian had retired from being a nanny. She lived on the eighth floor of a block of flats beside a canal and close to the Harrow Road, a flat bought for her by a grateful Saudi Arabian couple whose many children she had looked after once Romy had grown out of her. Marian did not think it was odd to have been given a whole flat in west London for nothing. It was God's will – and on top of that the family was very rich and she deserved to be rewarded. Acceptance was her duty, and that meant acceptance of the gift.

It also meant acceptance of her new charge: Jem. She said, 'I never thought I'd be taking on another little one at my age,' but she never complained.

Jem did not feel like a 'little one' but she did not argue because Marian seemed to know everything. This was an obvious and immediate contrast to Romy, who had often said 'I haven't the faintest idea, my darling. What do you think?' but Jem was prepared to concede at this point that it was reassuring to be taken under the wing of someone with certainty and direction. She wanted 'yes' or 'no' but not 'I don't know'. Everything Jem had been sure of up until now had vanished and would never come back but Marian, relentless and unheeding as a waterfall, brought curious comfort.

Frank was not mentioned often and never by name. He became 'that dreadful man' and Marian sounded when she said it as if she had put something disgusting in her mouth by mistake. Meanwhile, Jem did not know how to say 'Dad' without the word creating a shocked silence after it like a dropped saucepan lid, so she stopped saying 'Dad' altogether.

She remembered everything about their journey to London, right down to the smell of chips on the ferry. Marian's car was small and noisy. Jem rode in the front and sat on the wrong side because Marian's car was English. An English car in France meant that Jem was on the right side for seeing traffic coming towards them when Marian wanted to overtake:

'Anything coming?'

'Yes.'

'Near or far?'

'Far.'

'Miles away or quite near?'

'Miles away. Getting nearer. Quite near.'

This was the moment when Marian would usually pull out.

Into the boot they had stuffed three cardboard boxes: one of Jem's clothes, another of her books and a third containing Mimi the rabbit. Mimi had lettuce and water for the journey and holes punched into the top of the box for air.

'She had better keep quiet in there,' Marian said, 'or else she'll be arrested at the border and put into quarantine.'

74

Whatever 'quarantine' was it sounded something to avoid. Jem whispered instructions to Mimi in French before she shut the box. Only Gaston the knitted poodle, travelling on her knee, would be visible to the customs officers.

Marian did not speak any French at all which meant that Jem did all the speaking for both of them as long as they were in France. She also passed the money to the person in the booth when they needed to pay on the autoroute because she was sitting on the right side of the car for that. It was nice to feel useful.

'Never' became the word that rang in her head like a funeral bell. She would never see her mother again. She could not believe it. It was not that she didn't understand it – her mother was dead, like Milou and the chickens, and she knew what that meant – it was just that she didn't believe it. How could 'never' be attached to something essential? It was like saying 'never' to breathing or food.

In the middle of the journey they stopped in Beaune for the night. They ate supper in a brasserie and stayed in a hotel. Gaston came along but Mimi stayed in the car.

In their shared room Jem discovered that Marian knelt beside the bed to pray before she got in. Jem had seen praying in pictures and films but not in real life. It felt not quite right to watch, just as it had felt not quite right to watch Marian getting undressed, putting on her nightie and cleaning her teeth, but at the same time it was hard to concentrate on her book – even though it was *The Island of Adventure* and one of her favourites.

After a minute Marian opened one eye and caught Jem staring over the top of her book. 'Why don't you pray too?'

Jem did not know what to say. She wriggled her toes under the sheet.

'You don't have to,' Marian said, 'but it will help.'

Jem put her book face down on top of the duvet. 'Help what?'

'Help with the sad feeling.'

This sounded good. 'What would I say?'

'You could ask God to look after your mother in heaven, and you could thank Him for your life.'

Jem was not at all sure about God and even less sure that she wanted to consign her mother to heaven. That sounded a lot like goodbye. The idea that the person who was still so present and alive in her mind had gone somewhere as indistinct as heaven was shocking. It was worse than being told she had been fired out of a rocket into outer space. Also, if God existed and He was in charge – reluctantly Jem awarded Him a capital H – then He was the one who had taken her mother away and the reason why she was here in a hotel room with Marian and not in her own bed at home. How could she thank Him for that?

She did not say any of this because she feared it would be rude – as rude as insulting Marian herself – but Marian seemed to guess at her thoughts.

'Don't worry about God,' she said. 'Let God worry about you. You'll come to Him when you're ready.'

When Jem woke up in the night she did not know where she was. This was bad enough, but when she remembered it was worse. Much worse. Everything that had happened crashed around her ears as if the hotel were collapsing in an earthquake. She felt panicked. *Where is Mum?* Dead – but she must be somewhere. She could not be nowhere. Not knowing where was frightening and awful. Jem wanted to sick up the contents of her head to get the dreadful feeling out. Now she had forgotten to breathe and thought she might faint. Perhaps she would die. A noise like the sea filled her ears. Then she remembered praying. *Dear God —* (The blood thundered in her ears and her heart crashed in her chest.) *— please look after Mum. Please look after me.* After a second or two the terror subsided and she could hear Marian's gentle breathing, up and down, regular and calm, from under the covers in the next-door bed. She listened to this until she fell asleep.

6

It was traditional for the Griffins to eat lunch on Christmas Day at Hala, a Lebanese restaurant on Edgware Road. They were well known there – so well known that Kathleen's signed photograph hung on the wall, alongside other actors she described as 'perverts and dinosaurs'. It was traditional also for Lester, Annie and Becka to join them and this year Becka's half-brother Rex was visiting from Paris.

Lauren drove to the restaurant with Walter next to her and Kathleen behind with Sonny. Because of his eyesight Walter was not allowed to drive any more. Kathleen was already too drunk to drive and Sonny had not yet passed his driving test – or rather, had not made any attempt to learn to drive. He had been given money for lessons and had spent it on other things.

'Like what?' Lauren was irritated by her brother's laissez-faire attitude to pretty much everything.

'More important things,' Sonny shrugged.

'Are you going to be one of those selfish fuckers who never learns to drive?' Lauren eyeballed him with a savage glare in the rear-view mirror.

'Maybe.' Sonny had learned long ago not to rise to the

bait. 'As long as I can get one of you chumps to drive me around, why should I?'

When Lauren tried to wind Sonny up it usually put her into a rage. Now she flipped her right indicator on and swung furiously past an orange light onto Adelaide Road.

'Why are you going to Swiss Cottage? It'd be quicker by the park,' said Sonny.

'When you learn to drive,' Lauren said, changing crossly up a gear, 'you can choose the route.'

'*Excusez-moi.*' Sonny raised his palms and his eyebrows. '*Gardez vos culottes.*'

'My pants are fine, thank you very much—'

'Lauren! Slow down.' Kathleen was rootling in her handbag for a mascara wand. 'I've got to do something about my face.'

'Can't you do it when we get there? You've had all morning to doll-up.'

'I was *busy* this morning.'

'Busy getting drunk?'

'What's it to you if I have a drink on Christmas morning?' Kathleen peered into a tiny mirror and started prodding at her eyelashes as they descended a straight half-mile of Finchley Road. When she had finished and was screwing the lid back on she said, 'I have to look my best for Mahmoud.'

'Why, Mum? *Why* do you have to look your best for Mahmoud? Are you hoping he'll ask you out on a date?'

In the back, Sonny got the giggles.

'Because if I don't' – Kathleen licked the end of her eye pencil – 'he'll take my picture off the wall and replace me with some young bit of stuff.'

'Don't say "bit of stuff" like that, Mum, it's horrible and sexist.'

'How can I be sexist? I'm a woman.'

'Would you call Sonny a "bit of stuff"?'

'Oh, Lauren, do stop lecturing me.' Kathleen snapped the lipstick away. 'Walter? Tell her to stop lecturing me.'

But Walter was staring out of the window. He heard but did not listen to his family squabble around him, so used to the sound that he could have fallen asleep to it and sometimes had. It was like the noise made by birds over the bird table: vehement yet harmless.

Recently, Walter had begun to feel invisible. His family used to stop bickering when he walked into the room, but now they behaved as if he did not exist. Some unspeakable and inverted logic dictated that the less he could see, the less he would be seen. He knew the quickest way to Edgware Road, but no one thought to ask him. The map of London was stamped on his memory as it was on their own – more so: he was oldest and had lived here longest – but he was just a passenger.

In the end, he supposed, he would not be able to see them and they would stop seeing him at all. If he did not take part then they would forget he was there, and at that point he might as well not exist.

He felt a sickening claustrophobia when his mind tunnelled deeper into this darkness and so instead he concentrated on Mike, who was sitting on his knee and gazing through the window, not vacant and unseeing like his master but with a fierce, trembling preparedness, taking in every dog, pigeon and human on the pavement, snuffling the glass with his wet nose, shifting his weight from paw to paw and digging his claws into Walter's trousers to keep his balance. Mike did not want to miss anything. *Look! Look!* Nothing escaped his notice. Reassured, Walter closed his eyes.

At the restaurant Annie, Lester and Becka had already arrived with Rex and were sitting down at the table. When Lauren saw Rex she felt her heart give a great heave like a boat on a swell. Four years ago she had gone to Paris for a hen weekend but had forgone the horrors of prescribed events in favour of spending seventy-two hours, all of them perfect, with Rex. Two weeks later Sonny found out from Becka that he was engaged. 'I hate to fuck up your day,' he told Lauren, 'but Rex is getting married. Some Swiss Miss named Clothilde. Pregnant. Been going out for a year.' Pause. 'D'you want me to go to Paris and knock his teeth out?'

There had been a long silence before Lauren replied, 'It was just a weekend. Not important. Nothing to be upset about. Forget it, will you? I don't want anyone finding out.'

The subject was closed and Rex got married, but his poor baby died before it was born.

Today his nose was buried in the menu when Lauren walked in and so she was able to turn away and busy herself with coat, scarf and bag. She wished she had washed her hair. She wished he would not make these random appearances. Why wasn't he in Paris spending Christmas with his wife? It did not seem fair that he should turn up here and ruin her Christmas lunch. He was only a half-brother to Becka – they had not grown up together. They were the accidental products of a shared father, and that did not count as family unless a kidney or a transfusion was called for. It was infuriating and unnecessary. It was rude of him to have come. She could not sit next to him – she had forgotten to put on deodorant and she could feel sweat breaking out under her too-warm polo neck – so she sat between Walter and Lester instead.

'Lucky me,' said Lester, pouring her a huge glass of wine.

Kathleen loved Rex and sat down next to him herself. 'And how's that lucky wife of yours?' she asked. 'Is she looking after you?'

'Not really.' Rex had grown up in California and in his mellow, amused accent nothing ever sounded too serious. 'She's run off to Geneva with some guy she dated at high school. She's having his baby in April.'

'Left you? How dreadful. Are you all right?'

'Fine. It's better this way. I was driving her crazy.'

'I can't believe you could drive anyone crazy,' Kathleen protested.

Looking up, Rex caught Lauren staring. 'You'd be surprised.'

Lauren swivelled her eyes from his face to the wall and took a big gulp of wine.

'I'm going to have a fag,' she stuttered to no one in particular. 'Order for me will you, Dad? The same as you.'

'I'll come too.' Rex got up and followed her.

Outside he lit her cigarette and then his own.

'I'm sorry about your wife,' Lauren said. It was easier here on the pavement where she did not have to look at him. 'Running off like that.'

'I'm not.' He puffed. 'Now I can take you out to dinner. Four years too late.'

Lauren glanced at him in surprise. Was he joking?

'Well? You free tomorrow?'

'What? Tomorrow?' She puffed on her fag and stared very hard at splots of chewing gum dried on the concrete slabs beneath her feet. 'Yes. Yes, I am.' When she looked up Rex was smiling at her.

'The upside of divorce,' he said.

Lauren felt as if someone had let off a firework over her head and she had been lit from above by a showering silver crown. She rubbed her nose to hide her illuminated face.

'Tomorrow would be fine.'

Back at the table Kathleen felt deflated. One moment she had been having a nice time with Rex and now she was staring at an empty seat. Sonny was talking to Becka and Walter to Annie, which left only Lester, who made her nervous. She knew he did not like her. She had tried every trick in the book but he, like Mike, remained uncharmed. She suspected he thought she was too silly for words.

Confirmation of this suspicion arrived when Lester said, 'I listened to *Hamlet* on the radio a couple of nights ago, Kathleen. I must tell you I was surprised.'

Must you? Really? 'Surprised how?'

'The most sympathetic Gertrude I've encountered. Perhaps something to do with Sonny playing Hamlet?'

Kathleen smiled a tight smile. 'I suppose you thought I'd be too stupid for Shakespeare.'

'No one is too stupid for Shakespeare. That's his genius,' Lester said crisply. It was a long way short of a compliment. Lester had been a professor of English Literature at University College London before he retired. 'I was surprised because it's the first Shakespeare you've done in the ten years I've known you – I thought you were wedded to television.'

'I'm wedded to the money,' said Kathleen. She lowered her voice. 'The truth is that I did *Hamlet* for Sonny. The theatre wanted him because they'd got me; they used my name to sell tickets. I'm a "veteran star", you see, and he's a "new face".' She waited to be told that she was not a veteran but Lester said nothing. How typical. 'What did you think of Sonny?' Fishing for compliments on Sonny's behalf was a better bet.

'Very natural.' Lester looked over at Sonny and Becka whose heads were almost touching as they leaned together over his telephone, looking at photographs. 'Just as he always is.'

Kathleen frowned. 'To make Hamlet sound natural is extremely difficult,' she said sharply. 'Sonny succeeded because of his talent—'

'And his talent is natural: it comes naturally to him. Acting isn't playing the violin or speaking Chinese – it's not a skill that takes ten thousand hours of practice. Shakespeare did the hard work; acting is simply the talent to convince.' Ignoring Kathleen's affronted expression he continued, 'And how is Mrs Peabody? Still going strong?'

For the last five years Kathleen had been playing the female lead in a hugely successful television drama that ran for an hour every Sunday night in the eight-week run-up to Christmas. Mrs Peabody, the eponymous heroine, was something like a Victorian female version of Robin Hood and presided over a gang of rebellious girls – her own Merry Women in place of his Merry Men. It was a smash hit:

saucy, entertaining and (for everyone but Lester) unmiss-able. The final episode of the series was always screened on Christmas Day.

'I've never watched an episode,' Lester was saying, 'but Annie and Becka enjoy it.'

'Six and a half million viewers last Christmas,' boasted Kathleen. She refused to be crushed by an intellectual snob with an ungovernable beard. 'If only *Hamlet* had the same pulling power.'

After lunch the Griffins stopped on the way home to give Mike a walk on the Heath. It grew colder and darker as each moment passed and there was an empty, finished feel-ing to the outdoors as if the birds had already settled on their roosts and the day was done.

Kathleen tucked her arm through Sonny's and Lauren walked beside Walter, making sure he didn't stumble in the gloom. Mike trotted in front of them, vanishing into the dusk between one lamp post and the next. He sniffed every-thing with the serious attention of a gardener amidst his roses. He was at his most self-important on the Heath.

Kathleen was still cross with Lester. 'He's always so snooty with me. Anyone would think he bloody wrote *Hamlet*.'

'Why do you care? You're a national treasure and he's a retired prof,' said Sonny.

'I pay *all* the bills and I work a damn sight harder than he ever did—'

'Yes, Mum.' Sonny patted her arm. 'You're marvellous.'

'It's not as if either Annie or Becka is such a towering intellectual.'

'Oi,' Sonny nudged her with his elbow, 'leave Becka out of it.'

'Do you like her? Really? *Really?*'

'She's kind and funny. She's my friend. Be nice.'

'Hm.' Kathleen was not convinced. 'What sort of friend?'

'I like Becka,' Lauren piped up. 'I like her and she likes you. Don't mess her around will you, Sonny?'

'I don't fancy her.' It was an automatic response and then Sonny remembered last night, after the pub. 'I mean I don't think I do.' He frowned. 'Do I?'

Lauren was treasuring her dinner date and Rex's smile like two presents she had not yet opened. She could not help mentioning his name.

'Nice to see Rex,' she said. 'Sad about his marriage.'

Sonny replied, '*Very* sad,' pointedly and with sarcasm.

'I knew they'd get divorced,' Kathleen said happily. 'No baby to keep them together, you see. They should never have got married.' As she spoke Kathleen remembered that Frank was dead. She felt giddy with relief all over again.

'I don't know why anyone gets married these days,' said Lauren. 'Completely pointless.'

'Aren't you glad we're married?' Kathleen took Walter's arm and squeezed it. 'Your old mum and dad?'

'Of course I am, but that's different. In those days it mattered.'

'"In those days"?' Walter interrupted indignantly. 'It wasn't that long ago.'

'Thirty-three years,' Kathleen said.

'Good Lord! That many?'

'Oh, *Walter* you know it is!' Kathleen pinched him. 'Don't be a toad.'

'But I love toads.' Walter bent to give her a kiss.

Sonny was not too old to be disgusted by one parent kissing the other.

'*God*. Must you?'

And thus – bickering, loving, laughing and teasing – the four made their way home.

7

Tonight, for the second time in her life, Jem broke her journey at Beaune. In her rush to leave Frank's house she had forgotten that it was Christmas. The motorway was empty and the town was deserted. Shops, cafes and restaurants were all shut. Not a soul walked the streets.

Jem drove slowly and aimlessly about within the town walls, looking for signs of life. She realised she had been hoping to find the same hotel – the one she had stayed in with Marian – but now that she was here it seemed impossible. Today she would be lucky to find anywhere to take her.

In the corner of a deserted square she spotted a lighted doorway. Over it a sign read 'Hôtel des Voyageurs' in curly, olde worlde calligraphy. She turned the car round and drove past the hotel again, peering in. Then she parked and turned off the ignition. For a moment she sat still, listening to the tick and sigh of the engine and watching through the windscreen a newspaper shaken to pieces and blown into the air by a scurrying wind.

For four hours on the road she had been remembering; it had made her forget she was alive. She might herself be a ghost: no one knew where she was. She could stay here for ever and no one would know.

She blinked and shook herself awake. Then she got her telephone out of her handbag, looked up the website of the Hôtel des Voyageurs in Beaune and booked herself a room using Frank's credit card. When she saw '*réservation confirmée*' she put her telephone back in her handbag.

Getting out of the car she discovered that it was cold enough to see her breath: proof of life. She locked the car and crossed the square to the hotel. Glass doors revealed a lobby painted orange and a shiny ficus plant as tall as she was. Low tables were spread with leaflets and magazines. It looked anonymous and characterless – it was perfect. She pushed open the door and went in.

The lobby was deserted but for a teenage boy who sat behind the desk at reception. He was watching something intently on his telephone and at the same time tracing absent-mindedly over the spots on his chin with his finger-tips as if he were reading Braille. When he heard Jem he looked up, dropped the telephone and stuttered, '*Bon soir.*' He blushed crimson with an unexplained shame.

Jem did not want to begin a conversation with anyone and so she spoke in English. 'Do you speak English? I've a reservation. The name is Martell.' She waited while he typed her name into the computer.

'*Oui, c'est ici.* It is here.' Having recovered his compos-ure the boy asked for her passport, copied down the details and handed her a key. 'Floor number four. Room number forty-two. *L'acenseur* – the lift – *est au coin.*' He gestured at the corner of the lobby.

'Thank you.'

It was oddly satisfying to get away with using Frank's credit card. Jem wondered how long it would be before someone cancelled it. But who? If she were the person responsible for registering Frank's death then why couldn't she keep it to herself and take from him what she could? It would be the sort of thing she read about in *Metro* on the Tube: 'Thieving Daughter Robs Dead Dad'.

Room 42 was extraordinarily hot and just as violent an orange as the lobby. It smelled of very old, very full ashtrays. Jem opened both parts of the window and stood looking out. This was the attic floor and from here she could admire the black silhouettes of steep rooftops, stacked like a deck of cards against the indigo sky.

Leaving the windows open she turned off both radiators. She decided to go out and get something to eat while the room aired. Downstairs the spotty teenager had been relieved at his post by a middle-aged woman who took Jem's room key from her.

'I hope my son was helpful.' She spoke excellent English. 'Did he explain about breakfast? And WiFi?'

Jem smiled blandly. 'Yes, thank you.' She backed away and escaped.

Outside in the square the spotty boy was fastening a motorcycle helmet under his chin, breath puffing into the cold air. Next to him a girl waited on a scooter, a long plait hanging down her back from beneath her helmet. Once the boy had climbed on and put his arms around her waist she revved the engine, clicked into gear and they buzzed away across the square. Jem watched the scooter's little red light zigzag out of sight.

She buttoned her mother's coat and set off, wandering from street to street around the town. Her boots clicked on the pavement. She saw no one; nothing was open; no lights were on and nobody was around. Once or twice a car passed her and its occupants turned their faces to examine her through the windows as if she were an unfortunate curiosity, wandering the streets alone when everyone else had somewhere to go.

She did see one man, middle-aged and smart in a long overcoat, who was leading a small and somehow unlikely looking dog slowly along the pavement. The dog was wearing a festive red collar and it appeared as reluctant as anyone might who had been dragged away from a cosy basket to go for a walk they did not need. The man was not paying the dog any attention; he was engrossed in a telephone call and smoking a cigar. It was plain that he was enjoying two favourite vices: smoking and telephoning his mistress.

In Somerset, at an address Jem had committed to memory but never visited, her married boyfriend, who was also her boss, was spending Christmas with his wife and their three young children. *Mr and Mrs Antony Peck, Bramble Cottage, Whetstone, Exmoor.* It was like an address from a children's storybook.

Jem knew everything about the Pecks' family Christmas. She knew that Antony's in-laws would arrive the day before Christmas Eve and leave the day after Boxing Day. ('Too long,' said Antony glumly.) She knew that there was a holly tree in the garden whose berried branches had been pruned for indoor decorations. She knew that empty stockings would be laid over the children's beds and replaced by their father with full ones. She knew that the family's two dogs, Ferris and Noodle, would be given their own miniature stockings filled with Bonios and chews. She knew that the eldest child, Robert Jonah Antony Peck, had already guessed the truth about Father Christmas while the youngest, Amelia Frances Peck, was too young to understand. Last but not least she knew that Mrs Peck would cook all of Christmas lunch without complaint before opening her Christmas present – gold and garnet earrings Jem had admired in their box – from her husband.

Jem did not know these things because she saw Antony at work every day, but because she lay next to him in bed while he told her about his life at home with his family. She did not forget a single detail. She thrived on the information – she lived for it. She did not like to hear too much about Mrs Peck (who was Caroline to her friends but Moomy to her family), but details of the home, the children, the dogs, the garden and the routine of family life were intoxicating and addictive. They made her sick but she wanted more. As she listened she conjured up images in her mind so detailed she might have been watching a film; she felt as if she were enjoying a delicious, unending dream which she could enter and exit at will. It all sounded so perfect; it was just what family life was supposed to be like; it was so totally, blissfully removed from herself and her experience. She knew everything and yet she was not present; not responsible; not committed. She was the family ghost.

If Jem was Antony's mistress, then what was he to her? She did not know. She did not like to think about it. He was not her partner, not her boyfriend, not her friend. She could be called his mistress but she did not want him for a master. Perhaps he already was: she came when he called, like a dog to the whistle.

When Christmas was over Antony would leave Bramble

Cottage and return to London for his usual midweek stay, kissing his adorable family goodbye until the weekend.

Children, parents, grandparents, aunts, uncles, nephews, nieces. Jem had none of these. 'All dead,' she told Antony when he asked. It was the answer he wanted – he had enough family to last him a lifetime, he said, which she supposed meant the right amount.

She worked in the same building as Antony every day but he did not see her there because she was the lowliest person in the office while he was the boss. This was literally true: she worked in the basement and his office was two floors up. She was the one sent out to buy sandwiches for meetings he was taking in the boardroom. The 'relationship', although Jem could not have brought herself to dignify it with the word, was all the more reassuring for being a cliché. It had even begun at the office Christmas party last year, which must be the ultimate in *Marie Claire* don't-dos.

Once a week Antony would come over to her flat and bring a bottle of wine, which he would then drink. Jem did not drink alcohol so he always drank the whole bottle. They did not have anything in common except work, and their experiences of work were too dissimilar to be a topic for discussion. Antony wanted to know what people in the basement were saying about him.

'Nothing.'

'Nothing?'

'Nothing.'

Sometimes she would make something up, to make him feel better, but she did not want to talk about the office because she wanted to hear about Bramble Cottage, the dogs, the naughty pony and all the little Pecks.

She had imagined that an affair with a married man would be exciting but in fact it was quite boring. Antony did not like to go out in case he was spotted by someone he knew, so their evenings were spent indoors. They would chat and he would drink and then they would have sex. It was more of an appointment than a date. Idly she sometimes thought she should be paid for her time.

Moomy had only one fault, it seemed: she did not want to have sex with her husband. Not since Amelia was born, and not much before that. Antony did not quite go as far as to say that the affair was therefore his wife's own fault but the implication was there. It sounded to Jem, although she kept this thought to herself, as if of the three of them Moomy had the best deal: a perfect home, children she adored, no requirement to work and little interference from a husband who had served his purpose. It made Jem wonder how different humans were from rabbits after all.

Wandering around Beaune in the freezing cold on Christmas Day was not a suitable moment for these reflections. There was never a suitable moment for these reflections – Jem did not like to think about Antony. If she were always to be self-possessed – intact like an egg in its shell – she could not risk any cracks.

Spotting a yellow light from a cafe window on the other side of the road she crossed to squint through the glass. Behind a lace curtain she could see a long, narrow room containing eight or ten round tables and a bar at the other end. Only one table was occupied: two men in their sixties sat watching television, one of them smoking and the other not, and between them sat a baby in a high chair, also watching television and holding an orange plastic spoon in his fist. The television hung from the ceiling in a bracket, like the ones showing train times at a railway station, and today was showing not football or rugby but *Mary Poppins* dubbed into French.

Jem lifted the latch and pushed open the door.

'*Bon soir.*'

The two men turned around in surprise. '*Bon soir,*' they both said together.

The baby swivelled around in his high chair to give her, like the others, an appraising look. Then he stuck his spoon in his mouth and sucked it before turning back to the screen to see what Mademoiselle Poppins was saying to Monsieur Banks.

The smoker asked in French, 'You want something?'

It was a useful moment to speak French and so Jem did. 'Something to eat. Is that possible?'

'We're closed, but—'

The second man shouted towards the back of the room, 'Marie?'

In response came a distant shriek. 'What is it?'

'There's a mademoiselle here wants something to eat.'

Sounding astonished Marie shouted back, 'Now? It's impossible! Tell her . . .' There was a crash of dropped saucepans. 'My God! Tell her to wait. I'm coming.'

The second man turned to Jem. 'The cafe is closed, but . . . ?' He turned his palms up and the corners of his mouth down as if anything was possible in this crazy world.

From a room behind the bar came Marie, swishing through the coloured ribbons of a plastic curtain and wiping her hands on her apron.

'*Qu'est-ce qui se passe?*'

'This young lady wants something to eat.'

'Now? Today? You know it's Christmas?'

'Yes. I've driven from Avignon. I haven't eaten. Please, if it's possible—'

'Well.' Marie pursed her lips and raised her eyes to the ceiling. 'An omelette?'

'Thank you – you're very kind.'

'Hm.' Marie sounded as if she knew this to be true but life would be simpler if it were not. 'Sit down.' She turned on her heel and disappeared back through the ribbons into the kitchen.

Jem sat at the next table. She watched the film in silence with her three companions and the baby swivelled occasionally in his seat to eye her with a round, brown gaze. After a few minutes the ribbon curtain shivered again and Marie produced a perfectly cooked omelette and a heap of tiny fried potatoes.

'Thank you,' Jem said. 'And thank you for letting me—'

'It's nothing. A glass of wine? A cognac?'

'A Coke?'

'Certainly. Papa? A Coke for Mademoiselle.'

The smoker got to his feet and fumbled behind the bar for a bottle of Coke and a glass. Marie flopped down into an empty seat, poured herself a glass of wine and lit a cigarette. The baby thumped his spoon on the plastic table of his high chair and gurgled at his mother. Marie smoothed his fringe away from his eyes with her thumb.

'*Mon poulet*,' she murmured.

'*Joyeux Noël*.' Jem saluted them with her Coke glass and then she ate up her omelette.

They watched the film in silence, all the way to the end. When it was over, Marie would not take Jem's money. Jem did not know what to do, so she stood awkwardly saying thank you until she was shown out of the door by Marie's father.

'It's nothing.' He waved a hand. 'Goodnight.'

Walking back to her hotel, Jem realised that they had taken pity on her. She must seem a pitiable figure: no father, no baby, no old friend and no cheerful cafe in which to watch television at Christmas. No home and nowhere to go. She wanted to turn back and tell them, *I have a brother. Tomorrow I'm going to meet him.*

IV

On Boxing Day in the late afternoon Kathleen said to Sonny, 'Will you jump up and shut the shutters? I would but I'm—'

'Too lazy?'

They were sitting on the sofa watching *Raiders of the Lost Ark*. Walter dozed in his armchair. Mike slept on the floor. Lauren had retreated to her flat for an hour or two of peace and quiet. Kathleen and Sonny had eaten most of an extra-large Toblerone that Lauren had given Walter for Christmas. Both were now sunk into a calorific stupor.

'What did your last slave die of, Mum?'

'Disobedience.' Kathleen poked her son in the ribs with the Toblerone box. 'Go on. It's depressing looking out at the dark.'

'Yes, milady,' said Sonny. It was what the housemaid said to Mrs Peabody in Kathleen's television programme and Sonny liked to imitate her obedient and grateful tone: 'I ain't never had no educayshun, milady. You've done everyfing for me, milady, taking pity on a poor girl wot had nuffing.'

He levered himself off the sofa, went over to the bow window and began to unfold the shutters. He liked the

99

ingenious way their many straight slats, hinged together, covered the curved glass. As a child he had always volunteered for this chore and invariably pinched his fingers.

Tonight, peering out of the window at the street, he said with mild surprise, 'There's a woman standing outside our house. She's looking right at me.'

Kathleen dragged herself more upright on the sofa. 'What woman?'

'I don't know,' said Sonny. 'About my age. Maybe one of your nutty fans. Bloody hell' – he backed out of view – 'she's coming up the steps.'

Kathleen said, 'I'll deal with this.' She got to her feet.

Walter woke up. 'Whosis? Whassat?'

Before he was answered the doorbell rang and Mike jumped up, growling.

Kathleen turned on him. 'Shut up.' She was suddenly panicked. 'Sonny, sit down. I'll get the door.'

'I can do it, Mum—'

'I said *sit down*.'

Walter and Sonny caught her tone and looked at her but Kathleen ignored them and hurried to the door. She knew who this would be – it was not premonition or suspicion but certain knowledge: she had been tracked down by Frank's daughter who would be standing on the step. The only question was how to get rid of her. She opened the door.

She was completely unprepared for how similar Jem looked to Sonny. She gaped, recovered herself and asked, with a pantomime of innocence:

'Can I help you?'

'Are you Kathleen Griffin?'

'Yes.'

'I'm Jem. I'm Frank's daughter. We spoke on the—'

Abruptly Kathleen stepped outside and pulled the door behind her, closed but not quite shut, so that they were both crammed together on the step.

'What do you want? Why are you here?'

'I—'

'*Yes*, I knew your father. So what? It was *years* ago. You can't just turn up at my house at *Christmas*, when I'm here with my *family*, out of the *blue* . . .'

Kathleen did not want to stop speaking. If she left space for Jem to fill she might have to listen and after that there would be nowhere to hide.

Jem did not wait for a pause, interrupting with, 'This is important.' She spoke quietly. 'I wouldn't be here if it was just . . . what you think.'

'What I think?' Kathleen adopted a tone of self-right-eous indignation. 'And what *do* I think? You'll have to tell me because I have no idea what you're talking about.' Her outrage sounded so genuine she almost believed herself.

'Can we—'

'What? Go somewhere? No. Talk? No. Can I let you in? No. There is nothing to—'

'Frank died of a heart condition,' Jem interrupted again, 'and it's hereditary. He could have passed it on to me – or to any child he might have had.' She left a significant pause. 'That's why I'm here. I had no choice. I had to come.'

Kathleen had been robbed of speech. She shut her mouth. Her mind was racing.

'It killed him out of the blue,' Jem went on. 'His heart split open. The doctor told me that there's a genetic predisposition.'

'*Genetic?*' Kathleen repeated the word in a whisper.

'They want to scan me. My heart. They asked if I had any children. Or siblings.'

Kathleen said nothing.

Jem searched her face carefully and then said, 'Do you understand what I'm telling you?'

'Of course I do.' Kathleen was beaten. She said clearly, as if she had taken the witness stand and decided to confess, 'You're here because of my son. You know about him. Frank is his father.' She had never said these words aloud before. 'You've come to warn me. To warn him.'

And there it was, all laid out like meat in a butcher's shop.

There was a long pause in which they both seemed to be listening out for the echo of what had been said. At last Kathleen broke the silence.

'How long have you known? How long did Frank know?'

'I found out yesterday,' Jem said. 'I think Frank only realised the night before he died. When I got to his house I found pictures of Scott Griffin on his computer. And of you. He'd heard you on the radio—'

'It was *Hamlet*.'

'And he was coming to find you. He died at the airport.'

Kathleen's eyes widened. 'On his way here?'

'I think so, yes. There's no way to be sure.'

Kathleen closed her eyes. 'It doesn't seem fair,' she whispered, more to herself than to Jem. 'Why couldn't he have died not knowing?' Then she opened her eyes and said more vehemently, 'And why couldn't you have stayed away? Why can't you leave us alone?'

'Scott's my brother. I had to warn him.' Jem wondered as she spoke if she meant 'warn' or 'meet'.

102

'He's not your brother and he's not Scott. He's Sonny and he belongs to us.' Kathleen was becoming frantic. 'There's nothing wrong with him. Go away. Leave us alone.'

'There might be. You don't know. Not for sure.' She waited. 'You have to tell him. Then he can decide what to do.'

'You're a liar. You're making this up.'

'You don't want it to be true but it is. He could *die*. You *have* to tell him.'

'No.'

Kathleen shook her head as if Jem were nothing more than an irritating noise she did not want to hear. She had it in mind to escape: to shut the door in the face of this crisis, go back into the sitting room and say it was only someone who had got the wrong house, the wrong family and the wrong idea. That it was someone wanting money or to sell them a mop. There must be a way out – to be caught today after so many years was just not fair; not allowed; not possible. She could not let this woman, this stranger, press the nuclear button on her family.

'No.'

She shook her head again, but this time with decision. It was final: she would leave this situation out on the street like the rubbish, where it belonged. She pushed the door open to go back into the house—

And met Sonny on the threshold, come to see what was up. He was standing right there, facing them both.

'Mum? What's going on?' He looked from Kathleen to Jem. 'Who are you?'

When Jem saw him the words fell out of her mouth like marbles. 'I'm your sister.'

There was a breathless, ringing silence as if the conductor's baton had stopped the orchestra at *fortissimo*.

Sonny smiled and laughed. 'Right.' He looked at his mother. 'Is she nuts?'

Again Jem said, 'I'm your sister.' She could not take her eyes off him. 'Can't you see it?'

'No.'

Kathleen intervened, trying to push Sonny back into the house. 'Stop it.'

'What the fuck?' Sonny was looking at Jem. 'You're crazy, right? Deluded.' He tapped his temple with a forefinger.

Jem did not budge or even look away from him for a second. 'Ask your mother,' she said.

Kathleen said, 'Sonny . . .' She put out a hand to take his fingers in hers.

'*Ask* her.'

In the face of this, Sonny faltered. 'Mum?'

'What's going on?' Walter had appeared in the doorway. 'Who is this?'

Kathleen swung round to look at her husband.

'Walter.'

His name left her lips as an exhalation – the sound of surrender. She was cornered like a fox in a drain.

'It's true,' she said, holding Sonny's hand and looking up at him. 'You are. She is.'

'She is *what*?' Walter was confused and impatient.

'I'm his sister.'

After Jem had spoken something like a shock wave spread out to touch Sonny and Walter. Both men trembled minutely and invisibly. Neither could speak.

104

Then Sonny snatched his hand away from his mother and Kathleen grabbed Jem by the wrist and pulled her into the house. 'Come on, then. Come in.' She shut the door and faced them. 'It's true. I had an affair and I got pregnant. Walter is . . .' But she could not say it: *not your real father*. 'The man was called Frank Martell. He was her father.' She nodded at Jem. 'He's dead. He died on Christmas Eve.'

Jem was still looking at Sonny. 'Your real father died of a heart condition. You might have it. That's why I came. I had to warn you.'

'Real father?' Echoing her, Sonny found his voice. He glanced at Walter and then away. 'How long have you known?' he asked Jem. 'About me?'

'I found out yesterday. Frank died and I went to his house. He'd found you on the internet.'

'It was *Hamlet*,' Kathleen said to Sonny. '*Hamlet* gave us away.'

'He heard you both,' Jem said, 'and then he must have looked you up.'

'And I look like him? I look like this person?' He was astonished, staring at Jem. 'Do I look like you?'

'Yes,' Jem said simply.

'*No*.' Kathleen was still protesting, even now. 'You look like *me*.'

Sonny turned from Jem to Walter. 'Not like you.' He had just understood. 'We're not related.'

It was a cliff and he pushed Walter off it.

Walter said nothing. He was leaning ever so slightly on the door frame and he looked completely undone of his usefulness, like a scattered newspaper or a squashed cardboard box.

Kathleen broke in wildly, 'No, Sonny, wait: Walter is your *parent*. Frank is not. He was not. Walter brought you back here from the hospital. He kissed you goodnight. He taught you to ride a bike. He's been here with you every day of your life . . .' This was the bit she had rehearsed, over the years – the bit when she tried to persuade them it didn't matter. She looked between the two men, desperately, but they were looking at each other as if they had both seen the same ghost. 'Stop it,' Kathleen said. She was frightened. 'Say something.'

It was Jem who spoke. 'I should go. I should leave you—'

'No.' Sonny turned to her. 'Not yet. I don't know anything yet.' He rounded on his mother. 'All this time you knew?'

'Not about the heart. I didn't know about that.' Kathleen began pleading. 'What was I supposed to do? Get rid of the baby? If I had told you' – she turned to Walter – 'you would have left me.'

'Don't you dare!' At last Walter spoke, making them jump like a thunderclap. 'Don't you dare try to blame me.'

'I'm not. I . . .' Kathleen did not know what to say next and so she burst into tears, sank to a chair and put her face in her hands. Mike went up to her and tried to lick her face. Tears made him anxious. 'Go away, Mike.' Kathleen pushed him away and so he retreated and stood behind Walter, tail softly waving with worry.

No one moved for a minute. No one said anything. Sonny was looking at Walter, Walter at Kathleen and Jem at Sonny. Kathleen hid her face.

Eventually Sonny said, 'Did you always know?'

At the end of a horrible pause, which was an admission in itself, Kathleen lifted her face and dried her eyes. 'Yes.'

'But you didn't think you'd get caught.'

'No. I tried to forget.'

'Forget?' Sonny was incredulous.

'It was easy. No one knew.'

'It's called denial,' Walter said. 'It's not called forgetting.'

Kathleen stood up, taking a step towards Sonny with one hand out, beseeching him, but as she came near he stepped back, away from her, shaking his head.

'Stay away from me,' he said. 'Don't come near me.'

'Sonny, please . . .'

'No.' He turned to Jem. 'Who was he? Your father?'

Jem said carefully, 'I barely knew him. He lived in France and I was brought up in London. We weren't close.'

'How old are you?'

'Twenty-five.' Jem paused and then added, 'Nine weeks older than you. I saw your age online.'

'Nine *weeks*?'

Faintly Kathleen said, 'I need to sit down. And I need a drink.'

'No.' Sonny – inquisitor and executioner – shook his head. 'We talk here. Tell me who he was.' He waited. '*Tell* me.'

Kathleen put the fingertips of one hand up to her forehead. She sat down again and closed her eyes, her face half-hidden by her hand. 'I was in France, making a film. I met him there. We had an affair. It lasted two weeks. I never saw him again.' She took her hand away from her forehead. 'That's it.'

'Except it wasn't,' Sonny said, 'because then there was me.'

Walter said, '*Yellow Afternoon*. The man on the telephone.' But no one was listening to him.

Sonny said, 'And what about *this*?' He pointed at his own chest – at his heart – and tapped at his breast pocket with his forefinger. 'My heart. What about that?'

'I told you. I didn't *know* about that.'

'I could be dead. I could have died.' He turned from incredulous to enraged in an instant, as if he had been smouldering and now caught fire. 'How could you? How could you?' he shouted.

Jem had not heard a man shouting at a woman for a long time. It was not something she had missed. She stepped away from them, towards the door, and as she did so Walter stepped forward to separate Sonny from Kathleen.

'Enough,' he said. 'That's enough. Calm down.'

'Calm down?' Sonny turned on him. 'You've no right to tell me what to do. Never again.' He jabbed viciously into the air in front of Walter's face with a forefinger. 'You can fuck off.'

But now Mike was growling in a low persistent voice. He had come to stand between the two men and to rumble at Sonny like a motorbike at a traffic light: *I mean business.*

Sonny said, 'Mike, shut up, it's me—'

But Mike's growl turned into two loud barks: *Watch it.* He stood his ground.

Sonny shrank a little and retreated. 'All right.' Quietly to Walter he said, 'I can't believe you're defending her.'

'I can't believe I have to defend her from *you*,' Walter's retort was equally quiet.

'Why aren't you upset?' Sonny's voice cracked. 'You don't have a son any more. Don't you care?'

Walter blinked. 'You are my son. This changes nothing.'

But Sonny shook his head. 'It changes everything. Don't you see?' And then he laughed, bitterly, 'Of course you don't. You can't.'

In the awful silence that followed a key turned in the lock. Lauren pushed open the front door and came in. She looked from one to the other.

'Who's this? What's going on?'

'Ask them,' Sonny said. 'I'm going out.'

'No. Wait. Sonny—' Kathleen tried to stop him.

'Get out of my way.'

He pushed past them all, out of the door and down the steps.

Sonny realised straight away that he was going to get very cold. He didn't have his jacket, which was hanging on the back of the kitchen door, nor his wallet, which was in the jacket pocket. He was unprepared for leaving home. With this in mind, he trotted up the street to Becka's house but instead of knocking on the front door he jogged down the steps to knock on her basement bedroom window.

'Becka? Becka? Are you there?'

'Sonny?' She came to the window. She was combing tangles out of her wet hair. 'What's going on?'

'Something. Everything. I don't know.'

Becka turned the lock and pulled up the sash. Sonny stepped in over the sill and sat down on the bed. He rubbed his head and got up again. He looked at the floor and then at the ceiling.

'What's going on? Just tell me, will you?'

'Mum says I've got another father. Not Dad.' He put

both hands on his head in amazement, hearing the words. 'Not Dad.'

'Shit.' Becka put a hand on his shoulder and pushed him down to sit on the edge of the bed. She sat down next to him and took his hand. 'Calm down. Tell me.'

'Mum had an affair. She got pregnant with me. She knew all this time. Someone turned up at the house, just now, and says she's my sister.' He blinked. 'She's the same age as me.' Then he remembered, 'Her father died of some heart thing. She says I could have it too.' He began to panic. 'I could die.'

'You're not going to die.' Becka put her arm around him. 'Just breathe for a minute, OK?' When his shoulders had stopped heaving she said, 'Is there a name for it? The heart thing?'

'I didn't ask.' Sonny stared wildly at her. 'I don't know.'

'Well, we need to find out. OK?' Becka held him at arm's length and looked into his eyes. 'I'll get Rex to go and ask. Stay here.' She got up and left the room. Sonny heard her going upstairs and calling, 'Rex? You there?'

Sonny stayed where he was, quite still. He looked around the room dumbly, like a baby left on its own in the few seconds before it starts crying. His wits were too scattered for him to be able to take much in beyond music and colour: clothes in heaps on the floor, clothes neatly stacked on rows of shelves, clothes on a long rail and even something soft and colourful pinned halfway through the sewing machine on a table in the window.

He had spent many hours of his life in here lying on the bed or sitting on the sheepskin beanbag on the floor, listening to music and smoking pot, giggling, floppy and stupid, unable to get up. He had once sat here after eating magic mushrooms and the walls had heaved and streamed with colour as if he had been trapped inside a kaleidoscope. On that day the colour and the closeness had been too much – he had gone to Primrose Hill and stared at the sky to cleanse his palate – but today the room was a snug little nest in which he was safely cocooned. He wondered if he could stay here for ever.

'Rex has gone to find out,' Becka said, coming into the room. 'You OK?'

'Maybe it's not true. Maybe the whole thing's made up. I mean, how does that woman know? For sure? It might all be a mistake.'

'What did your mum say?'

Sonny was silent.

After a moment Becka said, 'It doesn't matter who your father is. You're *you*. It doesn't make any difference.'

'But now I'm only half me. I don't know where the other half comes from.'

'Rubbish. You're not half Kathleen. You're all Sonny. Nothing's changed.'

'You're saying that to make me feel better.'

'It also happens to be the truth.' She smiled at him. 'I'm going to make us some tea, and then I'll roll a joint.'

Alone again, Sonny lay down on his back on the mattress and stared at the ceiling. The news sat in his chest like a half-swallowed pill that would not go down. He could neither digest it nor work out its weight and mass. Did it mean nothing? Or everything? Just now it felt as if he had been poisoned – *The potent poison quite o'er-crows my spirit* – but at the same time he was not sure he wanted, or

111

needed, ever to think about it again. Perhaps Becka was right. What difference would it make? Perhaps he could pretend nothing had happened.

When Becka returned she was carrying two mugs of tea. 'Yours has got sugar in it. You need sugar when you've had a shock. Sugar and pot.' Expertly she rolled a joint, heating a corner of chocolate-brown hash and crumbling it into a pleat of cigarette papers. 'This is strong stuff. For emergencies.'

After they had shared the joint Sonny felt leaden, as if he had sunk to the bottom of a swimming pool and was too heavy to swim back up. On the plus side the recent crisis had remained on the surface, floating like a leaf or a dead wasp, and from down here it seemed smaller and further away. He viewed it, blinking. He would lie down here for as long as he could. He could hear faint voices from the television but they sounded strange – swimming pool voices. He tried to speak to Becka but pushing words out of his mouth would be too effortful, like blowing bubbles in glue. Bubbles that would sink to the bottom.

But then he remembered his heart and panic burst like a porpoise toward the air. Lying on his back he placed his right hand on his breast as if he were taking an oath. Eyes wide, breathing shallowly, he felt for the steady *tick-tock* under his palm but found instead a boiling knot of netted fish. He tried to count but the sensation was muddled and faint. Was it always as faint as this? Always as muddled? He had never noticed. He had never cared or needed to. *Every moment I am alive my heart is beating.* It had always seemed amazing, but now it was terrifying. Did a heart not need to take a day off? To be serviced like a car? The more he thought about it the more peculiar and unlikely it was that it should be able to continue without incident, every day of his life. Eighty beats per minute made nearly five thousand in one hour. That was more than one hundred thousand in one day. He closed his eyes. Nearly fifty million in one year. He wished he had never smoked or snorted cocaine or run for a bus or eaten butter or bacon or roast potatoes. He imagined all his sins crowded in his arteries like rush hour on the Tube.

He managed to speak. 'I think I'm having a heart attack.'

Becka giggled. 'No, you're not. You're just stoned.' She propped herself up on her right elbow and looked over at him from her side of the bed. 'Sonny? Listen to me: you are not having a heart attack.' She put her hand on his arm and shook it gently, as if she were waking him up from a bad dream. 'Your heart is not going to go wrong today just because you found out it might go wrong one day. That would be crazy.'

'If this was a movie of my life I would have a heart attack right now.'

Becka laughed. 'Save it for the movie.' She kissed him briefly – casually – on the lips. 'Relax.' She lay down again next to him, holding his hand. They stayed like this until Lauren clattered down the steps outside the window and called out, 'Sonny? I know you're in there. Open up.'

After Sonny ran out of the door Lauren said, 'What the hell is going on?'

'Tell her,' Walter said to Kathleen.

'Do I have to say it again?'

'*Tell* her.'

'Your father is not Sonny's father,' Kathleen said to

Lauren. 'I had an affair.' She nodded in Jem's direction. 'This is Sonny's half-sister.'

When she heard this Lauren looked from her mother to Jem. Surprise turned to recognition. She could see it was true.

She managed to say, 'Who? Who is the father?'

'He's dead. He died yesterday,' Jem said.

'Frank Martell,' Kathleen volunteered. 'I met him in France. Making that film *Yellow Afternoon*.'

Lauren frowned, turning to her mother. 'But I was there,' she said. 'On that trip. I was *there*. I came on my own on the aeroplane. I made friends with the cook. Don't you remember?'

Kathleen seemed to shiver. She returned her face to her hands and said wearily, 'Yes.'

Walter came to life. 'Kath? Can I speak to you privately?'

Kathleen got to her feet unsteadily and Walter ushered her out of the hall and into the sitting room. He shut the door behind them.

'Sit down.'

'I want a drink,' said Kathleen. She beetled over to the table where the gin was kept. 'Don't you?'

'Yes. Whisky.'

Once they both had got a drink Walter stood in front of the window, looking out, and Kathleen sat in her usual spot on the sofa. She waited for him to speak but he said nothing.

Eventually she cracked and said, 'Walter, please. What do you want me to say to you?'

Walter cleared his throat. 'I'm going to ask you something and I want you to tell me the truth.' He turned around

114

to look down at her. 'I guessed you were pregnant, with Sonny. You didn't tell me. I guessed.'

In a small voice Kathleen said, 'I don't remember.'

'Yes, you do. You must.'

'All *right*, you guessed,' Kathleen admitted sulkily. 'How could you not? I kept being sick.'

'And crying all the time.'

'There's nothing odd about that. Lots of pregnant women cry all the time.'

'And drinking gin. I couldn't understand why you weren't happy. I was happy.' He shook his head. 'How could I have been so' – there was no other word for it – 'blind?'

'That's not how it was.'

'Yes it is. Why didn't you tell me? Why did I have to guess?'

'Because . . .' There was a little pause while she tried to think up an answer. Walter knew her so well he could almost hear the workings of her brain. 'Because I—'

'Because you knew it was Frank's baby and you were planning to get rid of it. And that explains the gin.'

'Walter! What a horrible—'

'I know it's the truth. You might as well admit it.'

'I won't admit anything. You're being a bully.' Kathleen looked firmly at the floor as she spoke.

'If I hadn't guessed, you would have got rid of him. I wondered why you were drinking and smoking when you knew you were pregnant, and the answer is you didn't care. You weren't planning to have the baby at all. Now I know.'

She looked up. 'What does any of this matter? We have Sonny. We wouldn't have Sonny without Frank.'

'We wouldn't have Sonny without *me*.' Walter pointed at

his chest. '*I stopped you from . . .*' He stared at Kathleen until she dropped her eyes to the floor again. Then he turned back to the window.

After a moment Kathleen said, 'I was terrified of losing you. I didn't know what to do. What should I have done?'

'You should have told me. You should have let me choose.'

'Choose? You would have left me with Lauren and a baby.'

'I would never have left Lauren.'

'You see?' Kathleen lifted her head and looked up at him with fierce indignation. 'If I'd told you we wouldn't be a *family*. We're a *family*.' She thumped the arm of the sofa. 'I *know* I did the right thing: you love Sonny and you have me to thank for that.'

Some of the air seemed to go out of Walter. 'Aren't you sorry?'

As if the failure to comprehend was all his Kathleen said deliberately, 'Sonny would not exist without Frank. How can I be sorry? Why should I be?'

Walter did not answer for a moment and then he said, 'If you won't understand, I won't explain it.'

He turned back to the window.

Lauren said to Jem, 'But he's *my* brother. I know he is.'

'Half yours and half mine.'

'But . . .' Lauren was frowning as if somehow she could prove Jem wrong. 'But you don't know him. You look like him but you don't know him.'

Lauren was frightened. She had been Sonny's sister for every minute of his life and yet she had nothing to show for it while this woman, a stranger, could have proved her kinship by standing next to him. Anyone could see there was a likeness. Quick as the fall of a blade Lauren had lost him. She was shocked. There seemed to be nothing else to say.

There was a ring on the doorbell and it was Rex.

'I came straight over,' he said to Lauren. 'Becka told me. Are you OK?'

'How did Becka know?'

'Sonny's there. With her.'

'With *her*? What for? We need him here.'

'Leave him. Let him come back when he's ready,' said Rex. 'It's a shock.'

'Of course it's a fucking shock.' Suddenly Lauren was furious. 'Don't tell me how to look after my own brother.'

'I'm trying to help.'

'Why? It's got nothing to do with you.'

'I should go.' Jem sidled towards the door.

'No.' Lauren rounded on her. 'You started this. You stay. I'll fetch Sonny.'

And so she ran up the street and clattered down the steps outside Becka's window.

'Sonny? I know you're in there. Open up.'

For the second time, Becka pulled up the sash.

'You've got to come back,' Lauren said to Sonny. 'You can't just sit here and get stoned.'

'This isn't happening to you,' Sonny said. 'I decide what I do.' He was sitting on the edge of the bed and he did not get up. He could not get up.

'It's all of us. It's the whole family.'

'No.' Sonny pointed at his chest. 'Me.'

'What about Mum and Dad?'

117

'Dad?' He gave a horrible, flat laugh.

'Sonny—'

'Go away. Leave me alone.' He would not say any more.

Back at home Lauren found Rex in the kitchen alone.

'Where's she gone? Jem?'

'She wrote everything down: address, phone number and the name of the heart thing.' Rex waved a folded piece of paper. 'Then she left.'

'You should have stopped her.' Lauren felt like a sheep-dog in charge of some very disobedient sheep.

'Lauren . . .'

Rex tried to put his arms around her but she pushed him away.

'You should have stopped her.'

'I'm trying to help you.'

'Stop saying that. You're not helping. The only thing you've ever done for me is break my heart into a million tiny fucking pieces.' There, she had said it. 'Now please go away.'

Rex looked as if he wanted to say several things. Instead he picked up his coat and left. As soon as he had gone Lauren sat down on the bottom stair in the hall and put her face in her hands. For a few minutes she made noises into her fingers which could have been rage or despair. Then she rubbed her eyes with her fingers and her cheeks with her palms and stood up.

When she opened the sitting-room door to check on her parents she found her father looking out of the window and her mother sitting on the sofa. They looked static, as if they had been positioned by an artist for a portrait entitled

'Bad News', but Walter turned when he heard the door open.

'Lauren?'

'Yes.'

'Good.' He seemed relieved. 'Where is—?'

'She's gone.' Lauren looked from one to the other. 'So you haven't killed each other.'

'No.' Walter managed a thin smile.

'Have you made up?'

'No.' The smile vanished.

In a tired voice Kathleen said, 'I'm going to lie down.' She stood up and shuffled to the door. 'Will you come?' It was a plea to her husband.

'No.'

'Please, Walter?' Kathleen sounded as if she might start crying again.

'No.'

Kathleen hesitated. She did not want to be alone. She asked Lauren, 'Where's Sonny?'

'At Becka's.'

'Perhaps I'll go over there and—'

'Just leave him alone,' Lauren cut in. 'He doesn't want to see any of us.'

And so Kathleen crept away alone, upstairs.

When she had gone Lauren stood in front of the fireplace and lit a cigarette. Holding it in her left hand she pressed the thumb and index finger of her right hand against either side of her forehead and squeezed her skull between her fingers. After pinching as hard as she could for twenty seconds she released the pressure. Then she turned to her father.

'Well, Dad. Are you all right?'

Walter turned the empty whisky glass around in his hand, feeling its ridges with his fingertips. 'Why didn't I guess?'

'No one would.'

'Perhaps I wasn't looking. Perhaps I couldn't see.'

'No, Dad.'

'I should have known. I *could* have known.' Walter shook his head. 'I just didn't want to.'

'Don't be—'

'My God!' All of a sudden he was floundering in a strong current. 'I've got to get out! Out of this house.'

'I'll come with you. We can walk Mike.'

'No. I want to be on my own.'

Walter went to the pub. It was the same pub that Sonny and Becka had visited on Christmas Eve. He ordered a double whisky up at the bar from the landlord, Richard, to whom he was well known. He drank it in one gulp and ordered another, which he watered down and took to a seat near the fire. The pub was busy but not crowded: three women sat with a bottle of wine between them; a group of young Australians, rowdy and homesick, shouted and slapped their palms on a table covered with empty glasses; a row of men sitting up at the bar might have grown like toadstools out of the carpet.

Walter held his glass between both hands. He sat hunched and unblinking, staring at the blue flames, little more than ribbons, tepid and insubstantial after the orange crackle at home.

He tried not to think about anything. He only came to the pub if he wanted to get away from his wife – perhaps once a fortnight he might come here for an hour or so, for the peace and quiet. Sometimes he and Lester sat here together and spilled crisps down their fronts, drinking. This pub, unlike any other in the neighbourhood, had not been revitalised, or even vitalised, in living memory. It was a drinkers' pub – there was no food on offer besides Quavers, Walkers crisps and salted peanuts. Snacks to make drinking more palatable, or necessary. Walter could not remember which one was supposed to be worse for him. It was the sort of thing Lauren knew: 'Not those, Dad. Eat those if you must.'

Kathleen used to come here but now she preferred to drink at home. She was a person people recognised off the telly – she could not be anonymous if she drank in public, and definitely not if she drank too much which she usually did. She did not like to be observed and how could she not be? Telephones and cameras were everywhere. It was unfair that Mrs Peabody, a fictional character, should be nationally adored for being exactly the sort of character one might find in a pub, drunk on gin at three in the afternoon, but if the actor who played her were to follow suit she would be disgraced.

Walter wondered if she was unhappy. Had she always been unhappy? No – he shook himself – he would not allow himself to think like this. He would not count backwards, for example, and remember the year before Sonny was born. He would not try to think of what he must have been doing while Kathleen was having her love affair. Was it love? He would not think about that. He swallowed the rest of his drink. She had been in France. The film was *Yellow Afternoon*. When she came back he had not suspected any

121

betrayal. Why would he? There had been no crisis. They had carried on as before. He had discovered the pregnancy and had been overjoyed – more delighted than she. Now he knew why.

It was not the idea of infidelity which sickened Walter, who was both realist and romantic, but the fact of impregnation: another man's sperm had fertilised his wife's egg and produced Sonny whom he, Walter, had taken for his own blood relative, his only son, and nurtured to adulthood. When he had put his hand on Kathleen's belly and felt Sonny's kick it had been the kick of a stranger's child. He churned inside. The deception disgusted him. It was not a question of loving Sonny or not, it was a question of having been tricked: the baby had been a cuckoo. He felt a savage fury.

With the pull and slam of the pub door came a rush of cold air and Walter blinked. Where was he? In the pub, two double whiskies down. It was time for another. He would have to go to the bar. Some whisky would make him feel worse, but a lot of whisky would make him feel nothing. Before he could move there was someone standing next to him: Lester.

'Lauren sent me,' Lester said. He shoved his hands into his coat pockets and rattled the keys and coins within to signify sympathy. 'Another of those?' He nodded at the empty glass.

Part of Walter wanted to cling to Lester and weep like a toddler. The other part said, 'Maybe one more large one.' He slid the tumbler over the table. He was drunker than he had thought. In his thoughts he was sober. Speech less so. 'You've heard my news I expect?'

'Yes. Odd business. We can talk about it if you like, or not.' Lester shrugged off his coat and dumped it on the banquette. 'Back in a tick.'

Kathleen was the next person to exit 36 Beech Road. She snuck up the street and knocked on Lester's front door. She wanted to see Sonny and she would not let Lauren stop her.

Rex answered the door. When he saw her he smiled. 'Boy are you in trouble.'

'Don't you take anything seriously?'

'No. Looking for Sonny? He's locked in the basement with Becka and a lump of hash the size of my head.'

'Stop it. Let me go down and knock on their door.'

'No,' said Rex, '*I'll* go down and knock on their door. You stay here.'

He left her in the hall, which was tiny enough to feel like waiting in a cupboard lined with coats. Grateful to be swaddled Kathleen leant against a puffy jacket and shut her eyes.

When he came back upstairs from the basement Rex said, 'Not right now.' He saw her face fall. 'I'm sorry. It's too soon – and he's probably blitzed. Leave it until tomorrow.'

But Kathleen was stricken. 'He said no?'

'Is it possible your son has never told you to fuck off before? Really? You poor old thing. I used to tell my dad to fuck off all the time and one day he did – he ran off with Annie and they had Becka. So I guess it all worked out in the end.' He put an arm over her shoulders. 'Come in. Come and chat to me instead. I'm drinking red wine and I guess you'd like some.'

Kathleen had realised halfway through this speech that

Rex was already drunk. It suited her fine – she wanted to be drunk too. She followed him into the kitchen where he slopped wine into a second glass and handed it to her. Then he refilled his own glass and offered her a pack of cigarettes.

'Smoke?'

'But I've given up.'

'Bad luck.'

'Well, go on then. I mean if I can't smoke now then when can I, for God's sake.'

Rex lit the cigarette for her and they sat down together on the sofa in the kitchen.

'Where's Annie?'

Rex exhaled a gust of smoke towards the ceiling. 'Gone to see her sister in Balham.' He called it Bal-Ham. 'Aunt May. Like in Spider Man.'

'I've met her. She's got a Rottweiler. She brought it to dinner.'

'That's her.'

'She's not your aunt. She's Becka's aunt.'

Rex raised an eyebrow. 'Are you really in a position to split hairs?'

'And where's Lester?'

'In the pub with your husband. And where's Lauren?'

'No idea.' Kathleen was not interested in Lauren just now. 'Oh, Rex, will Sonny ever forgive me?'

'I doubt it.'

'Don't joke!'

'Of course he will. Everyone will.' He waved a hand expansively. 'The whole world. No one could stay cross with you for long.'

Kathleen cheered up. It was nice to have Rex to herself and if he carried on like this she would feel less unloved.

Pouring more wine Rex asked, 'Who was the guy anyhow? Sonny's father?'

'Frank Martell.' Kathleen stubbed out her cigarette. She was already feeling drowsy and foolish from the wine and it was a great deal better than feeling anxious and depressed. 'I met him in France. I was shooting a film.'

'And?'

'It's hard to explain. I know it sounds terrible but I didn't even think about Walter.' It was easy to tell Rex the truth. 'I was abroad, working on a miserable film about a woman whose husband locks her in the attic and tells her she's insane. The director was a bully. I was lonely. I know it sounds pathetic but . . .' She looked down at her hands. 'I can't explain. I've never had to try.'

'You don't have to explain.'

'Then I met Frank and he was crazy about me. He thought I was perfect. He wouldn't leave me alone. At first it was wonderful – like a holiday. It was too easy: no one cared what I did. And then' – she shivered at the memory – 'I realised how stupid it was. How dangerous.'

Rex lit two more cigarettes and passed one over. 'And Walter never guessed?'

'I told myself that he knew and just accepted it, but that was just wishful thinking. He didn't have a clue. Why would he? I loved him – I never stopped loving him. It was weakness, not design.'

'You're weak. I'm weak. We're all weak. We're pathetic little worms. Walter is too.' He sloshed more wine into their glasses. 'He'll see it. He'll see that it could just as easily have been him, fathering a son with another woman, off on one of those trips of his, back in the day.'

In all the years since Sonny's conception Kathleen had never thought of this and now she blurted out, 'He'd better not have!'

Rex laughed. Then he said, 'I always thought Sonny looked like you.'

'Everyone said so.' Kathleen shrugged. 'We see what we want to see.'

'Then I saw Jem. It's unmistakable.'

'Yes.'

The admission was a relief and, somehow, like a final word: passing sentence.

After a pause Rex asked, 'What happened to him? Frank?'

'I don't know.' Kathleen drained her drink. 'I left. I never wanted to see him again. He . . .' She stopped and continued carefully, 'It ended badly.'

'He wanted more than two weeks?'

'He wanted everything.' Kathleen did not want to talk about Frank any more. 'Come on,' she waggled her glass. 'Open another bottle – unless there's somewhere you need to be.'

To her surprise Rex said, 'I was supposed to be taking Lauren out tonight, but I guess that's not happening.'

'Lauren? My Lauren?'

'You're surprised?'

'Well, no. I suppose not. Or . . .' She gave up. 'Yes, perhaps I am. You and Lauren? On a *date*? It's just that . . .' She stopped and wondered why it made her feel odd, to think of them out together. 'You're so relaxed, and Lauren wants everyone to be perfect.'

'That's not such a bad ambition,' Rex said lightly.

'But she's strict, Rex. At least she is with me. And she's dogged. Difficult about small things – she won't let anything go.'

'Yes.' Rex was smiling as if 'strict' and 'dogged' were his two favourite things about Lauren.

At that moment Kathleen felt a wave of jealousy and an impulse of which she was not proud: to talk him out of his feelings. She opened her mouth to continue but Rex, who must have sensed her tension and displeasure, spoke first.

'We spent a weekend together in Paris, before I got married. She was there for a hen night but she skipped out on her friends. It was . . .' He did not find the words to finish.

'She never mentioned it.'

'I don't think she told anyone – maybe Sonny. He gave me a couple of cold stares afterwards.' Rex swallowed more wine. 'It happened just after Clothilde told me she was pregnant. I thought she was on the pill and so we fought – I was an asshole, basically – and she ran off to stay with her parents for a few days. She said she was going to think about it but I knew she'd keep it. I knew I was fucked. Then Lauren turned up in Paris. I wanted to pretend there was no Clothilde and no baby. It felt like it was the last weekend before I started a life sentence.' He gave a grim smile. 'On Monday Lauren went home to London. Clothilde came back and told me she was keeping the baby. She moved in, we got married and that was that.'

'And Lauren?'

Rex exhaled air very slowly through his teeth like an old groom. Then he said, 'Lauren nothing. I never explained. Never called her.'

127

'You *are* an asshole! You should have called her, told her everything and said sorry.'

'Like you should have told Walter everything and said sorry?'

They looked at each other.

Then Kathleen spoke. 'We're either both terrible people, or neither of us is,' she said decisively. Then she frowned. 'Wait, does that make sense?' The wine had muddled her; it was a pleasant feeling.

'To us.' Rex lifted his glass. 'Pathetic little worms.'

They clinked their empty glasses.

'Worms,' agreed Kathleen. 'Now, how about that other bottle?'

The subject of this discussion had taken Mike for a walk. She did not know what else to do. She had tried to herd all the members of her family into the same room but they had found holes in the fence and slipped out one by one.

If she could not reconcile each to the other she did not trust them to do it for themselves but for tonight she gave up any hope of uniting them. She took to the empty streets with Mike. They walked slowly and in a roundabout way to the petrol station on Wellington Road where she could buy cigarettes.

Mike trotted in front, pausing every few yards to check for messages left by other dogs. At each corner he stopped and glanced around at Lauren, looking for the invisible and unconscious body language that would tell him whether to turn left or right or continue straight on. Lauren would not even look at him – sometimes she would try to fool him – but he was never wrong. 'Mike knows everything,' Sonny would often say, and it was true that each of them had at one time or another wept secrets into his woolly ears.

Out here it was as quiet as if it were four in the morning – everyone was tucked up at home watching television. Everyone but a fox, who slipped between some railings and onto the pavement in front of them. He stopped there, turned his head and looked. They looked back. Mike, who was nearer, bristled and lifted one paw as if he might at any moment give chase, but he had learned his lesson from previous encounters with other foxes and stayed put. The fox waited, a yellow silhouette under the street light. He cringed a little into his shoulders and twitched the white tip of his brush as if asking Mike, *Well? Are you coming or not?* For a minute it was a stand-off and then he dismissed them, stepping off the kerb and vanishing almost before he was out of sight. Mike stepped busily up to the place he had stood and sniffed it.

Lauren wondered why she felt such a terrible sense of loss. At the vanishing of the fox she could have wept, but Sonny had not vanished. He had not died, he was not ill and he had not changed. The news itself could not change him. It need not alter his personality or his character or make a material difference to his being whether his father was Walter or Frank or anyone else. Why should it matter at all? Why should she despair? But she did.

Her family of four had always divided into two pairs: Walter and herself one; Kathleen and Sonny the other. Lauren had always supposed that this division had been accidental – how could it have been otherwise? – and yet now she understood that similarities and differences, closeness and separation, had not come about by chance:

129

Kathleen had created Sonny for herself. She had made him her special child and she had done it in the knowledge that he was hers and not Walter's. *We're cut from the same cloth*, she would say. *We're peas in a pod.* It had not seemed sinister until today.

It was not loss itself but the premonition of loss that made Lauren wretched: it was impossible not to conceive the idea that Sonny would be spirited away to a foreign land by his new sister; that Lauren would lose him to this relative with an equal claim who was a perfect stranger. In her mind Lauren pleaded, *But I know him. I would know him in the dark. Isn't that something?*

At Wellington Road she headed south towards the petrol station, star-bright in the gloom. On the forecourt, beside those machines which fill tyres with air or vacuum Maltesers out of seat crevices, a silver saloon had been parked and its driver, a bald man in his late fifties, had gone to sleep. His head was lolled back on the headrest and his mouth was slightly open. It occurred to Lauren as she passed that Sonny's father might have been bald. Having thought of this she wondered about all the other things that Sonny might have inherited unwittingly from his father: hay fever, sleepwalking, an allergy to horses, his inexplicable dislike of Marmite and not being able to tell left from right. And even, perhaps, a defective heart. Could it be, she wondered, that everything she knew to be 'Sonny' was actually 'Frank'?

A few minutes ago she had thought she could cope; now she was certain she couldn't. Every reasonable thought in her head was suddenly drowned by a flood of panic that overwhelmed her. Who was her brother now? He had been replaced by an unknown man. If she tapped his shoulder in a crowd – 'Sonny?' – a stranger would turn to face her.

Inside the shop she waited behind two other customers. Christmassy music fizzed out of overhead speakers. The cashier was grey and underslept. Directly in front of Lauren a man held a thick packet of nappies under one arm. His telephone rang.

'I'm in the fucking queue,' he muttered into it. 'I can't queue any fucking faster.'

Lauren shut her eyes. It seemed imperative to remember that childhood trip to France because it was the only part she had played in the whole Frank business. *I was there. I was there.*

She remembered a bright outdoors and the house pitch-black when she ran inside. She remembered gutting a chicken – the puddle of grey intestines in her hand. She could recall impressions one by one like bright handkerchiefs from a top hat – the insolent taste of French milk; white cats lying in the dust; her feet slap-slapping up steps in a pair of striped espadrilles; a red drink spilled on a table – but she could not tie them together to make a narrative. What was significant she had never known, and now she would never guess.

V

The film was called *Yellow Afternoon* and Kathleen would be away for six weeks. The crew was small, the production was cheap and the script required only three actors: a man and two women. A handful of extras would complete the cast, all of them French and local to Provence where the film would be shot.

Kathleen had landed the lead role and was in carnival mood when she bounced into Walter's study and told him. He asked the one question she did not want to answer:

'What's the story?'

'Must I tell you? You won't like it.'

The film described the progressive breakdown of a woman diagnosed with depression and confined to an attic bedroom by her husband.

'A laugh a minute,' said Walter.

'It's an adaptation of a seminal feminist work,' Kathleen said importantly. 'A book called *The Yellow Wallpaper*.'

'I can't think why I've never heard of it.'

'Aren't you going to congratulate me before you start making jokes?' There was a small but sharp edge to her voice. 'I'm the lead and I'm going to be brilliant.'

Walter got out of his desk chair and kissed her. 'Congratulations. I'm very proud of you, Mrs Griffin.'

'Thank you.' Kathleen was mollified. 'You're just the sort of misogynist dinosaur the film is aimed at. We're going to stop you from thinking "mad wife" and make you think "controlling, bullying husband".'

'I can't wait,' said Walter tactfully. 'Now, can we go out and celebrate? I've been staring at contact sheets all day and my eyes have gone squiffy.'

'Better than that, we can go upstairs and celebrate – Lauren won't be back from school for a bit.'

Lovemaking initiated by Kathleen was always brief but enthusiastic – she did not need to be got into the mood because she already was. Kathleen's feelings about herself fed directly into her ability to enjoy herself in bed: when she was feeling fat and a failure she resented the whole picnic; when – like today – she was in Oscar-winning mood it was all as easy and fun as it had been back in the days before marriage and motherhood.

Afterwards they clung together among the pillows. Walter began to drift towards sleep and Kathleen returned to the day's favourite subject.

'It's a psychological thriller,' she said.

'Hm,' agreed Walter. He was almost asleep.

'Scary but clever.'

'Ah.' Walter's favourite film was *Trading Places*.

'The director's an American called Vincent Wexler.'

Walter issued a sleepy noise of derision into her hair.

'A Francophile, apparently. Young, clever and arty. Wants to be taken seriously.'

'With a name like that?'

He wanted to sleep but Kathleen was fidgeting.

'No one cares what you think.' She poked him. 'Walter? Walter? I said *no one cares what you think*.'

But he had gone to sleep.

In the bath Kathleen reflected that in fact the opposite was true: Walter did not care what anyone thought, and everyone – particularly his wife – cared what he thought. She wished she could be so blasé. He was not interested in her opinion of his work, his looks, his weight, his clothes, his new haircut or anything else about him. She was expected to be agreeable, available and non-interfering. With this he was content.

To be left alone was not, however, Kathleen's idea of contentment. She liked attention, she liked to be needed and she absolutely positively *had* to be wanted. It was vital to her well-being; fundamental; necessary for life. Recalling the urgency of their lovemaking she shivered with a sudden pleasure. Today had put her in a very good mood.

The very good mood was nearly spoiled by Lauren, whose bedroom she visited before going out to dinner. Lauren was in bed, reading. She would read all night if she were allowed. When Kathleen entered the room she looked up with her librarian's expression.

'Where are you going?'

'Out for dinner.'

'You're always going out.'

'Rubbish. Anyway, we're celebrating. I got a part in a film, did Ebba tell you?'

Ebba was the au pair, pigtailed and Swedish, to whom Kathleen had already boasted about the film. How could she not have passed the good news on to Lauren?

'No. What sort of film?'

'An excellent, grown-up, clever one and I'm the main character.' It was nice talking to a child – one was not expected to be modest – but Kathleen had forgotten for a moment that Lauren was naturally squashing.

'It hasn't been made yet. How can it be excellent?'

'Because I know about films and you don't. Anyway I'm going to France for six weeks. What do you think of that?'

'Six *weeks*?' Lauren looked even more disapproving. 'What about me? What about Dad? You're supposed to look after us.'

'Ebba will look after you. That's what she's for. Dad can look after himself.'

Lauren was so conservative, Kathleen thought with a frown. Her ideas about men and women were Victorian at best: she wanted her mother in the kitchen and her father adventuring abroad. Walter was allowed to go anywhere he liked for as long as he liked in the name of work, but if Kathleen wanted to work she was reproved for her vanity and told off for being neglectful. It was maddening. Where did children pick up these ideas? It occurred to Kathleen to sit down and deliver a lecture on the feminist principle but she did not want to crease her dress. Instead she took a different tack.

'Better still,' she said cleverly, 'Dad's got you. You're much better at looking after him than I am.'

This was convincing and Lauren's expression registered the compliment.

'And what about poor old me?' Kathleen decided to push her luck. 'I'll be all on my own in France with *no one* to look after me.' Having scored two points it was time to change the subject. 'What do you think of my dress?'

'Is it new?' Lauren did not like her mother to spend too much time or money shopping.

'No. I just haven't worn it for years,' Kathleen lied. 'See you in the morning. All right?' She blew Lauren a kiss from the door.

'All right. Don't get *drunk*.'

'So what if I do? You'll never know.'

'Yes, I will: you'll be in a horrible mood tomorrow.'

'Then you'd better stay out of my way.'

Kathleen banged the door shut behind her and swept downstairs in search of a drink. Lauren was too self-reliant and too serious, she reflected. Everything was work – even her teddy bears did not loll about on the duvet but were dressed in splints and bandages and laid out in a field hospital ward. A walk in the park with Lauren became a kind of exhausting safari that entailed the spotting, listing and naming of birds and animals. There was no aimless skipping about or kicking at piles of leaves. She filled innumerable notebooks with lists, adhered to a neatly copied-out time-table, folded her own clothes and wrote all her thank you letters on Boxing Day. She was disapproving – she did not know how to be frivolous. Kathleen dreamed of a second child who liked dressing up, play-acting, watching television in bed on Saturday mornings and who never wanted to go outdoors: an adorable moppet; a smaller version of herself.

Walter heard all these complaints in the restaurant.

'Lauren is perfect,' he said when Kathleen paused for breath. 'I won't hear a word against her. Now stop being boring and let's order.'

There were two words that would shut Kathleen up under any circumstances: 'boring' or 'ugly'. She stopped talking.

Walter raised his eyes from the menu and instantly the waiter appeared at his elbow. His ability to summon a waiter was one of Kathleen's favourite things about her husband. He did not have to raise his hand – or even his eyebrows – but drew them invisibly, like experienced sheepdogs, to his heel. She had seen other men wave the menu or clear their throats or say plaintively, 'Excuse me?', and she had pitied their wives.

Kathleen loved and admired Walter, but she feared his restlessness and his self-containment. Because he did not need her she could never be quite certain of him; she could never quite relax. To love him was to put herself at risk: if she was in a bad mood he would leave the room; if she lost her temper he would leave the house; if they had a falling-out he might go away for a month. What would stop him leaving her for good? If she went away, as she was about to do, he would not miss her. He would be fine. If, when she came back, she were to ask him 'Did you miss me?' she would see a slight, puzzled frown pass over his face as he wondered what she meant, or how that would feel. Politely he would reply, 'Of course,' but she knew it to be untrue.

Unlike Lauren, Walter did not want Kathleen to be a housewife. 'Work is freedom,' he said. 'Freedom from me; freedom from Lauren. Nothing is more important.' But how could she be married and free? Her well-being depended on him; as long as she loved him she was tethered to him. He did not understand because he did not feel the

138

same – he was self-contained, not dependent. If she wanted to be happy she needed not freedom but approval.

When he was away on a trip she could not help wondering if he would ever come back. What did she have to draw him? Even when she heard the front door open and he stood in front of her again, smelling of the dirt of another country, foreign coins spilling from his pockets and in need of a shave, she did not believe he had come back for her.

On location for *Yellow Afternoon* Kathleen discovered that Vincent Wexler expected a high price, namely her sanity, in exchange for the part in his film. 'To be credible,' he was fond of saying, 'you must believe the story you're telling.' At first she thought this was a director's note but gradually she realised it was an instruction: he intended actually to alter her state of mind until she thought herself both worthless and friendless. He wanted her not to pretend but to suffer; not to 'make believe' but believe. In order to convince, she must feel: confusion, humiliation, uncertainty, jealousy and paranoia.

Along with Vincent, his assistant Rocky and the two other principal actors Kathleen was staying in a 'mas', or Provençal farmhouse, rented for the duration of the shoot. The crew meanwhile – all French – had been designated a cheap hotel in Apt and the cinematographer, Jean-Paul Racine, drove in every day from the nearby vineyard where he lived.

Known as Rass, Jean-Paul Racine was eighty years old. He had officially given up film-making in favour of wine-making at the end of the 1970s but Vincent – slippery with charm when he chose to be – had lured Rass out of retirement with promises of creative freedom, a nearby location and short working days. Vincent had also impressed Rass and the rest of the crew by speaking fluent French – an unheard-of accomplishment for an American.

Besides Kathleen there were two other actors: a more famous contemporary, Bob Latimer, who was cast as her on-screen husband and a younger French woman, Ava Mathieu, who would play both nurse and housekeeper. It was an inventive trick of Vincent's that one actor should play the two extra female parts, thus exploiting even more comprehensively the fragile mental state of Kathleen's character, known only as 'Wife'. Wife believed herself persecuted, controlled and undermined by her faithless husband but he insisted that she was suffering a mental breakdown. He told her he had hired two women to take care of her, but she could identify only one. He talked about a nurse and a housekeeper; she saw only a lover. This was paranoia, he claimed, and only proved what he had been telling her: that she was losing her mind. Was she crazy? Had she been tricked? Should she trust her husband, or could she trust herself?

Adding credibility to fictional plots of treachery and betrayal was the real-life affair between Bob and Ava, begun almost as soon as they got off their respective aeroplanes from Los Angeles and Paris. Bob was a notorious philanderer and Kathleen had wondered if he would attempt to seduce her – she had even prepared a handful of light-hearted comments with which to rebuff him charmingly. She found herself more irritated than relieved when she caught him emerging from Ava's bedroom on the first morning.

'For Chrissakes don't tell Vincent,' Bob hissed when he

saw her – but of course when Kathleen told Vincent he made no attempt to conceal his satisfaction: anything that made Kathleen feel rejected and sidelined would help the film. Vincent could not have arranged the affair but he certainly backed it.

Kathleen began to wake at dawn, her stomach churning, dreading the day ahead. She dreaded the dozens of takes and retakes – walking into a room might take up a whole morning. She dreaded the crew's ill-concealed resentment – their sullen expressions and muttered comments – as the hours passed and nothing was achieved. She dreaded Bob and Ava whispering together, sharing cigarettes and even wrapped around one another in the narrow, concealing shade of a cypress tree. But most of all she dreaded Vincent.

He gave her neither encouragement nor praise, merely interrupting her with 'Not like that' or simply 'Again'.

'Again how? Differently?'

'Better.'

He would turn his back on her to speak cheerful, rapid French to his crew and then turn again to eyeball her in silence, while everyone waited, as if he were wondering what on earth to do with her. He might approach her and fiddle with her appearance – taking the clasp out of her hair, tugging this way and that at her clothes – before shaking his head in defeat and saying, 'It's just not working.' Several times he sent her away to change. 'Your clothes look wrong. Too tight.' One morning he said, 'You're sunburned. This red face' – he pinched her cheek – 'is no good to me.' In the heat of a bright midday he made her run upstairs so many times that she fainted. When she was revived he told her off for wasting everyone's time. 'This is what happens when you drink too much at night: we all have to pay the next day.'

Kathleen hated him. He did not treat anyone else like this and so she knew it was a deliberate ploy: to pick away at her confidence until she felt as much of a failure as the character she portrayed. Even knowing this, she hated him. He was a bully, he was in sole charge of their little circus and there was no superior she could complain to – the film's producer, Mitchell Peters, had greeted them all on the day they arrived and then flown straight back to Los Angeles. 'That's why he's the best,' Vincent said with a twisted little smile. 'Because he knows when to be here and when to fuck off.' Without Mitch, Vincent's control was absolute. No one else would even talk to her because he had told them to exclude her.

But then, as the days turned into weeks, she began to wonder. Had he? What if she were being ostracised because she was actually disliked? What if she were being criticised because she really was no good? Perhaps it was not Vincent after all; perhaps she deserved to feel like a failure. How could she tell? Where did his machinations end and her shortcomings begin? No – she shook herself – *no*. She was falling into his trap – these misgivings were not real, they had been cultivated: this was the effect he wanted. She was not going mad, it was his plot to undermine her. *The voice in my head is the voice of sanity, not lunacy.* But wait – wasn't that a line from the script? Was it something she had learned, or something she had thought?

Because Rass did not want to work late – '*J'aime beaucoup ma femme*,' he told Kathleen, '*et j'aime beaucoup mon lit*' – filming finished at eight and everyone dispersed. Back at their own house, and whatever the trials of their daily interactions, Vincent would expect Kathleen, Bob, Ava and Rocky to sit down with him for a civilised dinner.

Each night the five would gather around the large, stone table that stood outside the kitchen door. Candles flickered in the mellow dark and the cook brought food and wine, her espadrilles slapping fondly on the flagstones. Kathleen would soothe her frayed nerves with drink – at this stage of the day she was safe from Vincent, who ignored her entirely – and when she was quite numb she would slip up to bed, unnoticed. From her room with the windows open she could hear murmured conversation drifting up from below. The occasional burst of laughter would make her flinch. *Are they laughing at me?* She could no longer distinguish between the sound of people enjoying themselves and the sound of mockery; creeping night-time terrors plucked at her nerves and she could not sleep; with no friend to reassure her she would surrender at last to tears and, worst of all, to the bleak certainty of failure.

In London, halfway through Kathleen's shoot, Lauren began her half-term. It was only when Ebba telephoned that Kathleen discovered Walter was not, as she had thought, at home in London.

'Not *there*? Where's he gone?'

'I do not know. He did not say.'

'If it's bloody Sarajevo,' Kathleen said more to herself than to Ebba, 'I'll kill him.'

Ebba was not interested in where Walter had gone. Her mother had fallen downstairs and broken a leg.

'I must go home,' she said, meaning Sweden. 'My father cannot cope.' Her father was already in a wheelchair and now her mother would be too, at least for a while.

'All right, Ebba, calm *down*.' Kathleen was irritated beyond measure by the inconvenience of another person's crisis. 'Your timing couldn't be worse. And you can't take Lauren with you? Well then, I suppose you'd better put her on a British Airways flight to Marseille. I'll call them now and book a ticket on my Amex. She can fly as an unaccompanied minor and I'll get Rocky to meet her. Tell her to look out for a tall American man with a shaved head.'

Lauren, naturally, was delighted by such drama and thrilled by the unaccompanied flight. This was a much more fun way of spending half-term than sitting at home in boring old London with boring old Ebba. When Mum was away she had fun with Dad, but when Dad was away there was never any fun. Even the house seemed to go into hibernation.

She was met by Rocky at Marseille airport and transported to the house by air-conditioned Mercedes-Benz. She wasted no time when she arrived but immediately explored the house from top to bottom and made best friends with the cook, a young woman whose name Kathleen had failed to learn in three weeks. In the kitchen she was fed ice cream and shown how to make meringues. By the time Kathleen arrived home at the end of the day Lauren seemed almost surprised to see her.

'Mum! It's amazing here. I pulled a chicken's guts out. Romy showed me how. Romy's the cook. She's half-English and half-French. She grew up in Tangier, which is in Morocco, which is in Africa. Have you seen the cats?

They're *all white*. All of them. I've thought up names for them and written an alphabetical list. And there's a hammock and Romy says I can sleep in it one night.'

Kathleen gave Lauren a frosty hug. Having been taunted and bullied all day she was not in the mood to be generous.

'I see.'

Catching her tone, Romy said, 'I told her to ask your permission.'

Kathleen turned to her as if seeing her for the first time.

'Lauren has never asked my permission in her life,' she said. 'She takes after her father.'

'She tells me her father is a war photographer? He must be very brave.'

'So I'm told,' said Kathleen briskly. 'Come on, Lauren, let's go upstairs. This nice lady . . .'

'Romy,' prompted Lauren.

'. . . doesn't want to listen to you gassing on about nothing.'

She caught Lauren by the shoulders and pushed her towards the stairs.

'Come and see me again,' Romy said to Lauren before she left the room. 'When I was a little girl I used to spend all day in the kitchen. You're welcome whenever you like.'

As she herded Lauren upstairs to the bathroom Kathleen considered this idea and wondered if she might use it for her own advantage. Once Lauren was in the bath she went back downstairs to the kitchen.

'Did you mean it,' she began casually to Romy, 'when you said Lauren could spend all day with you? Because – the thing is – I haven't figured out what I'm going to do

145

with her while I'm working. She's not supposed to be here at all, you see, and I don't want to antagonise Vincent. I thought I might find a childminder in the village but' – she would resort to flattery if it would help – 'you've already made friends and Lauren seems so taken with you. Please say no if you want to.' She smiled brilliantly, meaning the opposite. 'I would hate to put you in a difficult position.'

'Of course she can – it's not difficult. It's easy.'

Romy was making mayonnaise in a large bowl: whisking with one hand and dripping oil from a jug with the other. Her fringe was escaping from its kirby grips and sticking to her sweating forehead. Kathleen wondered how young she was. She looked barely out of her teens.

'I love children,' Romy went on. 'Lauren can help me, there's lots of room, she can run around . . . we'll get on beautifully. You must concentrate on your work. It's why you're here.'

'Are you sure? Really sure? I'll pay you of course.'

'But it's nothing! Don't even think of it, really.'

Apparently looking after an eight-year-old girl was not such a terrible chore as Kathleen thought. Perhaps childcare, like making mayonnaise by hand, came easily to some.

'Certainly I must pay you,' she said. 'It wouldn't be right otherwise.'

When out of her bath and in her pyjamas Lauren was informed of this development and became wild with excitement all over again. Here was a chance to be useful and grown-up – it felt almost like being given a job. To be occupied in the kitchen all day with Romy would be much more fun than anything her mother could offer.

'It's called being a "sous chef",' Romy told her. 'It's a very important job.'

Kathleen, for her part, would have left her daughter with Pontius Pilate if it got her off the hook, but here was a solution she did not even have to feel guilty about.

At the end of the first day of this new arrangement Kathleen rushed back to the house.

'I came back to put you to bed,' she announced to Lauren. 'Are you all right? Did you have fun?'

'You didn't have to,' Lauren said. 'I can do my own bath and bedtime. I know how.'

Lauren did not like having being helped when she could do something herself, but Kathleen called this ungrateful.

'You could just say "thank you",' she said, 'instead of telling me off. I *rushed* back to see you.'

Lauren yawned. She could hardly keep her eyes open.

'What did you do today?' Kathleen asked.

'I helped Romy.'

'Was it fun? Did you have lovely things to eat?'

'Yes. I helped make the pasta and hung it up in ribbons.' She began scratching one of the new mosquito bites on her forearm.

'Don't do that.' Kathleen caught her daughter's hand and held it still like a butterfly she had trapped on a window-pane. 'Tomorrow I have to leave early. Will you be all right?'

'Yes.'

'Are you sure?'

'*Yes*. Stop asking all the time.'

'There's no need to bite my head off.' Kathleen dropped Lauren's hand and stood up to look down at her. 'I hope

147

you're more polite to Romy. She won't want to look after a rude little girl.'

But Lauren was not frightened of her mother. 'I am polite, and she's not looking after me. I'm helping her.'

'Don't be cheeky. Now go to sleep.'

'It's not time yet.'

'It's nine o'clock.'

'It's eight o'clock in England.'

'I said go to *sleep*, madam.' At the door Kathleen snapped off the light. She wished her attempts to be motherly did not always end in rage or disappointment, usually her own. Was it her fault? Was it Lauren's? Even as a baby Lauren had refused to breastfeed and, as soon as she was able, had tried to grab the bottle and feed herself.

Lauren's appearance in the household had the opposite effect to the one anticipated by Kathleen. She had expected irritation and annoyance, and she had rehearsed the apologies she would have to make, but everyone seemed both improved and cheered by Lauren's presence. Her enthusiasm was a tonic, her curiosity was infectious and her guilelessness seemed to cure the atmosphere of its sourness. At breakfast, yawning and muddle-headed in her pyjamas, she was something of a mascot. Vincent, always first down, would offer her a little bow.

'Good morning, Mademoiselle Griffin.'

'Good morning, Monsieur Wexler.'

Ava came next, tousling Lauren's hair with one hand. She and Bob maintained the illusion that they had not shared a room by coming separately to breakfast.

'*Bonjour, ma petite.*'

148

'*Bonjour*, Ava.'

When Bob appeared, last of all, he would stretch theatrically and give a tremendous fake yawn.

'Howdy, Lauren. Sleep well? Any more bug-bites this morning?'

'Hello, Bob. Five more on my legs and three on my neck, thanks for asking.'

Lauren was interested in all of them but fascinated by Vincent. She studied him as if he were an animal in the wild and wrote lists of his peccadilloes and distinguishing qualities in her notebook. She had no experience of an adult so peculiar – he was more like Willy Wonka or the White Rabbit or Peter Pan than a normal grown-up. His skin was chalk white and his hair a rich orange that shimmered in the sunlight like a cockerel's wing. He was allergic to strawberries, peanuts, bee stings and shellfish. He only ate white food: yoghurt, poached chicken and the whites of eggs but not their yolks. He suffered from asthma and carried little puffers about in his pockets, patting himself anxiously when he started to wheeze. He was afraid of water and could not swim – even a bath was beyond him. He drank Coca-Cola but only from a bottle, never from a can, and always through a plastic straw. Lauren pattered after him, questioned him ceaselessly and seemed not to be afraid of him. Even more surprising, he seemed not to grow tired of her.

At first Kathleen was relieved, but soon she was jealous. She began to wonder if Vincent was doing it on purpose. Was this another tactic to undermine her? When she heard Ava and Bob laughing at some childish comment, or Vincent patiently enduring another of Lauren's Q&A sessions, she felt even more isolated than she had before. How could they listen to Lauren rabbiting on? Vincent frequently walked off before Kathleen had even finished her sentence and yet now she watched him put down the daily call sheet, make a tent of his fingers and explain, in no apparent hurry, that his Jewish mother had been bundled away to America as a little girl and grown up to teach him French.

'And that's why I love France. Does that answer your question?'

'Yes. Thank you.'

'Any time.'

Was that rejoinder accompanied by a little, amused glance in Kathleen's direction? *Any time*. It was humiliating. He had made her feel that anything she said was a waste of his time and now *this*. Kathleen could not bask in Lauren's success but sat glowering in her shade.

It was a long and trying week, but at last it was Saturday and Lauren's last day. It was also her birthday and when Vincent discovered this at breakfast he magicked a 500-franc note from behind her ear, shivering it into existence between finger and thumb and handing it to her with one of his little bows.

At first Lauren was too astonished to say thank you.

'Lauren, where are your manners? Do you know how much money that is? How lucky you are?' Kathleen lowered her coffee cup. 'You must thank Mr Wexler properly.'

'Thank you very much,' Lauren stammered.

'You're very welcome. Thank you for coming to visit us.'

Lauren went pink. 'I'm going to show Romy.' She ran indoors with her money.

When she had gone Vincent said, 'I'm going to give you the day off, Kathleen. We'll manage without you and you can spend the day with your daughter' – he waved a beneficent hand like the Pope on Easter Sunday – 'doing whatever it is that mothers like to do with their little girls.'

'Day off?' Kathleen did not like the sound of this. 'What do you mean? Why?'

'Because it's Lauren's birthday. You both deserve a treat.'

It was his way of telling her what to do: to make it sound as if it was for her benefit.

'Treat?' Cup rattled into saucer. 'But what? What would we do?'

'Whatever Lauren wants. That's what treating someone means.' He was goading her.

'But . . .' Kathleen tried in vain to think of a 'but'.

'There's a problem?' Vincent glittered at the prospect of a tantrum.

'No.' Kathleen gathered herself. 'Of course not. No problem.'

'Aren't you going to thank me?'

Kathleen flushed. 'Yes. Thank you.'

Only now did he smile.

Kathleen was silenced. At first she fumed and then the crawling fears began to teem around her. He wanted to get rid of her, that much was plain, and they had most likely all discussed how to do it: Lauren was their convenient excuse. He was making her babysit to punish her for having Lauren. She was expected to be a mother but not allowed to be an actor. The only thing worse than spending the day with Vincent was being expelled from Vincent's presence entirely.

Having eviscerated a croissant onto the tablecloth, she got up, went indoors and climbed the stairs to her bedroom where she paced up and down, knotting and unknotting her fingers. After twenty minutes she heard the Mercedes start up on the gravel and she rushed down to the front door – she could not help herself.

'Vincent, please,' she begged, 'I don't want to take the day off. There's so much to do and I'd rather work. I'm here to work. Please?'

'You're overtired,' he said. His face was expressionless and his green eyes hidden behind huge dark glasses. 'You need a day off. We're all agreed.'

'We?' Kathleen was frantic.

'You need to decompress. Don't think about the film for the rest of the day. Enjoy yourself.' He got into the seat beside Rocky and buzzed the window down. 'Promise me you'll relax.'

'But . . .' Kathleen was nearly in tears.

'Promise?'

Tears were crammed behind her eyes, ready to fall. 'I promise' came out in a whisper.

Vincent smiled in triumph. 'Good girl.'

Rocky released the clutch and the car sped away, closely followed by Bob and Ava in their hired convertible. Kathleen stood alone in the sun on the white gravel. Her humiliation was total. The ground seemed to throb beneath her feet. She looked up at the sun. *You need a day off. We're all agreed.* They thought she was cracking up. Was she?

Blinking back tears of frustration she stepped from baking white sunlight into the inkpot cool of the hall and then, her pace quickened by rage, strode along a dim stone passage to the kitchen where she found Lauren and Romy in cheerful harmony, the latter kneading dough on a marble slab and the former dusted from head to toe with spilled flour.

Lauren looked up at her mother. 'Why haven't you gone?'

'Don't say it in that nasty way. I've got the day off. What happened to you?'

'I dropped the flour and it went poof. Why have you got the day off?'

'Because it's your birthday.'

'Because of *me*?' Frowning, Lauren considered the implications and became suspicious. 'What are you going to do?'

'I'm going to have a swim and then we are going on an expedition.'

'Who is "we"?'

'You and I.'

Kathleen could see Lauren thinking quickly.

'But Romy needs me. While the dough is *proving*' – it was a new word and she brought it out proudly – 'we're going to make ice cream.'

'I'll buy you an ice cream.'

'Not *eating* it, *making* it. That's different.' Lauren was desperate and desperation made her rude.

'This is supposed to be a birthday treat for *you*. I've taken time off work specially.'

'No you haven't. Vincent's the boss. He *gave* you time off. If you want to give me a treat leave me here with Romy. I'm busy. I'm not hungry. I don't want an ice cream and anyway I feel sick when you drive.'

In a sharper tone Kathleen said, 'I'm not asking you, Lauren, I'm telling you: this is what we are doing. Be ready in thirty minutes. I'm going to have a swim before we leave.'

'But—'

'That's enough!' To be continually answered back was

153

infuriating. Kathleen gathered herself for a blast of temper but before she could speak, Romy intervened.

'Lauren, why not take the day off? Even sous chefs do on their birthdays.'

'Do they?'

'Yes, sometimes, and anyway I'm making you a cake this afternoon. You can't help me with that – it would spoil the surprise.'

'Oh.' The cake was a pleasing thought. 'I suppose I could.'

'I'll manage without you.'

Grudgingly Lauren capitulated. 'Well, OK.'

Kathleen, her temper snatching at its bridle, said, 'So that's settled? Everyone's happy?'

'If Romy says—'

Kathleen overruled her. 'You don't need Romy's permission to do as I say. Put on some clean clothes and meet me in the hall in thirty minutes.'

Having kept her temper so far, or just about, it was imperative that Kathleen now exited the room. Without waiting for a retort she stepped out of the kitchen door, past the stone table and the remains of breakfast, quickly along the paths through the garden and down three scented terraces to the pool where she took off all her clothes and dived into the deep end. Up and down she swam, fast lengths of front crawl until her chest was bursting. When she had run out of puff she rolled over and floated on her back, arms outstretched, looking into the blue with vacant calm. After ten minutes she got out and shook water off herself, watching lizards scoot out of range across the hot limestone paving. Feeling cooler inside and out she wrapped herself in a towel and climbed the stairs to her bedroom.

Here she stood naked in front of the mirror and then reached for a dress she had bought in the flea market at L'Isle sur la Sorgue a few weeks ago – a long, pale, antique cotton with cap sleeves and delicate lace at the hem. She would wear this, and her hair in a ponytail, and no make-up today. It would be a holiday from herself.

Downstairs in the hall she found Lauren, who always bounced back quickly from an argument, trying to do a somersault over the banister. She had changed her clothes and put on a new pair of striped espadrilles.

'I'm ready. These are espadrilles.' She put out one of her feet for Kathleen to admire. 'They're a French sort of shoe.'

'I know.' It was irritating to be told things she already knew but Kathleen had determined to be serene. 'I used to have some myself.'

'*You* did?' Lauren was astonished. 'But when? How?'

'I bought them on holiday I expect,' Kathleen said, 'like you.'

'Mine were a birthday present. From Romy.'

'How kind of her.' Perhaps if she said the right things and pretended to be cheerful then the right feelings would follow. 'Maybe I'll get some espadrilles this afternoon,' she said playfully as they went out of the house to the car. 'Then we could have matching shoes.'

'*Maybe*.' Lauren looked doubtful. 'We could ask Romy where to get them.'

'We are not going to ask Romy anything,' Kathleen snapped before she could stop herself. Then after recovering she added, 'We are going to have a lovely adventure all by ourselves.'

In the hot car Lauren sat on her hands to stop her legs burning.

'My hands don't get as hot as my legs. Why is that? Mum?'

'I don't know. Stop wriggling.'

'It's the seat. It's hot-hot-hot.'

'You're making an awful fuss.'

'I'm *burning* that's why. Where are we going?'

'To Gordes.'

'What for?'

'Because it's a very pretty village.'

'How do you know?'

'Because I've been there before.'

'When?'

The questions were like balloons bursting and Kathleen closed her eyes briefly.

'Before you were born, with your father. We drove around the south of France on our honeymoon.'

Lauren was silenced. She could always be temporarily muted by information about her parents' lives before she was born – she did not really believe that they could have existed without her and found every detail about their previous lives absurd and incredible.

She could also, as she was now, be terrorised into submission by Kathleen's driving, which was fast and erratic. As they accelerated down the drive and swung out into the road she moved edgily about on her seat and put a hand on the door handle as if she were considering jumping out. Finally she blurted out:

'Mum! Too fast!'

'*I'm* driving, not you.'

Lauren was quiet, and when she was quiet Kathleen felt better.

'It's about a twenty minute drive I think,' she said. 'It'll be lovely when we get there.'

'I'm going to be sick.'

'No you're not. You're just trying to make me slow down.'

Surprised to find herself losing all today's battles Lauren gave up speaking and stared through the windscreen with her mouth tightly shut.

The route was exceedingly twisty and Kathleen glanced over at Lauren's white face several times as they approached Gordes, climbing the winding road up to the middle of the village, but Lauren, perhaps by sheer force of will, was not sick, and nor did she complain of being frightened. They parked at the western corner of the village in a dusty car park where a row of grumbling coaches signalled other visitors.

'Ugh,' Kathleen said. 'Tourists.'

'What are we?' Lauren asked.

'*Not* tourists,' said Kathleen firmly. She held out her hand for Lauren to take as they walked into the village together.

Lauren was relaxed now that the journey was over and skipped along in the dust, tugging at her mother's hand and peering over the wall at the edge of the road. 'I can see goats! And a fig tree! And a man fixing his car!'

Kathleen yanked her back. '*Stop* it. If I let go you'll fall off the cliff.'

'No I won't.'

'Walk properly next to me.'

'I'm not scared of heights. It's your driving I'm scared of.'

'You don't mind your father's driving and he's much faster than me.'

Lauren wrinkled her nose. 'I wish Dad was here. It's my birthday and he hasn't even rung up.'

'He won't have forgotten. He probably just can't get to a telephone.'

They were both silent, thinking about where Walter was and what he was doing. Being on a film set was like being on another planet – Kathleen had not looked at a newspaper for a month. When she thought about Walter she felt uneasy and frightened so she tried not to think about him at all.

Now her mood dulled again as if the sun had gone in. Like Lauren, she wished Walter were here. What felt like work to her would be fun to him: looking around the little town; stopping for ice cream and Orangina at a cafe; buying postcards and sending them home. But without Walter she felt nothing but tired. Self-pity nudged the headache in her temple. The sun was too bright and hot; the shade too cold and dark. They ought to sit down somewhere and have lunch but Kathleen did not want lunch with Lauren, she wanted a grown-up date: cold white wine and langoustines. *This* was not fair. *This* was not fun. If only she were at work she would feel at the centre of things but here she was no better than a hand-holding nanny.

Lauren was having similar thoughts. 'If Dad was here he would know what to do,' she said as Kathleen dithered on a corner.

'I know what to do.' Kathleen tried to sound decisive.

'We're going to buy a postcard and then sit at a cafe and write to your father.'

Lauren was pleased. 'Are we? Oh good.'

'Yes. Here's the tabac – you see it has that red thing outside that looks like a cigar. That's how you know.'

'It doesn't look like a cigar.'

Kathleen, who agreed, pretended she had not heard. 'We can buy a postcard here.'

Lauren rattled the door. 'But it's shut.'

'All right,' said Kathleen wearily, 'we can't.'

Peering at the sign, Lauren said, 'It opens at fifteen-thirty. "Ouvert" means open.' She had been learning French from Romy and took every opportunity to show it off. 'We can have ice cream first.' And she skipped away to choose a table.

Under a soothing umbrella things felt a little better. Kathleen ordered ice cream and a citron pressé for Lauren. She remembered a drink called a 'bicyclette' and ordered that for herself – Campari and white wine, just right for a hot afternoon. The village basked half-asleep in the sun, and the umbrella's fringe flicked in the warm breeze, making a pleasing sound.

Gordes did not seem to have altered since Kathleen's first visit. 'French life is a routine that will never change,' Walter had told her. 'Why would it? They know how to be civilised.' Back then, having just married him, Kathleen agreed with everything he said. He was not only a man and older than she was but he always sounded as if there was no doubt in his mind. Her only confidence was in her looks, more beautiful every day. 'Women are more beautiful as they get older,' Walter said approvingly. 'They are most beautiful in their thirties.' She hoped he was right about that. In any case, French men all turned for a second look as she walked past and Walter saw them noticing. *That* was the important thing. He held her hand tightly because, 'I daren't let go.' He was proud of her and she, in consequence, was proud of herself.

Yes, Mr and Mrs Walter Griffin had been delighted with one another that day. How glad they were to be together and, better still, married! Nothing could be better; no one could be happier. They spent hours over lunch and ambled back to their hotel for a long siesta. Lauren was born forty-one weeks later – noisy, blackberry-faced and upside-down – and today she was nine years old.

The waiter brought their drinks.

'Don't put in too much . . .' Kathleen began but it was too late: sugar poured from a canister lay at the bottom of Lauren's glass in an inch-thick sludge. 'See? Now you've ruined it.'

'No I haven't. I've made it delicious.'

Kathleen did not answer but drank her bicyclette and ordered another, wagging her empty glass at the waiter.

'What is it? I thought "bicyclette" meant bicycle.'

'It does, but it's the name of a drink too. It's for grown-ups. It's wine mixed with a bitter drink called Campari.'

'Sounds yuk.'

Lauren went back to hoovering sugary lemon-water up through a straw and kicking the chair legs with her feet. Kathleen reminded herself that this was a birthday treat. But where was her second drink? Mothers deserved a treat too.

At last the waiter, black-haired and sweating, appeared

again bearing another Campari concoction and Lauren's ice cream.

'*Voilà, Mademoiselle.*'

Lauren beamed. '*Merci beaucoup.*'

The waiter tucked their bill under the ashtray and withdrew, and Lauren busily tackled her ice cream, mixing balls of chocolate and vanilla in the silver dish until she had created a muddy gloop which she lifted quickly, teaspoon by liquid teaspoon, into her mouth. Kathleen watched her for a minute and then could bear it no longer.

'Lauren, that is a *disgusting* way to eat. Children don't behave like that in France. They are sophisticated and have good manners.'

'Sophisti-what?' Interested, Lauren looked up. She liked a new word. Under the table she swung her legs. 'What's it mean?' She crossed and uncrossed her feet rapidly at the ankle – it was one of her favourite fidgets – and in doing so bumped a table-leg sufficiently hard to tip over Kathleen's drink; they both leapt back but not before a crimson ocean had poured across the table and sloshed into Kathleen's lap.

'Oh, *Lauren*!' Kathleen jumped up. Her new white dress was soaked in scarlet. 'Look what you've done!'

It was impossible! This was France! French women did not spill drinks all over themselves and laugh about it the way some drunk girl might at the pub in England. Looking around Kathleen could see faces turned towards them – people looking, pitying and embarrassed, relieved it wasn't them or their daughter who had caused such a scene.

Lauren was staring at her mother with an open-mouthed expression that reflected to Kathleen the scale of the disaster. Seeing this, Kathleen was suddenly maddened with rage and without thinking she grabbed Lauren by the arm and shook her.

'You stupid little girl!'

'It was an accident!'

'Get away from me! Get out of my sight!'

Kathleen pushed Lauren away – a hard push; hard enough for her to stumble backwards, trip over her chair and fall on her hands and knees. In this position she burst into tears and then she picked herself up and ran.

'Lauren!' Kathleen yelled after her. '*Lauren!*' She watched Lauren's ponytail swing out of sight around the corner of the square. Then she rushed into the cafe where she was given a bundle of napkins by the smirking waiter. She dabbed at her dress but it was no good: the mark only seemed to get bigger and brighter and now blots of damp paper had stuck to it.

When she came outside again there was no sign of Lauren. Summoning the waiter to pay her bill she asked him, '*Avez-vous voir ma fille?*'

'*Vu,*' corrected the waiter. '*Avez-vous vu ma fille.*' He put her change on the table. '*Non, je n'ai pas vu votre fille.*'

It was defeat. Kathleen walked slowly back to the car. She was sure that Lauren would be following at a distance and she allowed her imagination to make it so – *there* she heard a striped espadrille scrunch in the gravel; *there* she glimpsed her daughter's little triangular face watching her from a corner – but even when she had got into the car and wound down all the windows there was no sign of her.

Before she set out to look for her she reflected on the day: a failure. She should never have tried to play mother, she should have left Lauren in the kitchen with Romy where she

162

preferred to be. Vincent had not wanted her on set and Lauren had not wanted to be stuck with her all day. How could it be any other way? She was neither actor nor mother but a failure at both. She leant her head back against the leather headrest and closed her eyes. She seemed paralysed by this latest catastrophe and unable even to lift her arms and legs. She had been vanquished.

Whether it was a few minutes or an hour later she could not have said, but she was roused by Lauren's shrill voice:

'That's it! *That's* the one. It's got a yellow sticker in the back.'

Kathleen got out of the car. 'There you are!' Here was Lauren and here too was an attractive dark-haired man she was leading by the hand.

'I got lost. This man was helping me.'

'I couldn't find you.' Kathleen crouched to hug her. 'Please don't run away again.' She placed her hands on her daughter's shoulders. 'Promise?'

'I didn't *run* away,' Lauren corrected her. 'You told me to go away.'

Ignoring this, Kathleen stood up. 'I'm so sorry,' she said to the handsome stranger. 'I hope she hasn't ruined your afternoon?'

'Certainly not.'

The man was smiling at her – appraising her. Despite herself she began to blush. She pulled at the short gold chain she wore around her neck, suddenly self-conscious, and found herself too nervous to meet his eye. His stare was heating her up like a two-bar fire. When would he stop? Her glance flickered over him: brown eyes, tanned arms and hands streaked with white paint. There was no wedding ring.

'Lauren tells me it's her birthday.'

'Yes – a good day for a tantrum!' Kathleen gave a light laugh and indicated the stain on her skirt. 'Just a silly accident.' She was feeling quite unlike the piteous creature of five minutes ago. 'I suppose she thought I'd be angry, so she ran off.'

'You *were* angry.'

'Only for a second,' Kathleen tinkled with laughter. 'I was soaked!'

'This is Frank,' Lauren told her mother. 'He lives here. He's English. He's building a house.'

'Rebuilding.' Frank smiled at Lauren and then at Kathleen. 'It was a wreck. It's nearly finished.'

'How lovely. It's beautiful here. I adore France and this is my favourite part.' Kathleen wished she had bothered with make-up this morning. 'Do you live here all year round?'

'Yes. For my work, really. I'm an artist.'

'How wonderful,' breathed Kathleen. She was gushing like a tap – she must stop speaking unless she could think of something sensible to say, but his gaze seemed to have emptied her brain of intelligent thought. 'It must be so peaceful and inspiring.' She sounded like a greetings card.

'Why don't you come and see the house? It's not far.'

'Can we?' Lauren looked up at her mother.

Kathleen did not want Lauren tagging along. 'Not today,' she said. 'We've no time.'

Lauren begged, 'Tomorrow? Please?'

'But you're leaving tomorrow.'

'Oh.' Lauren was crestfallen.

'And you?' Frank asked Kathleen. 'Are you leaving tomorrow?'

'No. I'm here for another fortnight. Lauren has to go back to school.'

'Well then,' Frank said, 'why don't you come on your own? Come any time. I'd rather have one visitor than none.'

'Well . . .' Kathleen pretended to think it over. 'I suppose I could try. If you tell me where it is.'

'Near Saint-Victor. Up the hill, past the castle and on for half a mile. Mine is the third turn on the right. Look out for two stone gateposts.'

'All right.'

'You will come?'

'I'll try.'

Now their eyes met at last and she could not tear her look from his.

Lauren broke the spell. 'It's not fair. *I* want to come. Why does everything fun happen without me?'

Kathleen looked down at her without sympathy. 'Poor Lauren. Say goodbye to Frank, will you?'

Lauren squinted up at Frank. 'Goodbye. Thank you for rescuing me.'

'*Je t'en prie*,' Frank said. 'Goodbye . . .' He shook Lauren's hand and turned to Kathleen '. . . and *au revoir*. I hope I'll see you very soon.' He passed his eyes over her once more, as if he were committing the image to memory, and then he was gone.

In the car on the way home Kathleen did not notice Lauren prattling on, and nor did she tear a strip off her daughter for disappearing. She did not in fact say anything. Without speaking she drove slowly and distractedly, nearly tipping off the edge of the road on several corners, while tugging with her thumb at her necklace. She did not want to abandon the little fantasy that was unfolding in her head: she went to Frank's house; he led her inside; he caught hold of her on the stairs and kissed her blindly, passionately, desperately . . .

'Mum are you drunk? You're driving so *slowly*.'

'What?'

Kathleen was not concentrating on driving but on remembering the way Frank's look had beaten down on her like the spring sun after winter, a luxurious thrill, a look she had felt and could still feel with her whole body as if she had been charged by a physical touch; as if she were a cat arching its back under its owner's hand. She did not want this sensation to fade; she wanted to extract every drop of molten pleasure from Frank's desire. She wanted to feel again the intensity of that gaze and to be sustained; to be transformed.

'Mum – *here!*'

A squeak from Lauren signalled the turn for their house.

Romy had made a birthday cake and decorated the table in the garden with flowers. The others were back from the set – filming had finished unexpectedly early today because one of Rass's dogs needed to go to the vet. Everyone was in a good mood. Even the dress, Romy said, could be salvaged.

'It's not ruined.' She examined the stain. 'I can dye it for you.'

'Would you? Really? You're a saint.'

Kathleen went upstairs to change and from her bedroom window she looked down on them all: Vincent sitting at the head of the table, his hair like a flame in the falling light; Ava fussing and flirting with Bob, her arms around his

166

neck; Romy standing apart, her hands on her hips and a tea towel thrown over her shoulder; Lauren kneeling on a chair and leaning forward to blow out her candles.

'What about waiting for your mother?' It was Romy's voice.

'Do I have to?'

'No!' This was Vincent.

Ava called out, 'One-two-three: blow!'

Lauren blew out her candles and everyone clapped.

From her eyrie Kathleen felt at last the serenity she had craved that morning. She was separate. She did not care. She watched Lauren cut the cake and then floated downstairs in a trance, not even sure if she touched the stone steps with her feet.

She preferred not to be noticed this evening and sat quietly, looking on. She did not feel the competition of yesterday, or every day for the last four weeks. She did not want to be noticed, and not being noticed made her think that she might as well be in Frank's house and making love for all the difference it made to anyone. She continued with her daydream: he would kiss her; he would say *I can't resist you*; he would press her against the wall and put a hand on her breast or draw up her skirt with one hand . . .

'Kathleen? Kathleen?'

Romy was offering a piece of birthday cake on a plate.

'No. I mean yes, of course, how delicious.'

Excitement made it hard to sleep, keeping her wakeful. Long after Vincent had wheezed past the door of her room and on up the stairs, pausing for a squirt from his puffer on the landing, Kathleen was still turning restlessly under the

167

sheet with her eyes wide open. Several times she sat up, punched the pillow into a more accommodating shape and lay down again. Once she said, 'Oh, no-no-*no*,' quietly to herself. She blinked at the ceiling for an hour. She listened to a nightingale in the garden, its unearthly, warbling song speaking of tragedy in a language she did not know. She lay on her side, facing the window, and waited for light. To the homesick and lonely, sleepless before dawn, everything seems impossible: marriage and its opposite; family and solitude; fidelity and faithlessness. When Kathleen could see the sky begin to turn from black to a cold grey she got up, pulled on a sweater and slipped downstairs and out of the kitchen door.

Night was over but it was still more dark than light; scattered objects took soft, grey shapes in different shades. Glasses and bottles stood on the table and a chair had been tipped over. Someone's shoes; someone's hat; a candle burned out in a tall, glass jar.

Walking away from the house and the table Kathleen drifted ghostlike along a narrow path between brushing borders of lavender. Clouds of scent, invisible but distinct, hung in the warming air. A bird shook its feathers on a branch above her head; another clattered through leaves before slanting away in the pearling sky. Steps took her from one terrace to the next until she reached the pool, where mist left a vanishing breath and the surface lifted and fell, stirred by departing spirits. Standing on the white flagstones Kathleen heard the first honey bee of the morning, winding past her ear on its way to breakfast. She stared down at the ground and then up at the sky. She closed her eyes.

The encounter with Frank had faded. With her eyes shut she could recall his face but the recollection did not summon yesterday's feeling – or even the feeling that had kept her awake last night, restless in the bed, imagining and imagining. That fever was gone; now she could recall an image but nothing more.

Today was a Sunday. With nothing to remind her of yesterday, it would go like this: she would take Lauren to the airport and commit her to the care of British Airways. She would tell her daughter to be good for the nice lady, she would wave goodbye and then she would come back to the house. She would go on as before until the last two weeks were done. There was nothing so hard about any of that.

And it was exactly what would have happened had it not been for Lauren. When Kathleen went into her bedroom to wake her for their drive to the airport she was met by a mutiny.

'I don't want to go.'

'You have to.'

'I hate London, I hate Ebba and I hate school. I want to live here with Romy for ever.'

'Stop being silly and get dressed. You've got to pack your bag and have breakfast and then I'm taking you to the airport.'

'I don't *want* to go.'

'Tough.' Kathleen yanked back the sheet. 'Get up and stop being a baby.' She dragged Lauren off the bed and onto her feet but Lauren went floppy, as if her legs had lost their stuffing, and refused to stand up. It was a maddening trick. 'Stand up. Stand *up*.' Kathleen tried and failed to put

Lauren on her feet. 'Why are you being like this? You wouldn't dare if your father were here.'

'If Dad was here you wouldn't be so horrible!'

This was all the worse for being true and Kathleen gave Lauren a smack.

'Ow! Stop hitting me! I wish you were dead and Romy was my mother.'

'Do you?' Kathleen was incandescent with rage. 'Well, I wish you'd never been born, you nasty *nasty* child.'

The pair stared at each other, eyes wide with disbelief. Then Lauren wriggled out of her mother's grip, rushed from the room and ran down the stairs in her nightie, leaving Kathleen empty-handed and clutching the air with her fists.

One by one she flung Lauren's clothes into her green nylon rucksack. *Horrible, ungrateful, vicious* – but it was no good: shame suffused her, an unbreathable fog, and she had to sit down and cover her face. She sat on the edge of the bed, the rucksack clutched against her, and waited for her heart to stop trying to punch its way out of her chest. She wondered how she would ever go downstairs and face not only Lauren but Romy, into whose shoulder Lauren would no doubt be shedding pitiful tears.

After chastising herself in the mirror – *Is that me? Did I do that?* – Kathleen trudged downstairs. In the hall she called wearily, 'Lauren? It's time to go.'

When Lauren appeared she was holding Romy's hand and looking not apologetic or upset but defiant. 'Mum,' she said, 'Romy is going to take me.'

Kathleen flushed. 'Romy does not want to spend her day off driving you all the way to Marseille airport.'

'I'm happy to,' Romy said. 'There's a *vide-grenier* in Lourmarin today and I can stop on the way back. It's a good place to pick up linen sheets.' She paused and then added, 'But if you would rather take her . . . ?'

Kathleen did not answer this but asked Lauren, 'Are you sure? You aren't going to have a tantrum halfway there and change your mind?'

Lauren lifted her chin. 'Not if Romy takes me.'

She had won and they all knew it. She eyed her mother with pitying hauteur.

Kathleen said, 'Here's your bag.' She handed over the rucksack. 'You'd better get dressed in the car. You don't want to be late.'

'OK.' Lauren took the bag.

'Goodbye, then.' Kathleen crouched on her heels. She put her arms around Lauren and felt the little girl lean briefly into them: a small concession. 'I'll see you in two weeks.'

'Bye.'

Outside the front door, Romy's car, a blue Renault 4, was waiting in the shade of a spreading fig tree. Lauren got into the front passenger seat, settled herself, shut the door and put her seatbelt on. Kathleen gave her passport and ticket to Romy.

'She's an unaccompanied minor so they'll send a chaperone. Should I give you some money? In case she's thirsty or something?'

'We'll be fine.'

Romy got into the driving seat. She put on a pair of sunglasses which had been resting on the dashboard, stuck one elbow out of the window and started the car. Then, remembering something, she leaned out to call to Kathleen . . .

'By the way – I think you met my husband yesterday. An Englishman covered in paint?' She smiled. 'That was Frank.'

'Frank? Your husband?'

'You're surprised?'

'Yes – no . . .' Kathleen was covered in confusion. 'It's just that you don't look old enough to have a husband.'

Lauren butted in. 'Mum, Romy's twenty-one. The law says you can get married when you're sixteen.'

'Thank you, Lauren,' Kathleen said. To Romy she went on, 'What a coincidence!'

'But, Mum, you don't believe in coincidence,' Lauren chipped in again. 'That's what you always say.'

'That's true.' Looking into the car at them both Kathleen felt jealousy, rage, frustration and disappointment washed away by a beatific calm. 'I don't.' Now it was her turn to smile. 'It must be fate.' Stepping back she released them and waved goodbye as they drove away.

After breakfast she showered, dressed and made herself up – but not too much. She wanted to look unadorned, as if she had woken thinking of him and come straight from her bed. Romy would not be back for two or three hours, Frank was only five minutes away and the others were asleep. Nobody saw how pretty she looked, nobody saw her drive away and nobody saw which way she went: through the village, up the hill, past the château and a right turn in between those two gateposts.

VI

Through her retirement home, well-versed in the proced-
ure, Marian arranged for Frank to be cremated.

'Quickly, please,' said Jem on the telephone.

Marian sniffed. 'Sooner the better. I'll do it myself if I
have to.'

There would be no funeral service and no memorial cere-
mony and no one, if Jem had her way, would be present.
She told Marian about Sonny.

'Your age, is he? That explains a lot.'

'Does it?'

'It explains what made that dreadful man – your father
– the way he was: he didn't get what he wanted. He wanted
that woman, whatshername, and he got you instead.'

Jem blinked when she heard this. It hurt. She had not
thought she could still be hurt by her father, but there it was.

'Kathleen,' she murmured. 'That's her name. You mean
he wanted Kathleen and he got me.'

'That's right.' Such things were perfectly straightforward
as far as Marian was concerned and she spoke as if hers
was the final word on the matter.

'You don't seem surprised,' Jem said. She felt faint in the
face of such certainty.

'Surprised?' Marian did her little snort-laugh, which meant 'you must be joking'. 'Nothing would surprise me about *him*.'

Having been a professional nanny for forty-five years Marian had seen everything that the unravelling family unit had to offer: affairs discovered, husbands fighting their wives, children weeping on staircases, dogs beaten and even a house set on fire. She had abandoned sentiment long ago and made a virtue of being unshockable.

'I hope for his sake,' she said of Sonny, 'that he doesn't take after his father.'

'You haven't met his mother,' said Jem.

This conversation took place on December 27th: the day after Jem confronted Sonny. She had woken with the understanding that yesterday, although justified, was irreversible.

This morning it felt as if Frank's body was the evidence of a crime she had committed, and it was therefore not only desirable but necessary to reduce him to ashes. She didn't want Sonny to see the body – she didn't want a concrete impression of Frank to form in Sonny's mind. Frank must remain a vague and flickering shape, like a figure seen in a flame, and therefore he must be got rid of. She telephoned Marian early, knowing she would be up because 'God loves an early bird', as she used to say. Sick days and lie-ins were not countenanced.

Sonny's first thought on the same morning was not of Frank or Jem but Becka: he woke up and found her wrapped in his arms. He was naked. She was naked. Unlatching his arms from around her he turned away carefully to lie on his back. He placed both palms on his head: *Oh no*.

They had fallen asleep on top of the covers, fully dressed. Hadn't they? But now he remembered waking in the night. She had woken too and they were both cold. They got under the duvet and almost by accident bumped into each other, shivering, and kissed. One kiss became many kisses and pleasure had run away with them: quickly they had undressed and made love almost blindly, as if they were still asleep and dreaming; as if this was the only moment and the end of the world was coming. Afterwards they had laughed quietly at the beauty of it.

Now the events of yesterday – not just Becka but Jem, Frank, Kathleen and Walter – burst over Sonny like a tropical downpour. He lay quite still as if winded. *Who am I?* He was frightened. When he could move he slipped out of bed, dressed and let himself out of the flat. It was early and still dark. Becka did not stir. On the street a ginger tomcat slipped past him on its way home.

Once inside his own front door he breathed a sigh of relief but it was short-lived: the kitchen light came on and here was Lauren, standing in the doorway with Mike at her side. They looked at each other. Mike was sleepy and yawning, his tail waving from side to side in greeting like the pendulum of a friendly clock. Lauren was still dressed in yesterday's clothes underneath a long overcoat of Walter's.

'Why aren't you back at yours?' Sonny whispered.

'Slept on the sofa.'

'Why?'

She shrugged. 'Felt like it. You?'

'Stayed at Becka's. I needed to get out. Can you blame me?'

'No.' Lauren yawned. 'No blame.'

She looked and sounded as if she had not so much slept on the sofa as lain down on it for a few minutes while for the rest of the night she stared out of the window, biting the skin off her lips. Sonny watched her pull a folded piece of paper from a coat pocket.

'Jem wrote down her number. And the other thing.'

Sonny looked at the name: *familial aortic thoracic aneurysm and dissection*. He was frightened again.

'This thing,' he said helplessly. 'I can't avoid it.'

'We'll deal with it together.'

But Sonny shook his head. 'It's not happening to you. It's happening to me.'

He was afraid. The signature on his portrait had been forged. He was not what he had been yesterday. He had been proved a fake. *Then who am I? What am I made of?*

'You're not on your own. You've got us.'

'But I haven't,' he said bleakly. 'Not any more.'

The threads that tied him to the planet – Walter, Kathleen, Lauren – had been severed. Jem was the only one left. He turned away from Lauren and trudged upstairs.

When he typed 'familial aortic thoracic aneurysm and dissection' into Google Sonny read that 'this condition, unless found and treated early, usually results in death'. After that he shut the laptop, showered and dressed with shaking hands. He waited downstairs for his mother.

When she appeared she was bleary with hangover, her skin pleated and her eyes vanishing. She had gone to bed in her clothes and they looked too small for her this morning, like a skin she needed to shed.

'What are you doing up so early?'

Sonny was vibrating with anger. 'You expect me to sleep? After what I learned yesterday?' His only aim was to punish her.

'Oh Sonny, please—'

'Please *what*?'

'Please wait until I've had a cup of tea before you start. I've got the most awful headache.'

'Headache? I could drop down dead at any moment thanks to you and you're complaining about a *headache*?'

'You don't know that there's anything wrong with you. You don't know.'

'I've just looked it up. According to the internet I'm going to die. If I do it'll be your fault. OK? Got that?'

'We'll get it checked out. We'll find a private cardiologist—'

'Fuck that! I'm going to A&E.' He grabbed his jacket and slammed out of the door.

Later, between appointments, he waited on a grey plastic chair in a smooth corridor on an upper floor of the hospital. He had switched off his telephone. It was warm and peaceful here. On the wall opposite his seat several leaflets were pinned to a noticeboard:

– *Need help to stop smoking?*
– *What to do if someone is having a heart attack*
– *Food and cholesterol: your choices*
– *How much alcohol is too much?*

This was the cardiology department and Sonny had never wanted a drink and a fag as much as he did right now.

Cocooned by the reassuring hum of hospital life around him, there was time to examine his feelings. He discovered he was hoping – yes, it really was hope – that the scan for which he was waiting would find something wrong with his heart. He did not want to die, but he did want to punish his mother. If he were found to be suffering from a life-threatening condition, the consequence of her long-ago treachery, that punishment would suffice.

More obscurely he wanted a specialist to find something wrong with him because he wanted the attention of specialists. He wanted to be worthy of specialist treatment. He *deserved* specialist treatment. He had always felt special, and now he might actually be special. It was a wonderful opportunity. When he anticipated the bad news he might be given (*I'm afraid it's serious. We're going to have to operate immediately. No, there's no time to make a telephone call*) he felt specialness warm him from beneath like a heated car seat. He would travel into the operating theatre on a gurney; Lauren and Walter and Kathleen would look down on him with worried faces; he would face the surgeon's knife with courage. Picturing this, he felt positively heroic – and what's more, an operation would clean him of genetic defects. He would return home restored to himself.

It was disappointing when his heart turned out to be perfectly ordinary.

'For now.' The cardiologist was brisk. 'Come back in six months. We'll have another look.' She was the sort of woman one did not disobey. 'Any sort of aortic enlargement – that's a bulge inside – and we'll operate. If you experience discomfort, pop in and see us.'

'Discomfort' was not, Sonny believed, an adequately

descriptive term and 'pop in' did not convey sufficient urgency. He asked precisely what to look out for.

'Chest pain.'

'Isn't there any warning *before* chest pain?'

'Sometimes. Not always.'

And so he returned home unsatisfied. 'She said I was OK *for now*,' he told his mother in a threatening tone. That night he lay awake and wondered whether he could feel the beginnings of something that might turn out to be chest pain. He cursed his mother in the dark.

The next day, December 28th, he met up with Jem. They arranged by text message to meet on the top of Primrose Hill, as if they were starring in their own romantic movie. Sonny was nervous. He did not tell anyone what he was going to do but left the house quietly, taking Mike as an alibi.

On top of the hill Jem waited, looking at the view, and Sonny was almost beside her when he said her name and she turned around. It was like catching his own image on CCTV: *that person looks familiar*. Then she smiled and it was easy.

They walked around the perimeter of Primrose Hill until Mike had tired himself out. Then they sat outside an expensive cafe on Regent's Park Road and made one cup of coffee last for an hour and a half. An electric heater beamed red above their heads and Mike lay flat on the tarmac under its glow.

Sonny noticed everything about Jem: her grey woollen coat; the five gold studs in her left ear; the tip of her nose turning pink in the cold; three freckles in a line below her jaw; her scuffed black boots, and especially her profile,

179

which he did not just notice but recognised. He felt excited, almost as if he were falling in love. He wanted to tell her all the best things about himself.

'I have to go,' Jem said eventually. 'I have an appointment.'

'With the doctor? About your heart? I had mine yesterday.'

'No,' Jem said. 'Not that.'

She did not explain and Sonny wondered about a boyfriend. He felt jealous; he did not want to be parted from her.

He asked, 'But your heart is all right?'

'So far,' said Jem carefully. She could not explain that she did not want to find out: *I cannot be like my father. I will not allow it.* Sonny would not understand.

'Good. Because I wouldn't want you to drop down dead just after we've met.' It was easier to make a joke than say, *Don't go.*

Jem laughed. 'I'll try not to. Walk me to the bus stop?'

On the way they passed a mirror in a shop window and stopped to look at their reflections, shoulder to shoulder.

'I can see a likeness,' Jem said. 'Can you?'

'Yes.' Sonny wanted to make much of it. 'It's obvious.'

'Strange yet familiar.' Jem put her face next to his.

Sonny could feel her hair, her cheek and the softness of her coat collar. The sensation almost made him shiver. What was this? He would have called it desire had she not been his sister.

They walked up the hill again and waited for a bus on Adelaide Road, sitting beside one another on the red bench with Mike resting gingerly on his haunches.

'You're my only living relative,' Jem said.

'Really?'

'Really.'

Sonny felt a weight of responsibility, but also pride.

When the 31 bus came into view, hissing and bouncing up from Chalk Farm, they got to their feet and Sonny said desperately, 'When will I see you again?' He had not wanted to ask – it sounded pathetic – but he could not help himself.

'Soon.' Jem rested in his arms for a moment and kissed his cheek. Then she turned for the bus and was gone.

Jem had to go home because she was expecting Antony, but when she got there she found not Antony but a woman, a stranger, outside the front door of her block of flats, pressing an angry forefinger against the doorbell for 8J.

'Are you looking for me?'

The woman turned. She seemed a strange shape in the half-dark but as she stepped closer Jem realised it was because a sleeping baby was strapped to her chest and her overcoat was buttoned up over the bundle. Of the baby only a face – closed eyes and black lashes – and a red woollen hat were visible.

'Are you Jem?'

'Yes.'

The woman advanced on Jem with a contained, righteous fury. She was in her thirties: dark-haired and a beauty. She pointed the angry forefinger at Jem's chest and when she spoke she used it to emphasise each word, jabbing her finger near enough almost to touch.

'Leave. My. Husband. Alone.'

Jem was so shocked she stepped back. She could not speak.

'D'you understand me? You little slut?'

Jem opened her mouth but nothing came out.

'Leave. Him. Alone.'

The finger jabbed again, three times, and the baby slept on, undisturbed, and Caroline Peck, known as Moomy, beautiful and a tigress after all, turned on her heel and walked away down the street. Jem was left staring, her heart crashing in her chest.

Sonny walked back into a silent, unlighted house. In the hall there was a large mirror, into the frame of which were tucked scraps of paper that had gathered over the years like prayers on a cherry tree:

coffee – milk – bin bags
Sonny where is my BIKE ??
Mike has NOT been out
GONE TO PUB
emergency vet 07789 414250

Among these Lauren had left a sad little note: *gone home*. No capital letters and no goodbye.

Sonny's home tonight felt closed against him like a shut-up shop into which he had crept after hours. Walter and Kathleen were not sitting by the fire. There were no lights on downstairs to draw him into the sitting room or kitchen. Perhaps they were not even here; perhaps they had fought, separated and left the house empty. Sonny did not know anything any more, and he did not know who to ask. He wished he had brought Jem with him. He wished he could take her everywhere, like a talisman or a shadow. He did not want to be without her again.

He fed Mike and let him into the garden. Standing on the step he looked up to see a light glowing behind the blind of his father's study. So he was here, but he did not want to be seen. Well then, Sonny did not want to see him. No one but Jem.

Kathleen was not at home because, like Moomy, she had gone to see Jem. Unlike Moomy, Kathleen could not have justified her visit but Kathleen did not let a little thing like self-justification stand in her way.

She had looked in Sonny's telephone when he was in the bath that morning and found his messages to Jem, and hers to him, arranging their meeting on Primrose Hill. She felt hot with jealousy, as if she had uncovered an illicit affair. It was *wrong*. All this secrecy was *wrong*. This liaison of her son's was *wrong*.

Having picked over his telephone she turned to his wallet and found inside a folded piece of paper in what she assumed was Jem's handwriting:

07973 756 990
8J Canal Side, Lock Road, W9
familial aortic thoracic aneurysm and dissection

Kathleen put the piece of paper back where she had found it, folded into the wallet like a billet-doux. She froze when she heard the sound of splashing – Sonny was as sloppy as an otter in the bath – and then she sneaked away downstairs and wrote '8J Canal Side' on the back of her left hand where she wrote important things she needed to remember. Almost at once she worried that Sonny would read it and so she tried to wash it off under the kitchen tap. At this moment Walter caught her.

'What are you doing?'

'Walter! You gave me a fright. I'm not doing anything. Not a thing.'

'Yes you are, Lady Macbeth.'

It was a joke but Kathleen was not in the mood. 'Oh *Walter*, go away and leave me alone.' She was getting crosser and more flustered by the moment. 'I've got too much to worry about without you coming in here . . .'

Walter was not going to stand for this. 'Isn't it time you worried about us?'

'What on earth is that supposed to mean?' But then Kathleen decided she did not want him to answer and so she went on, 'I'm worried about Sonny. He's the one who needs me.'

'I'm worried too.'

'It's me he needs. He's my son.'

It was a terrible thing to say and she only said it to end the argument, which it did: Walter was silenced. They were both silent, looking at each other in amazement. *Has it come to this?*

Walter was the first to recover. 'I'm going to pretend you didn't say that,' he told her quietly.

'Of course you are,' Kathleen said. Her mouth seemed to be running away with her like a car rolling downhill. 'It's what you do, now. Pretend you haven't heard. Pretend you haven't seen.'

Walter gave a humourless laugh that was more of a sigh. 'You're going to turn on me? Now?'

'Oh, Walter.' She felt not anger but a desperate sadness as if he had already died and she were speaking to his ghost on the battlements. 'Where have you gone? You're still alive, aren't you? You haven't abandoned me, have you?'

'Kath—'

'Don't stand there and do nothing for the rest of your life. *Our* life.'

Walter said, helpless and desperate, 'But I'm going blind.'

'You're not blind today.' She put a palm on his cheek and looked into his eyes. 'Are you?' She waited but he said nothing and so she tried again. 'I need you, Walter. Work was everything to you, but you are everything to me.'

Still he was silent.

'Say something.' She wanted to stamp her foot. '*Say something.*'

Facing him, she could not hold back her tears and so she ran away, out of the house and down the street.

'Don't go.'

But Walter spoke to an empty space.

Canal Side turned out to be a ten-storey block of flats in a corner of London hitherto unexplored by Kathleen. She asked the taxi to drop her at the opposite end of the street so that she could drink a large gin in a dark corner of the conveniently situated Lock Road Tavern. After two of those, pub measures being the measly offerings they were, she had braced herself to her task. She made her way to the dank-looking block at the end of the road and rang the bell for 8J.

Jem took a moment to answer and when she did her voice

was wary, as if she thought the person on the street might want to come up and bite her arm off.

'Who is it?'

'Kathleen Griffin. Can I come in?'

A pause and then, 'Eighth floor. There's a lift.'

When Kathleen got into the flat she found it much larger and nicer than she had imagined from the lift. She waited to be told where to sit and asked what she wanted to drink but Jem said nothing beyond 'I'll put the kettle on' and so she stood in the kitchen with her coat still on and looked out of the window. The long view south, orange and black on a winter's evening, seemed to contain every possible method of travel into and out of the capital: canal, motorway flyover, railway lines, Underground station and even an apparently endless line of aeroplanes winking towards Heathrow.

'What an exciting view,' Kathleen said, 'and isn't it quiet up here. I'd never have guessed how nice it would be from the outside.'

'That's what everyone says. Will you have a cup of tea?'

'What about a real drink?'

'I don't have anything to drink. I mean any alcohol.'

'What? None?'

'I don't drink.'

Kathleen raised her eyebrows. 'Tea, then, with milk and sugar.' She watched Jem make a pot of tea. 'You're not like him, you know,' she said after a minute. 'You look a bit like him, but you remind me more of your mother.'

'You're trying to flatter me.'

'It's a compliment, yes. All of us – out in France, working on that film – we adored your mother. She was the only good person.'

'And yet you slept with her husband.'

'That's right.' Kathleen had decided, since her evening with Rex, that giving up smoking could wait. She had bought cigarettes and matches in the corner shop and now she got these out of her handbag. 'Without wishing to patronise, love affairs are impossible to explain or justify. You may be too young to realise this, but I promise it's true. One simply doesn't think about collateral damage.'

Jem thought of Moomy, but to agree would be to give ground and so she said instead, 'You can't smoke in here,' as she passed Kathleen a mug of tea.

'Really? Why not? Is there a baby?'

'No. I just don't like smoking.'

'Good heavens, aren't you strict.' Kathleen put her cigarettes away.

'Tell me why you're here and then you can go home and drink and smoke yourself to death for all I care.'

Kathleen could not help laughing. 'You haven't inherited your mother's charm.'

'Don't laugh about my mother,' snapped Jem. 'You don't have the right. She was too good for you even to talk about.'

Kathleen did not understand. 'She was? *Was?*'

'We're not going to talk about my mother.' Jem was fierce.

'But that's why I'm here. I want to know what happened: to your mother; to Frank; to that house in the woods. If your mother is dead, then when did she die? Did your parents stay together? Did Frank . . . ?' She stopped. She could not risk going further.

Jem was watching her. After a silence she said, 'You want me to clear your conscience.'

Kathleen flushed. 'No. I want to protect my son. But from what, I don't know.' Without a cigarette she wrung her hands. 'From the past?'

'From the future,' Jem said, understanding. 'From me.'

For Sonny the pleasure of the day had ebbed like the light after sunset. Now he stood in the garden looking in vain for stars in a London sky. When his telephone grumbled in his pocket he unearthed it with more despair than hope.

It was a message from Jem: *Just had a visit from your mother.*

Sonny looked at it for a moment and then typed, *I want to get away from her. Just us for a while.*

After a few seconds his telephone bloomed into light with another message: *Want to come with me to France?*

His heart leapt: *Yes.*

VII

The next morning, December 29th, Kathleen got up before either Sonny or Walter and left the house. She found her car and drove it to a coffee shop close to the top of Rosslyn Hill where she parked on a double yellow line and bought a cup of strong coffee to take away. Then she got back into the car and drove a little further to the very top of the hill above Hampstead Heath where she parked beside a curious and artificial-looking concrete-lipped pond. Here she carefully settled the coffee cup on the dashboard and got out her telephone. She wanted to make telephone calls that no one would overhear.

She wanted to find Frank. He had died at Heathrow airport, she knew that much, so she telephoned the nearest hospital to Heathrow.

'Good morning, this is reception, how can I help you?'

'Can you put me through to the morgue?'

If she had heard that line spoken on stage she might have laughed, but the person at the other end of the telephone merely redirected the call without comment.

Then another voice: 'Yes?'

'I'm looking for someone. Someone dead,' she clarified. 'Frank Martell? I'm his solicitor.' She had decided that the

189

instructions of a solicitor were more likely to be obeyed. 'I need to know which funeral directors have taken his body and where to.'

'I'm sorry, madam, I can't help you with that.' The speaker's voice contained in it all the rush, bother and regret of arriving back at work on the first morning after the Christmas holidays. 'You need to speak to a family member. They'll have made the arrangements.' Kathleen could imagine this young woman putting down a takeaway cappuccino, taking her coat off, dropping it onto a chair, pushing her hair out of her eyes and wishing she had not picked up the telephone.

'The family is complicated,' Kathleen said. 'There's a *feud*.' She tried to sound important, busy and slightly bored, as if this was the least of the items on her to-do list for this morning. 'The daughter arranged for the body to be removed without consulting her father's new wife. The stepmother. They don't get on. That's why I've been instructed to make this call.' If she made it sufficiently confusing then surely the other woman would capitulate if only to get Kathleen off the line.

'It's not the sort of information I can give out.'

'Yes, you can. I know you can. I'm a *solicitor*. This information is not protected by any law that I've ever heard of.' At least the last bit was true.

There was a pause, which to Kathleen felt like her toe in the door.

'It's not a privacy issue,' she gabbled on. 'How could it be? The man's already dead.'

'Can't you ring back later? I've only just got in.' The woman became peevish. 'It's not even eight o'clock. I've been away over Christmas. My desk is all upside-down. My computer's still asleep.'

'Later will be *too late* . . .' Kathleen did not explain why but left the ominous sentence hanging like a rope end over a cliff. 'Why not just wake up your computer now? It'll take you less than a minute and then I'll be out of your hair.' *Out of your hair?* It was the sort of thing a man would say.

'Oh, all right.' A deep sigh, a long pause and at last the clatter of typing fingernails. 'Here we are: J. and D. Price and Sons, Cromer, Norfolk. They came and took him away. All right? And it was Texel House Retirement Living who rang up and arranged it, on behalf of the family. And that's all you're getting out of me.'

'It's all I need.' With a small feeling of triumph Kathleen ended the call and tossed her telephone back into her handbag. She opened the window a crack, lit a cigarette and sipped her coffee.

On a good day the view from this spot was spectacular but today it was unpromising. At present the air outside the car was a grey flannel blanket, studded with the blurred orange glow of street lights. A spiritless January sun must have been struggling at the horizon but there was nothing to show for it. In the car, cocooned by the weather and the dim, involuntary morning, Kathleen sat and drank her coffee.

She did not often sit alone with nothing to do and she did not often drive herself. When filming *Mrs Peabody* she was collected at home and driven to the set by a chauffeur-driven Mercedes. Her driver was called Jim. She knew everything about him, and he about her, because he had been driving her to and from *Mrs Peabody* on every working day of the annual six-month shoot for the last five years. The journey took half an hour in the mornings and a little more in the evenings because of the traffic, and they sometimes came this way but not often. It was quicker to go Finchley Road – Brent Cross – Mill Hill – Borehamwood than fiddle around at the Spaniards Inn where she was now. The traffic here was always a slow bleed.

Jim lived in East Finchley. He was younger than Kathleen but his three children were older than her two. They all had sensible jobs: dental hygienist, tax inspector and car mechanic. 'What I say is, there's always teeth, taxes and cars that need looking after,' Jim said. He was a practical man. He approved of Lauren. 'Smart girl,' he said. 'Head screwed on. Got property.' He meant that ridiculous bedsit. 'Can't go wrong with property.' He was less convinced by Sonny. 'With all due respect,' he said, 'acting's not *reliable*. You can't *rely* on it. But having his mum on the telly will give him a leg up.'

Clever, sensible Lauren had been a grown-up since the day she was born. Her success, therefore – her independence, her own little flat and her career ('Line Producer: Lauren Griffin') – was the fulfilment of expectation and not a remarkable surprise. Kathleen knew that she should feel proud of Lauren. When Annie said, after this or that programme, 'We saw Lauren's name in the credits. You must be so proud!' Kathleen would smile and say, 'I'm proud of *both* my children,' but this was not the truth. The truth was that she could not feel proud of Lauren because it would mean, for that moment, that she had neglected Sonny.

Worrying about Sonny was a pleasure which could, if she let it, take up all the hours that Kathleen ever spent alone. Sometimes she worried about him in the car, sometimes in the hairdresser, sometimes when she took off her make-up at the end of a day's work and sometimes while she waited for the kettle to boil in the morning. It was a subject she never grew tired of; a worry she never wanted to do without. She could have sat here all day, worrying about his feelings and his future. As long as he was not grown up and not sensible she would worry.

But to worry today was not the pleasurable indulgence that it had been last week or for the previous quarter-century. She had never really had anything to worry about; she had done it just for pleasure. Now she had actual, present concerns that could not be answered, the chief of which being: how long before he loved her again? They had never fallen out before. As Rex had guessed, Sonny had never told his mother to fuck off. Why would he? They were friends. They had always been friends. Not to be his friend would be worse than not to be alive: she lived for Sonny.

A tap at the window disturbed her. Here was a parking officer in his nasty uniform, tapping at his watch. She mouthed at the window, 'All right, *all right*, I'm going,' and started the engine.

Texel House was a large, white, Edwardian villa which must have started life as a grand hotel: two-dozen glimmering windows faced the sea and the bib of tarmac on which Kathleen parked had once no doubt been a lawn for tea and croquet. Now there was a sign, *Slow Please*, and a line of thin yellow firs, ankle-height, struggling to make a hedge.

Through the ground-floor windows of the house, built especially large to take in the view, Kathleen could see elderly people in wicker chairs, hunched into their shoulders and blinking like little birds in a coop. She felt a shiver trickle down her spine – she was never at her best with the very young or very old.

Her telephone told her: 'You have arrived.' She checked her appearance in the mirror and made a face at herself when she saw it. Ugh. All this drink and worry was not doing her appearance any favours – she had better quit both before *Mrs Peabody* began filming again in February. A magpie cackled at her from a leafless tree as she reluctantly got out of the car.

Behind the desk at reception was a woman wearing a label reading BETH.

'Can I help you?' She looked up and when she saw Kathleen her face changed. 'Ooh it's you,' she said excitedly. 'From that programme. Whatsit. Mrs Thingy.'

'Yes, that's right, hello, I hope you can help me, I've come about a funeral arranged by you? For a man called Frank Martell? Someone here called the undertakers. He died in London. Near London.'

Beth was flustered by a celebrity visitor but she tried to pull herself together and shuffled some papers about. 'Let me see. Now then.' Having calmed down she consulted her computer. 'Oh yes. Marian Frost. The deceased was the father of her adopted daughter, if I remember rightly, and she asked us to arrange the cremation for her.'

Adopted daughter? Kathleen was entirely confused but she tried to look as if it all made perfect sense. 'Yes, that's right. Marian Frost.'

'Let me see.' Beth looked at a clock on the wall beside her desk. 'Twenty past twelve.' Now she checked a laminated

Activities Chart pinned up beneath the clock. 'She'll be doing Zumba in Activity One until twelve forty-five. You can wait here. Is she expecting you?'

'No.'

'Not a problem. Are you a relative?'

'No.'

'Friend?'

'She doesn't actually know me.' Kathleen was becoming nervous. Must she answer all these questions? And truthfully? 'I know Frank's daughter, Jem. I used to know Frank, you see. I wanted to . . .' She could not think what else to say without sounding like someone who should not be let into the building. 'I was just passing.' *Just passing?* No one would believe that. Cromer was halfway to Amsterdam but nowhere else. She decided to stop talking altogether.

Being on television sometimes had its advantages.

'I'm sure she'll be thrilled to see you,' Beth said. 'Anyone would. We all love your programme.' She blushed. 'Take a seat. Marian won't be long.'

Kathleen waited in reception. She leafed through an old copy of *House & Garden*, trying not to think about germs, and watched the clock. She wondered if anyone could bring her a double espresso – one coffee in London and another at the Welcome Break near Stansted airport was not enough. A strong smell of fish pie was seeping out of the kitchen and she began to feel queasy. Whether it was the smell of the food or the thought that one day she would end up in a place like this—

'Kathleen Griffin? You're here to see me?'

A very small woman had appeared in front of her. She was wearing a tracksuit and white gym shoes with Velcro fastenings. She must have been about eighty but it was hard to be precise beyond the obvious accoutrements of an elderly person: white hair, wrinkled face, leaking eyes and a Kleenex balled into her sleeve.

'Do I know you?' She had a mousetrap quickness about her. 'Am I supposed to know you? I can't remember everyone.'

'Marian Frost?'

'I know who *I* am,' she said briskly, 'it's *you* I'm asking about.'

'I . . .' Kathleen stood up because she thought it would be polite but now she was talking to the top of Marian's head. She sat down again. 'I knew Frank Martell. That's why I'm here. I knew Frank before Jem was born.'

Marian's eyes flashed. 'You're the woman who had the baby. Frank's boy. Jem told me about you.'

'Yes. I suppose I am.'

'Well.' Pursed lips. 'Fell for him, did you? Or was it the other way around.'

'I—'

'Vanity. Men. The weak ones are easily got.' She glanced Kathleen over. 'You must have been just the type to turn a man's head, back in the day. Actress, aren't you? I've seen you on the telly. The one about the prostitutes.'

None of this was polite but Kathleen took issue only with the last. 'They're not prostitutes,' she said indignantly. Then she shut her mouth, swallowed, breathed in and out and started again. 'Mrs Frost—'

'Miss.'

'Miss Frost, I'd like to talk to you for a few minutes. It's for my son, really. He's . . . he's confused at the moment.'

196

'That's what happens if you go sleeping with men not your husband,' snapped Marian. 'People end up confused.'

How curious this is, Kathleen thought. *I am being told off.* She could not quite believe it. What's more she must accept it; she would accept it. For the first time in this whole Frank business she was prepared to be judged: if she were to be hanged, drawn and quartered in this hot, smelly room she would bear it with a good grace.

'I know,' she said. 'They do. Is there somewhere we can go and talk?'

'What for? He's being cremated this afternoon. It's too late for digging up bodies.'

'It's not Frank I care about,' said Kathleen. 'It's my son.'

But Marian was looking out of the window at seagulls circling over the car park. 'He was a dreadful man,' she said. 'A bully. I pity your son being related to him. He'd have been better off never finding out.' Then she brightened. 'We can go to the cafe on the front. I go there with Jem when she visits.'

'But are you allowed out?'

'It's not a prison,' said Marian hotly, 'it's called Retirement Living Advantage Gold. I own my own flat and I can come and go as I please. I'm not one of those mad old biddies locked up and forgetting her birthday.'

The cafe on the front was called Splash Point Café and it looked temporary, as if it had been thrown up overnight for a film shoot. It was a building that seemed too flimsy to survive weather of any kind, let alone the batterings of a wind blowing over the sea from, Kathleen supposed vaguely, the Arctic. It was a wooden cube, wrapped in clapboard and painted the colour of pistachio ice cream. Its large square windows wore white-painted frames. Outside tables and chairs were slick with a cold, desperate rain that blew into Kathleen's and Marian's faces. It was the sort of place Walter would have loved, particularly on a filthy day like this.

Marian had changed for her outing and was wearing a tiny angora cardigan, a woollen skirt, thick tights and a coffee-coloured coat. Her feet were tucked into shiny rubber boots. Beth had lent them a huge umbrella with 'Standard Life' written on it and under this, held fast by Kathleen, the two women shuffled from the car into the cafe. Kathleen shook the rain off the umbrella and they sat down at the only empty table. It was warm and rather damp indoors and suddenly quiet, out of the wind.

Marian asked for tea and a muffin and Kathleen, who would have paid a hundred pounds for a gin and tonic, ordered coffee. She wondered how to get the ball rolling but she needn't have worried: Marian did not pause, except to sip tea, for their allotted hour.

'I was nanny to Jem's mum, Romy. Romy Casta, she was born. Her father was French, a businessman, very smart and polite, never raised his voice when he was at home, which wasn't often. Her mother was English, a bit scatty – not a natural mother. I answered an advertisement and they interviewed me in a lovely house in Chelsea. Mrs Casta was as big as a barn that day – the baby came three days later and they called her Romy. They told me to pack and we all went to live in Tangier: me, Mr and Mrs Casta and Romy. I'd never been abroad and suddenly I was in Africa!'

Kathleen made sympathetic and encouraging noises that could have been 'Well I never.'

'Very smelly, dirty place. But they lived in a big house on the old mountain, that's what they called it, that looked out to sea. It was a pink villa with the paint all peeling off on the outside. Been in Mr Casta's family for years, they said. Shabby – but pretty, mind you, with a big garden and steps going down to the water. There was a cook, a maid and a gardener – all foreigners, jabber-jabber all day – and me. It never got too hot, what with the wind, and the garden was shady with grapes and whatnot all growing over your head. Lovely it was.

'They wanted Romy to have an English nanny – they wanted her brought up properly. They wanted her to fit in when she went to boarding school in England. Mister was very *French*,' Marian leant heavily on the word, 'if you know what I mean.'

Kathleen took this to mean badly behaved.

'He'd slip in and out the house and she never knew where he was going. Mrs wasn't supposed to ask – French rules. And she used to go off to town and come back with stray dogs. She collected them. There might have been a dozen at the house, fighting and mating and having puppies in the garden. Romy always tried to tame them, bless her, but she just caught fleas for her trouble.'

'But when did Frank come along?'

Marian blinked. She had been far away, travelling the backwaters of her memory, and now she was tugged back into the cafe.

'I'm coming to that.' She sipped her tea and crumbled a bit of muffin between her fingers. 'Well, they grow up these children, and you can't help that, and they don't need a nanny and on you go. So when Romy went to boarding

199

school in England I went back to London and I worked for a lovely family from Saudi Arabia, Faisal they were called but not a Mr and Mrs, they were a Prince and Princess, and we lived in a great big house on Hamilton Terrace in St John's Wood and I had my own rooms in the basement with a separate entrance, very nice I must say, and Romy, bless her, would come and see me from school. She didn't like to go home to Tangier so she'd come for half terms and the odd weekend, right up until she finished her exams. Then she met Frank, the minute she left school. She wrote and told me. Said she'd met someone older.' Marian pursed her lips and then un-pursed them to continue. 'Brought him to meet me. Well. The moment I laid eyes on him I knew he was Bad News. She was so young she didn't know up from down but it was plain as the tail on a dog. Charming, I'll give you that, but . . .' She shook her head and tutted. 'He was teaching art in a secondary school and living in a dingy house that he shared with his deadbeat friends. And he was twenty years older than she was! Or near enough. And he didn't have any savings, and he didn't visit his poor old mum who was dying of cancer, and he didn't speak to his brother because his brother had got the family money and he hadn't. Ugh. He had no heart. Selfish. Mean to Romy and mean inside, and she was just a child and couldn't see it.'

'So they got married?' Kathleen prompted. 'And had Jem?'

'I'm coming to that.' Marian did not like to be hurried. She looked at the ceiling as if the interruption had completely destroyed her train of thought. 'Where was I? Oh yes. So she rang me up and told me about the

200

engagement and I said congratulations. To be civil. Then I worried about it and I decided I'd write her a letter and tell her to be careful and not rush into anything, especially babies. Then I wrote to Mr and Mrs Casta, her parents, asking if they knew him at all. I never got a reply, not from her or them, but she must have shown my letter to Frank because next time he saw me he *hated* me. Looked at me daggers. Called me nasty names. Of course I don't mind about that sort of thing – lesbians and that – but he meant to upset me.'

She pulled the Kleenex out of her sleeve, blew her nose into it and then pushed it back into its hiding place.

'That was when she told me they were moving to France. Romy had money you see, money from her father, and that's how she bought the house in France. They were going to start a B&B because some book or other had got a lot of people visiting the area. Something about a year in Provence.'

'That's what it was called.'

'What's that?'

'That's what it was called: *A Year in Provence*.'

'That's what I said. But the house never got finished because Frank was good for nothing but drinking, so Romy got work as a jobbing cook and kept them both.'

'That's how I met her. She was cooking for . . .'

But Marian was not interested in listening, only talking, and continued over the top of Kathleen.

'She always loved cooking – she learned in Tangier. She could spend all day in the kitchen with her mother's cook, what was her name? Something foreign. Wore a thing on her head.'

She wafted her hands over her hair to indicate, Kathleen assumed, a hijab.

'Then Romy sent me a picture of a baby, and that was Jem. She sounded lonely. It can be difficult, a first baby, so I asked for a bit of holiday and I went to visit. It was January, I remember, and the house was not at all suitable for a baby. Freezing, draughty, no hot water and stone floors everywhere. Made me come out in hives just counting up the number of ways a baby could hurt herself, and little Jem only a month old. I kept telling Frank to stoke up the fire and get the water nice and hot but he wouldn't. Of all the new fathers I've ever worked for,' she buttoned and unbuttoned her lip again, 'he was the worst by a long chalk. Me and Romy got dreadful chilblains. I was on at him all the time, nagging, because she wouldn't. She was frightened of him. Then one night he went out and came back drunk and woke up the baby and she started crying. Romy went down and tried to shush him and he walloped her. He didn't know I was on the stairs, but I was, so I rushed down and gave him an earful but it was no good, he was bigger than me and he got me by the arm, chucked me outside and locked the door. I thought I'd freeze to death – he left me out in my dressing gown and Romy had to smuggle me in when he'd gone to sleep. In the morning he took me to the railway station and left me there. I said to Romy, "Come with me. Come now. Stay here and he'll kill you – or he'll kill the baby." But she wouldn't come. It was the last time I saw her.'

Marian looked down at her hands, clasped on the tabletop. Her face suddenly collapsed under the weight of a great, long-ago sadness that had never been cured.

'I wrote from London. Begged her to leave him. Told her

to come back and live with me until she got on her feet.'
Another pause. The longest yet. 'Then she was dead.'

Kathleen felt a chill.

'What do you mean? Dead how? Dead why?'

'Didn't you know? Frank caught her trying to leave him and he killed her: drove the car into a tree. That's why I took Jem. I was sixty-three, and Jem was nearly nine, and I've been mother and father to her from that day to this.'

When it was time to leave the cafe Marian became confused. Sitting there and talking of the past, she had lost her place in the present; the idea that she lived in a retirement home beside the sea near Cromer in Norfolk seemed to appal her. Kathleen insisted it was true and watched the news sink in slowly, like news of a sudden death.

Marian looked around the cafe and said, 'But . . . but . . .' As if woken from deep sleep she was disordered. 'I want to go home,' she told Kathleen. But when they got to the car park at Texel House she said, 'This isn't home. I want to go *home*.' Big tears leaked out of her eyes and rolled down her face. She hung back, dragging at Kathleen's hand like a dog at the vet.

Kathleen did not know what to do. 'It's all right,' she said, even though it wasn't. 'We're here. This is where you live. You'll be fine once you're inside.' She spoke in an especially loud, clear voice, like a presenter of children's television. 'Everything's fine. We've had a nice trip, but it's time to go home now.'

'No, no, no.' Marian shook her head.

Once Kathleen had tugged her inside Beth came out from behind her desk and took over. 'Come on, Marian. They're playing a nice game with balloons in the lounge. Don't you want to join in?'

'No, no, no.'

But 'no' carried no weight here at Texel House and Marian was led inexorably away. Kathleen stared down the corridor after her and as soon as it was decent, or perhaps just a moment before, she turned and rushed for the car.

In a lay-by not far away she parked and smoked a cigarette. She wondered if she would get dementia. Perhaps she had it already. Perhaps soon she would need her lines fed into an earpiece like Marlon Brando in his later years. Perhaps she would get as fat as he had.

In light of 'Then she was dead' it seemed wrong to worry about getting fat or even dementia. At least she would live long enough for either, or both. Romy had not been given the option. Feeling a sudden and urgent need to be at home with the living – *It's too late for digging up bodies* – Kathleen dropped her cigarette butt into one of the many empty coffee cups that littered her car and set off for London.

Arriving back in Beech Road after her day trip Kathleen opened the front door to be met by the unmistakable silence of an empty house. She was certain even before calling up the stairs that no one would answer, but she called anyway:

'Sonny? Walter?'

The house sat quiet, the air unmixed.

In the sitting room Kathleen made herself a drink and then, when she had fetched ice from the freezer, she tried to get Sonny on the telephone and, having failed, tried Lauren.

'I don't know where Sonny is,' Lauren said. 'I've been

working. Someone's too sick to work on the Amundsen thing so tomorrow I've got to—'

'You haven't spoken to him? With everything that's going on?'

'Haven't you? Since you're the one who's worried.'

'I've been somewhere for the day. Out of London.'

'What about Dad? Where's he?'

'I don't know. Probably at Lester's. It's not your father I'm worried about.'

'You don't say.'

'There's no need to be catty, Lauren. Sonny has been meeting up with Jem, did you know?'

'Surely you aren't surprised?'

'Not surprised, I suppose.'

'What, then?'

Worried. Anxious. Afraid that I've lost him. 'I don't know,' she said. 'I just want to know where he is.' Anything else would sound peculiar.

Two doors up she found Walter eating takeaway pizzas with Lester, Annie and Rex. Mike was stretched out on the floor but he did not move beyond rolling his eyes at her. Kathleen was the only person he did not get up for.

'Oh, it's you,' Walter said lightly when he heard her voice. 'You were gone when I woke up this morning. I thought you'd left me.' It was the sort of joke he would never make.

'I've been somewhere for the day. Out of London,' Kathleen replied automatically. 'I can't find Sonny. Do you know where he is?'

'No. Have you tried—'

'Ringing his phone? Yes, of course I have.'

She could not help snapping at him. It was somehow an affront that he should be here eating pizza with the neighbours while Sonny was who-knew-where. Now she had let her feelings show in her voice and they were all looking at her.

'I know where he is.'

This was Becka, who had appeared in the kitchen doorway. Her arms were folded tightly around herself and she had the bee-stung look of one who had spent the day in tears.

'You do?'

'He's gone to France with his new sister. I went round to your house,' she nodded at Kathleen, 'and he answered the door. He was all excited – he thought I was her. He was nervous. He had a bag packed. You were both out and he wanted to go before you got back. I caught him out, basically. Then this car drew up – it had French number plates – and in it was, you know, *her*.' She swallowed and shrank her fingers into the cuffs of her jumper. 'He told me not to say anything and then he got in the car and they left.'

Kathleen looked at her in silence, but not for long.

'They left? They *left*? And that's it? He's gone?'

Becka shrugged. 'It's all I know.' Whatever Kathleen said could not hurt her; she had no further capacity for hurt today. Sonny had turned on her. *Why are you hassling me? I've got enough shit going on without you giving me a hard time.* Yes, that was enough for one day.

Kathleen could not decide where to direct her anger but Walter was the safest option so she spun on her toes and faced him.

'And where were you?'

'I don't know. Swimming?'

'Swimming!' Hadn't she always known that no good would come of swimming?

'This is not my fault, Kath,' Walter said evenly.

No one was eating. Annie's look was concern and Lester's was plain interest. Rex was balling a wad of kitchen roll between his palms and looking bemused – as if he thought she had gone barking mad.

'If Sonny wants to go away with his sister,' he said calmly, 'then why not?'

Annie agreed with him. 'It's perfectly natural that Sonny should want to get to know Jem,' she said. 'It would be surprising if he didn't.'

'But he belongs to us! He doesn't need anyone else!'

The words screeched overhead like a flock of parakeets and they sounded crazy – she sounded crazy, she knew she did.

After a pause Rex said, 'Maybe you're wrong.' He aimed his balled-up kitchen roll at the bin and in it went: slam-dunk. 'Maybe he does.'

Now they looked from Rex to her with the same quiz-zical faces as if their opinion was one opinion and the fault was all hers. They looked as if they could perfectly well understand why Sonny would run away and never come back.

'He's my son!' It came bursting out. 'My son and not yours!'

After this there was nothing to add and so she left.

VIII

The sentence which Lauren began to her mother that day on the telephone: 'Someone's too sick to work on the Amundsen thing so tomorrow I've got to' – should have ended – 'go to Norway.'

The 'Amundsen thing' was a TV biopic about Roald Amundsen and 'go to Norway' meant flying to Svalbard to take over from the current line producer who had come down with shingles. Lauren rang her father.

'I don't want to leave you with Mum if she's freaking out.'

'She's not,' Walter lied. 'She's fine and I'm fine. You must go. Work is important. What would I do in your place?'

'You would go.'

'Well then.'

Lauren was not convinced, but it was permission and so she went.

On a Monday morning two and a half weeks later she flew back to London. She had left Longyearbyen airport in Svalbard the day before and flown via Tromsø to Oslo and then to Copenhagen where she had spent the night in an airport hotel before flying back to Heathrow. From

Heathrow there was the small matter of a train, the Underground and a bus journey that took her to her front door in Kentish Town. Once inside the door of her building she climbed four flights of stairs past six other flats to the topmost landing where she slid her rucksack off her shoulders and unlocked the door of her little home.

As she opened the flat door she was already anticipating the joy of a cup of tea in her own mug, a shower under her own shower and dressing in her own clean clothes. She was brought up short by a sight so unexpected it was almost incredible: her mother, curled up in bed and apparently asleep. Lauren stood in the doorway and stared. Then she widened her astonished gaze to take in the room. She had left it neat and now it was rudely dishevelled: clothes thrown over the furniture, pots of face cream on her desk, empty bottles of gin beside the door, dirty glasses in the sink and emptied ice trays upside down on top of the fridge.

'Mum?' Lauren was too furious to be polite. 'What the fuck?'

Kathleen woke up and rolled over to face the door.

'Good heavens,' she said when she had registered Lauren standing there. She sat up. 'I don't know how you put up with living in one room like this. The idea that anyone can walk into one's bedroom at any moment—'

'What are you doing here? How did you get in?'

'Sonny had a spare key. I found it in his room.'

'What about Dad? Where's Dad?'

'I can't live with him at the moment!' It came bursting out.

'Can't? You mean you won't. You being here is not the solution. It's not your way out.'

'This is a difficult time for all of us, Lauren, and you're being very selfish.'

'Does Dad know you're here? Does anyone?'

'Jim does. He picks me up and brings me back. He's picking me up' – she looked at her watch – 'in a minute.'

'And you're expecting me to live where exactly?'

'Beech Road of course. You've got your old room and you're much better at looking after your father than I am.'

But Lauren wasn't going to fall for that old trick.

'Oh, no.' She shook her head. 'No, no, no. I'm going to see Dad. When I get back I expect you to be gone.'

Chewing at her chapped bottom lip and muttering incantations Lauren trotted down all the stairs in the building and unchained her bike from the railings outside. She cycled as fast as she could to her parents' house, a journey which took ten minutes, most of it uphill.

It was one of those winter mornings when London goes back to sleep after the rush hour. The streets were quiet, the air was not rippled by noise or activity and the unmoving sky was the colour of a wet sheep. On Beech Road occasional noises rang out in the clothy air: a slammed car door; a dog's excited bark; a child's scooter rolling over pavement cracks. Overhead, hidden in that low-hanging fleece, an aeroplane rumbled in a slow circle.

Lauren noticed none of this – too furious with her mother and worried about her father. She chained her bike to a lamp post, ran up to the glossy front door of number 36 and put her key in the lock. Once she had pushed the door open she stood for a moment listening.

'Dad?'

211

No answer. The house smelled of burnt toast. Mike appeared, woolly and black, wagging his tail and rolling his eyes.

'Hello, boy.'

Lauren petted him briefly and straightened up but he would not let her go, circling her legs and whimpering, telling tales of woe.

'What have you done with him?' Lauren asked. 'Where is he?'

Mike put a demonstrative paw on her knee, looking up. *We can't talk here. Let's go to the park.*

She called louder, 'Dad?'

'Who's that? Who's there?' Walter came shuffling out of the kitchen into the hall.

'It's me. Lauren.'

He had grown a beard – or rather, an untidy fuzz had spread over his chin like mould over cheese. He was wearing pyjamas which seemed too big, or perhaps he had shrunk – the cuffs of the pyjama shirt hung over his fingers and its collar rested loosely over bony shoulders. His voice was different: querulous. Lauren looked at him, shocked.

'Lauren? Really?'

'Of course it's me. Who else?' She put her arms around him and kissed his bristly cheek. 'Are you all right? I've just seen Mum.'

'Where is she?'

'Fast asleep in my bed.'

'There? But why would she . . . ?' He blinked. 'I didn't know. Where have you come from? Turning up out of the blue like this – you gave me a fright. You should have rung first.' He rested his knuckles on the hall table as if standing still and speaking were too tiring to bear. His pyjama bottoms, Lauren noticed, did not match the top.

'But I never ring first.'

'You *should*. It's polite. I would have . . .' he waved his hand to indicate either 'tidied up' or 'vanished completely'.

'When did Mum leave?'

'I don't know.'

'Two days ago? Three?'

'I said I don't *know*.'

The last word was shouted as if Lauren were deaf. In response Mike began howling, his mouth an 'Oo-Oo-Oo' and his nose pointed at the ceiling.

'Mike. *Mike*.'

Lauren put a soothing hand and Mike came over and sat on her feet so she could not take a step without him: *Don't go*.

'What have you done to Mike? He's a nervous wreck.'

'Leave him alone. Leave me alone. You can't just walk back in and start interfering and asking questions. You might as well go back to . . .' he frowned '. . . wherever you've come from.'

The smoke alarm went off in the kitchen.

'Bugger that thing!' He shouted over the noise. 'Going off every five minutes!'

Beetling away he picked up a broom, clambered up on a chair and started bashing at the kitchen ceiling. Mike turned circles on the floor beneath him, barking. With her hands over her ears Lauren observed them.

'You've both gone mad,' she observed. Then she grabbed Mike by the collar, posted him out of the garden door and shut it behind him. 'You go out there,' she said. 'You' – she meant Walter – 'get down from there before you break your neck.'

She took the broom away from him and helped him down to the floor. Then she climbed onto the kitchen table, stood on tiptoe and pressed the button on the smoke alarm until the noise ceased. From her vantage point on the table she looked down at the mess of the kitchen.

'Bloody hell. What have you been doing in here?'

Walter was defensive. 'I wasn't expecting anyone to just *burst in*.'

'I'm not "anyone".'

Walter crumpled like a paper bag. For a dreadful, horrifying moment Lauren thought he was going to cry. She had never seen him cry. She held her breath.

'No, you're not anyone,' he muttered as he composed himself. 'You're not anyone.'

Lauren hopped down from the table, put the broom back in the corner of the room and opened the garden door to let Mike back in. Worried, silent, he threaded through their legs like a nervous sheepdog.

'Good boy,' Walter said. 'We've been fending for ourselves, haven't we, Mike?'

Mike gave Lauren a look of mute appeal: *Help us.*

'There was an argument. Your mother threw a glass at Mike. In the morning she was gone.'

'When?'

'A few days ago. A week? Perhaps a week.' He looked stricken, as if totting up the days had created an appalling total. 'And all the time she's only been down the road. Has she left me, then? She has left me.' The words were out before he could stop them and tumbling down the cliff face

214

like so many rocks. He shut his mouth tight to prevent further accidents and took a seat at the table.

'No she hasn't.'

'Why do you say that? She isn't here and she isn't coming back.'

Lauren sat down next to him. She felt exactly as if she were being pressed into the ground by an invisible thumb.

'Why didn't you call me?'

'What for? You were away working. Work comes first.'

'No it doesn't. Not this time.'

'What could you have done?'

'I could have come straight back and looked after you.'

'Straight back from the middle of nowhere? How?'

It was not an accusation but a statement of fact with which Lauren could not argue.

'I know what it's like,' Walter went on. 'It was the same with me. And anyway, I don't need looking after.'

'This is impossible.' Lauren was beginning to feel less desperately sad for her father and more desperately sorry for herself. She did not want to be selfish, but it did not escape her notice that she was trapped. 'You need Mum.'

'I don't have her. I don't need her.'

'Don't be ridiculous.'

Walter raised his voice. 'Don't call me ridiculous.'

He thumped his fist on the table, the dog barked and then there was quiet.

Carefully Lauren said, 'I'm sorry. That was a stupid thing to say.' She put a hand on his shoulder, gently. 'All right?'

Walter did not answer. He was blinking at the floor. Mike looked from one to the other. Lauren rested her hand for another few moments. Everyone kept still.

Then Walter cleared his throat and said, 'All right.'

'Why don't you go and have a bath and get dressed? Then we can go out.'

'Out?'

'Yes. Out. We can have some lunch and take Mike for a walk. OK?'

'Very well.'

'Do you,' Lauren hesitated as she asked, 'do you want me to help you shave?' She wondered if he could not see to shave himself. It had not occurred to her before today.

But Walter shook his head. 'No thank you. I'm growing a beard. Much easier.'

'OK. I'll make some coffee while you get ready.'

Obediently Walter nodded. Going slowly upstairs he called down, 'Don't clear up. Hear me? I don't want you to.'

'I wouldn't dream of it.'

But as soon as he was out of sight Lauren cleaned up the kitchen, put a pile of dirty clothes in the washing machine, hoovered all the rooms on the ground floor, opened the post, fed the dog, filled the bird feeders, watered the plants and peered at the food in the fridge, throwing some of it away. Once she heard Walter shut the bathroom door and put on Radio 4 very loud, as he always did when he got into the bath, she went upstairs, hoovered his bedroom and changed the sheets. He was only using one side of the bed, she noticed.

Walter reappeared downstairs just as *You and Yours* started.

'I can't bear that bloody awful programme,' he announced.

He smelled of Trumper's West Indian Limes and looked younger and somehow brighter under his crown of fluffed-up white hair. Even the beard appeared more organised.

'I told you not to clear up,' he said, looking around. 'I can manage perfectly well.'

'I know you can.' Lauren passed him a cup of coffee. 'Where's Lídia anyway?'

'In Portugal for six weeks. Her granddaughter's having that operation to straighten out her feet, remember? And Lídia's gone to help out.'

'What about Lester? Hasn't he rung?'

'He might have. I didn't answer the telephone.'

'Didn't he come round?'

'Possibly. I didn't answer the door.'

'Haven't you left the house? What about swimming?'

Walter would not answer but stared out of the window as if he had never seen anything so interesting as a blue tit pecking at a bird feeder.

After a minute Lauren gave up. 'Come on, then.'

She handed him his scarf, helped him into his coat, put the dog on a lead and then all three walked together to a cafe on Haverstock Hill.

With Lauren taking charge Mike relaxed and remembered how to behave like a normal dog: cocking his leg, lunging at pigeons, growling at a cat on a wall and eating something disgusting out of the gutter. At the cafe he sat on the pavement and watched people go by while Lauren and Walter took shelter under a heat lamp. Walter ordered *linguine alla puttanesca*.

'And a very large napkin,' he said. 'I'm a messy eater.'

'Signorina?'

217

'Just a Coke, please,' said Lauren.

'Red wine,' said Walter. 'Large glass.'

While they waited Lauren smoked and read out bits of the newspaper. She did not mention Kathleen or Sonny. When his food came Walter squinted at the plate and then ate everything very quickly, making a great deal of mess in the process.

'Fantastic Mr Fox,' said Lauren. 'When was your last proper meal?'

'What an impertinent question.' Food and wine had brought some colour to Walter's cheeks. 'Define "proper"?' He was feeling better.

'Anything else for you guys?' A young, cheerful waiter had come to take Walter's plate.

Walter frowned up at him. 'We are not "guys",' he said, 'and I will have a double espresso.'

Lauren smiled. 'Perhaps I'll have a glass of wine after all.'

Once he had emptied two sachets of sugar into his coffee and stirred it with a teaspoon, round and round for half a minute, Walter cleared his throat and put the teaspoon beside the cup on the saucer. He had decided what to say.

'Your mother and I could not agree about Sonny,' he said. 'About what to do. I thought we should let him alone – let him come back from France when he was ready – but your mother wanted to go and fetch him. She wouldn't drop it.' He sipped his coffee. 'She called him repeatedly, by which I mean obsessively, but he didn't answer and wouldn't ring her back. He did, however, send an email explaining that he wanted to get to know Jem, by himself and without our interference.'

218

'Mum's interference,' said Lauren. 'I don't think he meant you, Dad.'

'Either way it seemed to me understandable, but not to your mother. She couldn't bear to let them alone. Sonny didn't know what sort of person Frank had been, she said. What would Jem tell him? She was almost hysterical – up all night crying and so on. I asked her to tell *me* what sort of person Frank had been but she said either "I can't" or "You won't understand". It was all she would say, over and over.' His expression was bleak. 'One night,' he continued, 'she decided it was all my fault. Gin may have had something to do with it, or perhaps she was right: perhaps it is all my fault.' He looked surprised at himself and then carried on, 'She shouted, Mike barked at her and she threw her glass at him – she missed, of course, but it smashed on the floor and gave us all a fright. There didn't seem to be anything to say after that. Mike went under the table, Kath sat down and I just stood there. Then she went upstairs and shut herself in Sonny's room. I cleared up the broken glass – or tried to – and in the morning she was gone.'

When Lauren thought of him waking alone on that morning and all the ones after it she felt as if her heart had been split all the way down the middle like a boiled lobster.

'Why didn't you ring her? Ring me? Ring someone?'

'Because I don't need your pity or anyone else's.'

'What about Sonny?'

'Sonny will come back when he's ready. He's not gone for ever.'

There was a silence. Lauren drank her wine and put out

another cigarette carefully in the ashtray. Walter turned his glass on the tablecloth, holding the stem between finger and thumb.

'I'll be dead soon,' he remarked, 'and none of this will matter.'

'Not "soon",' Lauren reproved him. 'One day.'

Walter smiled. Then the smile faded. 'I should have been more vigilant,' he said. 'I should have been prepared.'

'Prepared for what?'

'For all this. You see, back then I didn't like to be at home all the time. I got bored. Not with you or your mother but with the walls of the house and the post on the doormat and putting out the rubbish on the right day and the man in the newspaper shop saying hello every morning . . .' He stopped for breath; gave the wine glass another turn. 'Just bored.'

'You shouldn't have to be *vigilant* when it comes to your wife. Isn't that what marriage vows are for? Removing the need for vigilance?'

'Your mother didn't have an affair because she wanted to ruin my life. It wasn't a malicious act, but a forgetful one. She loves to be loved.'

Lauren shook her head. 'You're too easy on her.'

'You're too hard.' Walter smiled. 'But then you've always been on my side.'

They both considered this point, now poignant, for a moment in silence.

Lauren asked, 'Do you think we four have separated for ever, down a fault line that always existed?'

'Separated, yes,' said Walter. 'For ever, no.' It was his turn to be robust. 'I'm not getting divorced at seventy-four.

Very undignified. If your mother doesn't come back I shall have to go all the way to Kentish Town and fetch her.'

Following this statement of heroic intent he invisibly summoned the bill.

And so Lauren moved back into her childhood room, next to Sonny's on the attic floor, while Kathleen continued to occupy the studio.

Lauren sent Sonny a message: *Mum's moved out. I'm looking after Dad.*

She received one in return: *Not my problem. How was Greenland?*

She wrote back, *It was Norway, thanks for asking, and it was cold.* Then she deleted the message without sending it. What was the point?

Walter did not want to see anyone but Lauren insisted on Lester, whom she rang up at the end of that first day. She told him to come round in the morning and take Walter swimming as usual.

'I don't think Dad should sit in the house all day,' she said.

'Kathleen *gone*? Gone where? To live at your flat? Good heavens, she must be desperate.' Lester's surprise was incontinent. 'I rang the telephone, I rang the doorbell, I tried to look in through the window and I shouted into the letter box. I thought they must have gone away.'

'She has. He hasn't.'

'Well, thank heavens you're able to take over.'

The invisible thumb pressed Lauren a little deeper into the ground.

'Yes,' she said, 'isn't it lucky.'

'I hoped they'd gone away together to sort things out.'

'The opposite.'

'Is he all right?'

'Not really. Will you take him swimming in the morning?'

'Of course.' There was a murmur in the background. 'Annie says you must both come over for dinner.'

Lauren said, 'That's so kind,' but she knew Walter would not agree to an evening out.

And so every morning Walter went swimming and every evening Lauren cooked dinner and then they played chess. Lauren turned down two jobs because they would have meant going away. Without them she did not have anything to do. She felt like a dutiful vicarage daughter from a nineteenth-century novel. When Walter fell asleep in his armchair and she sat smoking beside the fire she wondered whether her life would remain like this as long as he was alive. Then she wondered, with an equally small degree of interest, whether she would mind if it did.

One gloomy afternoon at the beginning of February, Becka contrived to bump into Lauren on the pavement. She had kept an eye on the street until she saw Lauren cycling past and then she popped out of the front door and trotted down to the pavement in a manner that she hoped looked casual.

'Hi, Lauren. How are you?'

'All right.' Lauren was bent over her bike, which was in a rebellious mood and did not want to be tied up. 'Fed up with this frigging bicycle.'

'I just wondered . . . have you heard from Sonny?' Saying his name, Becka blushed. 'It's his birthday soon. Isn't it?'

'Yes it is. No, I haven't.' Lauren did not notice Becka's blush because she was trying to chain her bicycle to its usual lamp post. 'Come *here*, you fucker.' At last she got it in a choke hold and snapped the padlock shut. 'I think he's gone off his old family. I expect he's celebrating his birthday with the new one.' She straightened up. 'Have you? Heard from him?'

'No.'

Becka looked down at her shoes, hiding her face from Lauren in case *I slept with your brother* was written all over it. Why would Lauren care if she knew? Of course she wouldn't. No one would. She herself should not care. It was one night! There was nothing to care about. If only she had not, for a moment in the middle of the night they had spent together, allowed herself to believe that Sonny felt the way that she did. It had been the happiest moment of her life and it was hard to forget but she had to.

Shutting her mind from it she said to Lauren, 'And how about you? Are you OK?'

'Me?' Lauren was taken aback. No one had asked her this. 'Fine.'

'Really?'

'Yes.' She frowned. 'Fine.'

'What's going to happen? Are your parents getting divorced? Is Sonny ever coming back?'

Opening her mouth to say *I don't know* Lauren found she could not speak. If she spoke she would break down, and she could not break down. For a moment she was completely paralysed and then she blinked and bent to her bicycle again, removing the white light from the handlebar and the red light from behind the seat. She fumbled to switch off both lights and then dropped them into her coat pockets. At the end of this pantomime she found she could speak again in her normal voice.

'I don't know,' she said.

Becka did not reply but continued to watch Lauren's face with an interest so keen it was almost invasive. Lauren felt as if she were being peeled like an onion. She could not meet Becka's eye.

'I'd better go,' she muttered.

'OK.'

Becka stepped forward but Lauren could not risk being undone by a hug and so she dodged sideways and backwards.

'I'll let you know if I hear from him.'

Once she was inside the front door Lauren leant against it.

Walter called, 'Is that you? Come in here and tell me what you think—'

'I'm just going upstairs for a minute.'

She went up to Sonny's room and sat on the bed. She stayed there until Mike came up to find her.

He pushed his nose at her face. *What are you doing up here, crying on your own?*

'I'm not. I'm coming.'

And she got to her feet, blew her nose and went downstairs to make supper.

IX

Two weeks after the beginning of their affair, Frank told
Kathleen he wanted to leave Romy. He also wanted Kathleen
to leave Walter and then the two of them could run away
together. They would live somewhere else, he explained,
and be happy. It was simple: he had never loved anyone like
this; he could not live without her; his marriage was over.
She must feel the same.

They were in bed and in a state of languid bliss after
making love, their bodies tacked together by sweat. Kathleen
was drifting in and out of a delicious doze, perfectly sated
and perfectly happy, when Frank began to outline his plans
for their future.

Smiling, she responded sleepily, 'Frank, you are silly.'

'You think I'm joking? About this?'

Now she lifted her head and looked at him. Could he be
serious? She felt suddenly too naked. She dragged herself
into a sitting position and tugged the sheet up over her
breasts.

'It's just such an odd thing to say when you know it's
impossible,' she said. 'We said this was just going to be an
affair.' She was a little bit irritated. She had been nearly
asleep and he had disturbed her. 'That's what we agreed,

two weeks ago.' A crease had appeared between her eyebrows.

'That was two weeks ago.'

'But it can't be anything else. We're married. To other people.'

'We don't have to be married. People get divorced.' Frank rolled onto his side so that he was nearer to her. He propped himself up on an elbow, took her hand and kissed it. 'I want more. I want everything.'

Every day for the last fortnight Kathleen had managed to slip her leash, even if only for an hour, and visit Frank. It might be after lunch, when the sun was highest and the light was too fierce and everyone took a siesta, or in the evening when Rass went home and filming stopped for the day.

Romy was too busy to notice. What with shopping, cooking, laundry, cleaning and changing sheets she did not have any free time in the day to go home and catch her husband in bed with Kathleen or anyone else. Sometimes Kathleen might loudly pretend that she had spent the missing hours visiting a nearby church or village in case someone had noticed her absence, but Frank said there was no need to pretend.

'Romy trusts me,' he said.

'Because she's a good person. Too good for you.'

Frank did not approve of comments such as this. He could not bear any imputation that he was behaving badly. He wanted to believe that he and Kathleen had been fated to meet, that they could not help themselves and that they existed in a bubble beyond the reach of the real world, as if they were sharing a dream. Kathleen knew all this was

226

nonsense but she did not disagree because it was so lovely to pretend.

Each day when she arrived Frank was there to kiss her thoroughly as soon as she got out of the car. He was always at the door, as if he had been listening out for the wheels. The house was well hidden from the road and from its neighbours and so there was no need to hide. He told her he had stopped leaving the house in case he missed her, a comment she took for a joke. Once he had kissed her he would lead her into the house and upstairs, not to the bedroom he shared with his wife but into the next-door room. Kathleen did not care where they had sex but Frank did not want to make love in his marital bed.

'It wouldn't be right,' he said.

This made Kathleen laugh. 'None of it's right,' she said. 'Doing it in a different bed doesn't make it any less wrong.'

Frank winced. He did not like to be reminded of right and wrong. He stopped her mouth with a kiss.

The room they used was unpainted and likely to remain unpainted as long as Frank was distracted by Kathleen. The lovers lay under a ceiling patched by pink and green flaking plaster. The bed was an antique and therefore very small but this did not matter because they were not sleeping but only making love, drinking wine, telling each other their funniest, best and favourite stories and making love again – if there was time. Kathleen was always careful not to be late. It pleased her to give Vincent the slip, but she dreaded the thought that he might catch her.

I want everything. This sort of remark, offhand or not, was unacceptable. Considering how to respond, Kathleen extracted her hand from Frank's grasp and picked up her watch from the bedside table. She looked at the time and said lightly, 'I'd better get going.'

'Not yet. I want to talk about this.'

'About what? Your ridiculous idea?'

She noticed his whole body tighten in anger. He hated not to be taken seriously.

'You can't go until you've heard me out.'

'Can't I? I'll go when I like, thank you.'

There was a silence while each registered the other's mood. Kathleen marshalled her thoughts. She did not want a row, but nor could she allow him even to contemplate a future that contained her. She must be firm: he must know for certain that she was not persuadable.

If he had listened to her two weeks ago then he would know how unreasonable he was being. She had told him she would never leave Walter. Why had he not heard her? She supposed he had been too busy getting her clothes off. How tiresome this was. Tomorrow would be their last afternoon and if he made a fuss he would spoil it. She did not want to argue but to lie here and bask like a cat in the sun.

'Listen,' she said, 'we're not discussing this because it's not going to happen. We've known each other for two weeks. We're both married to other people. What about Romy? What about Walter?'

'I can leave her. You can leave him.'

'I most certainly will not. I love Walter. I respect him and I like being married to him.'

'Respect him? How can you? You're lying in bed with me.'

'This is nothing whatever to do with Walter. How can he be hurt by what he doesn't know?'

'You wouldn't be here if you were happy at home.'

Kathleen frowned. 'I am happy when I'm at home, but I'm not at home right now. I'm on location, I met you and we're in a bubble. You said so yourself.'

'I don't want to be in a bubble any more. I want it to be real.'

'No.'

The word came out sharply because Kathleen was alarmed. The last two weeks had been a delicious, indulgent, secret holiday – there was nothing more satisfying than making someone adore you – but if Frank had fallen in love then he had ruined it.

'Can't we just enjoy our last two afternoons? Please?'

'They don't have to be the last two afternoons. We could have a whole future.'

'Stop it.' She was getting tired of this. 'I said *no*. How many times do I have to say it?'

But he ignored her. 'I know you love me,' he said. 'I can tell. I wouldn't feel like this if you didn't love me.'

But I'm an actress, Kathleen thought. *It's my job to make you love me.* She tried another tack. 'What about Lauren?'

'Lauren? You can't pretend you care about Lauren. You haven't given her a moment's thought in two weeks.'

Kathleen's eyes widened when she heard this. She realised he was prepared to be nasty.

'If you're too scared to tell Walter about us,' he said cleverly, 'I'm not.'

Not content with having annoyed her, now he was making threats. It was outrageous and also a little frightening.

'You won't persuade me to leave my husband by threatening me.'

'I'm telling you I love you!' It was almost a shout. 'How can that be a threat?'

'If you loved me you wouldn't be yelling at me and telling me what to do. Is this how you treat your wife? Do you love her too?'

Frank leapt off the mattress as if he had been scalded. 'How dare you!' His face was knotted and furious. His fists were balled. He looked as if he wanted to drag her off the mattress and throw her down the stairs.

Eyeing him, Kathleen realised she did not know this man at all. He was as good as a stranger and she was naked and in his bed. This sudden knowledge was dreadful. She had thought him foolish for neglecting reality but she had done it too: she had invented a personality for him, one that suited her, and she had given him a two-week shelf life. What this man was really like – and what he would do to get what he wanted – she had no idea. She had never been afraid of a man before and wondered what to do. Rolling away from him she got up and started looking for her clothes. Now the bed stood between them. Speaking softly, she did not meet his eye.

'I don't want to fight,' she said. 'I don't like fights.'

This was not quite true but it was true that she did not relish the idea of a physical fight with a man twice her weight and a foot taller than she was.

'Everything was perfect a minute ago, but now . . .'

She let the sentence hang in the air. She longed to get out. Where were her knickers? She felt for them under the sheet at the foot of the bed, turned them right side in and put them on. Then she put on her bra and hooked it together behind her back.

'Perfect?'

Frank's anger had flared and died and the word was almost a sob. He slumped at the edge of the bed, took a pillow in both arms and held it against his chest like a teddy bear. He was struggling to contain himself.

'How can it be perfect? I love you. I'm married to someone else. You love me. You're married to someone else. What's perfect about that?'

Tears were even more alarming than anger. What on earth could she do with him? This was the sort of dreary discussion one might expect at the end of an affair but not after two weeks. She longed to be back at the villa and under the shower, or in front of the camera and working, or swimming lengths in the pool or indeed anywhere but here. She thought of Walter, whose only crime was to be too independent. She had certainly learned her lesson.

'Frank, you can't love me. You just think you do. You barely know me.'

'I do. I love you. I understand you. I know you.'

'You don't.'

'You're kind, funny, beautiful, sweet—'

'I'm *not*. "Sweet"? How absurd! I'm none of those things. I've just been . . .' She could not say it: *pretending*. 'This was supposed to be fun,' she said. 'It's not fun right now.'

'I can't go back to the way things were. I can't.'

'You have to. You can't *make* me leave Walter.'

'If I tell him about us, then—'

'You wouldn't dare.' She must stamp on this immediately with a heavy boot.

'I love you. You don't love me.' He was weeping.

'Not right now, no.'

Kathleen picked up her dress off the floor, shook the dust off it, stepped into it and pulled it up over her shoulders. It was the same dress that Lauren had ruined, but clever Romy had dyed it scarlet and now the stain was invisible. The woman was a marvel.

'I've been having fun,' she said briskly, 'and that's all. I don't want anything else and nor should you.'

'Don't patronise me!' Frank flared again, standing up and throwing the pillow down.

Kathleen jumped in fright but she managed to recover and laugh charmingly.

'Darling Frank! You do look funny standing there with no clothes on looking furious. You're like a little boy who won't get into his bath.' She wondered how much he had drunk before she arrived. 'Don't be cross. Please?' She stepped around the bed, took his hands and pressed herself against him. 'Let's not squabble.' She stood on tiptoe and kissed him lightly in the corners of his mouth. 'Don't you know I adore you? Can't you tell?'

Frank was trembling at the edge of violence. He closed his eyes to hide the tears of mortification and disappointment that had sprung there. He could not move for fear that he would fight or weep, he did not know which. After a moment he breathed again, slowly, and surrendered. He inhaled Kathleen's scent, keeping his eyes shut. Into her hair he whispered, 'It's not enough.' Kathleen did not respond. Perhaps she did not hear.

Feeling him give way in her arms Kathleen patted his shoulder in approbation and stepped back. She had won.

'That's better,' she said, soothing him. 'Now I really must go.' She could not wait to get out.

'Will I see you again?'

'As long as we have no more of this nonsense.'

'Please?'

'*That's* more like it.' Kathleen kissed him squarely on the mouth, approving him. 'Come and wave me off?'

Frank realised then that she was relieved: she had de-clawed him, put him back in his cage and now she could pet him safely. The realisation was sickening.

When she had gone, and he was alone, and the house was quieter and emptier than it had been before she came, the rage returned. It smouldered like an underground fire – a fire that might burn for miles, for days, for years and then find a way out. She had ruined everything, and in the face of this lifelong ruin there seemed nothing more or less to be done than get drunk.

With this in mind Frank finished a second bottle of wine and opened another and then another, sitting outside the back door as the light faded and the stars pricked the sky, one by one, until they teemed in their scornful billions, looking down on him.

I am alone. She does not love me. She will not save me.

He would be here still, twice as drunk, when his wife came home.

Frank was right: it was not the same for Kathleen. She felt enlivened and invigorated even in his absence; she drove home in high spirits and she did not mope and pine without him. She luxuriated in her time with him but also afterwards back at the villa when she was alone. Here she lay in the bed, drowsy and sated as a leopard in a tree. To be adored was bliss, and she retained the feeling far into the night just as her skin retained the sun's heat long after sunset. She was replete.

It might be true to say that she preferred the afterglow to the actual experience: being with Frank was not as luscious as having just left Frank. Recalling him was the purer pleasure. This truth coasted over her mind like a seagull over a beach and then away out to sea. She did not want to retain it.

To lie in her dim, cool, blue-tinted bedroom at the villa and remember the sensation of Frank's hands on her body – *that* was pleasure. The memory alone was enough to stir her on the bed and thrill her inside and out. When she closed her eyes and recalled the look she had seen in his – the urgency and the surrender – she would be nourished and blissful in a cocoon of remembered sensations. Then she would fall asleep.

She had never felt like this with Walter, because Walter had never worshipped her – for a decade he had kept her guessing: did he love her? Was he bored? Would he leave her for someone else? Someone younger? More clever? More serious? One of those ugly, well-informed and courageous women he met in his line of work? Within the space of a fortnight she had become as essential to Frank as oxygen. It was a powerful intoxicant.

In the morning Kathleen breakfasted with Vincent while the others slept. Vincent ate his egg whites and took his vitamins in silence. He was preoccupied: today was the last day of the shoot. Kathleen, who did not want to talk to him anyway, pretended to read the *International Herald Tribune*

234

and wondered whether Frank was thinking about her and if so with what degree of feeling.

When she ducked into the kitchen for orange juice she found Romy retching into the sink.

'Poor you,' she said sympathetically. 'Hangover?'

'No, not that.' Romy shook her head, still hanging over the sink, the cold tap running. 'I'm sorry — do you need something?'

'I'll get it myself.' Kathleen began slicing oranges in two and pressing the halves face down on the electric juicer. 'I'm going to miss this machine,' she said. 'Such a luxury. Have you got a bug? Do you want to lie down in my room?'

'It's better now.' Romy splashed her face with water and dried it on a tea towel. 'It doesn't last long.'

Kathleen went stone cold all over as if a jug of icy water had spilled inside her. She stopped juicing the oranges and turned to look at Romy.

'I'm pregnant, you see,' Romy, smiling, went on. 'Just a couple of months.' She was happy and confiding. She was trusting. 'Too soon to tell anyone.'

'Even your husband?' Kathleen's mouth was dry.

'Oh no,' Romy laughed. 'I told Frank weeks ago. He's barely mentioned it since. I think he's in denial.'

'Yes.' Kathleen put down the orange she was holding and put her hand on the back of a chair to steady herself. She suddenly thought she might be sick as well, all over the oranges. 'I mean, possibly.'

Noticing, Romy said, 'Are you all right?'

'Yes. Fine.' She swallowed. 'Congratulations. How exciting.' She tried to sound enthusiastic. 'When you stop feeling sick you'll feel wonderful.'

'I hope so. I wish Frank were more excited.'

'He will be. It's different for a man.' Particularly, she thought to herself, if he is sleeping with another woman. 'Have you been trying?'

'Yes and no.' Romy smiled. 'I've wanted a baby for ever but we really can't afford to. Frank wants to wait. He's not earning at the moment. He's supposed to be finishing the house. He's an artist, you see. He gets distracted.'

'I see.' Kathleen started babbling to hide her confusion. 'Lauren was an accident – I didn't even notice. I was sick a few times but I thought it was hangover. Then one day I was looking in my handbag for a lighter and I pulled out a Tampax. I thought, "Hello stranger," and I realised I hadn't needed one for ages.' She had told the story fifty times and had it down pat. 'We were a bit casual, I suppose. I was doing *Measure for Measure* at the time – playing a chaste and virginal nun – and babies were the last thing on my mind.'

'Babies are *always* on my mind,' Romy said wistfully. 'I've been desperate to have one and now – oh!' She smiled with pleasure and hugged herself. 'When the house is finished I'm going to run it as a *chambre d'hôte* and Frank can paint, but he's been . . .' She stopped.

Kathleen swallowed nervously. 'Been what?'

'Oh, just typical Frank.' She began what sounded like a well-rehearsed apology on his behalf. 'Distracted.'

Indeed he has, Kathleen thought. She did not feel remorse, only indignation. Frank was a shit and had wronged them both.

'It was one of the reasons for coming here,' Romy went on. 'I bought the house with some money my father gave me. We've been doing it up bit by bit, but it's taken longer than we thought.'

'Distractions, I suppose?' Kathleen tried to keep the edge of sarcasm from her voice.

'Yes. There are plenty of people coming here because of that book, *A Year in Provence*, but Frank's got to finish the bedrooms. There are three above the studio but at the moment they're only fit for the mice. And I have to work in the meantime because of the money we owe the bank.'

'I'm sure he'll settle down,' Kathleen said automatically. 'There's nothing like a baby to make a man grow up.' Now she felt sick for having come out with such an awful platitude. She wanted to stop her mouth and stop her ears. She thought of Walter. What would he think of her if he knew? He would think her immoral. She *was* immoral.

Romy spoke, making her jump.

'You must finish your breakfast. I'll bring the juice. I'm feeling fine now.'

'All right. And congratulations again. You'll make a wonderful mother.'

It was the only truth Kathleen had spoken. She hoped it was as convincing as the lies.

Today was their last day on the film, tonight her last night at the villa and tomorrow she would fly home. She did not need to see Frank again.

She had known he was a cheat, of course. She was one herself – she could not pretend to be shocked by that. But Frank had deceived *her*: his lover as well as his wife. She had not suspected him of that. He had discovered his wife was pregnant and embarked on an affair. Two weeks later he had proposed abandoning his pregnant wife for his married lover. Was he fantasist or monster? Yesterday he had alternated threats with sentiment. Today Kathleen saw him differently: he was unbalanced. He had said he would tell Walter and now she believed he might.

For a moment she pictured herself a lonely divorcée, no one courting her but a penniless Frank, no house but only a horrid little flat, no company but Lauren, no money to pay for childcare and no work because soon she would be over the hill and past it.

Why had she not conjured up this vision two weeks ago? It might have put her off. She could not now recall what had made the affair irresistible. Instead she could see the future so clearly it was painted in technicolour – or rather, in the drab tints of a bedsit in Kentish Town.

At the end of the day cast and crew were condemned, by tradition, to having what was called a 'wrap party' – by everyone except Vincent, who hated jargon. He had not once said 'action' or 'cut' in six weeks, instead saying 'OK' for both. Today, when he finished, he did not say 'It's a wrap' but only 'OK' and then when nobody moved, 'I guess that's it.'

There was a moment of silence while it sank in. Then there was relief and hugging and soon the crew – half-a-dozen men and women, all French – began packing their kit into aluminium trunks and black nylon bags. The three actors, redundant at last, rushed back to the villa to start getting drunk.

When Kathleen arrived at the house there was a telephone message on the hall table in Romy's loopy handwriting: *Walter phoned.*

Kathleen found her in the kitchen preparing food for the evening.

'You spoke to Walter?'

'Yes.' Romy wiped her hair off her sweating forehead with a tea towel slung over one shoulder. 'He said he was flying home tomorrow.'

Kathleen felt a rush of pleasure and excitement. 'Did he say where he was?'

'No.'

'Did he leave a number?'

'No.'

'Did he say anything else?'

'Yes: he asked how you were. I said you were beautiful, too thin and very tanned.'

'Did you?' Kathleen was pleased. 'Anything else?'

'No.'

'Thanks, Romy.' Kathleen gave her an envelope stuffed with cash. 'And this is for looking after Lauren.'

Romy glanced inside and said, 'But it's too much.'

'It's not too much. You looked after me as well. I want you to have it, and I want you to keep it.' She paused and wondered how to say next what was on her mind. 'Don't give it to your husband.'

Romy laughed. 'Whyever not?'

'I'm serious. Don't let him know you have it. Every wife needs some running away money.'

'But I'm not running away.' Romy gave her a quizzical look.

'I know.' She could not make her understand without making her unhappy. 'Of course not. But keep it for a rainy day.'

'Thank you.' Romy tucked the envelope into the front pocket of her apron. 'You've been so kind to me.'

'No, I haven't.' Kathleen shook her head. 'You think everyone is kind, but we're not.'

It occurred to her then, as it had not before, that she should tell Romy everything. When that momentary impulse had passed she forced herself to laugh as if their whole conversation had been nothing but silliness and jokes. Then she went out into the garden to get drunk.

She was not quite the last to bed: she left Vincent stretched out on a cushioned lounger under a fig tree.

'That's a daybed,' she told him fuzzily. 'Not a night bed.'

'I like it here. I'm waiting for the nightingale.'

'Darling Vincent.' The film was over and she felt quite fond of him. She bent to kiss his cheek before tottering indoors and upstairs where she passed out.

She did not know what time it was when Frank woke her. He was sitting on the bed fully dressed, looking down at her and holding her hand. It gave her a fright.

'Frank? For God's sake. What are you doing here?'

'I had to come. I had to see you.'

When he spoke she could smell the drink on him. Confusion turned to alarm. She sat up. She had never seen him outside his house and now here he was and she knew it was wrong, as if she had bumped into a bull outside its paddock.

'How did you get in? Did anyone see you?'

'It doesn't matter. Nothing matters. I had to come. I can't let you go—'

But Kathleen had remembered yesterday and she interrupted him: 'Romy's pregnant. You didn't tell me.'

She touched her forehead with her free hand. Her head ached. Everything she had wanted to forget by getting drunk came swarming over her like angry wasps. It was painful and she wanted to cry, but more than that she hated him. He had ruined everything. The affair was spoiled and ugly.

'How could you? How could you say those things to me when . . .'

Frank had stiffened. He gripped her hand more tightly; too tightly.

'How did you know?'

'She told me. She's so happy. You're disgusting. I feel sick when I think—'

'What difference does it make? You've got a child and you still—'

'I'm not the same as you. It's not the same.' She pinched her head with her fingers. It ached so much she could hardly see. 'Get out,' she said blindly. 'Go home. I never want to see you again.'

'No.' This was said with a certainty that made Kathleen look at him in surprise. 'You don't get to tell me what to do.' He grabbed her by the arm and pulled her out of bed in one quick movement. 'I'm going to talk and you're going to listen.'

'*Frank!*' She hissed at him – she did not want to wake anyone up so she dared not shout. 'Let me go!'

She tried to pull her arm out of his grip but he was strong – she would not have guessed how strong. She wriggled and kicked but he held her pinned in his arms like an awkward

241

parcel, half-carrying and half-pushing her out of the room, down the stairs and into the garden. Once they were outside he hurried her down to the swimming pool, holding her by one wrist.

'Stop it! Frank! Have you gone mad? Stop it!'

She scolded him but he took no notice. When he had got her as far as the swimming pool he let her go but stood in front of her as if he were guarding the exit. The edge of the pool was behind her. They were both out of breath.

Kathleen was wearing only a nightie and her feet were bare but she gathered herself and said, 'How dare you. You're a brute. I'm going back to the house and if you try and stop me I'll scream the place down.'

She made as if to push past him but he caught her arm. When she turned in surprise he slapped her hard across the face.

'I don't care how much fucking noise you make,' he said. 'Scream your head off if you like. I've got nothing to lose.'

Kathleen was stunned. She lifted a hand to her cheek just like she had seen in the movies – she had never been hit before and was surprised by how much it hurt. But more than hurt and more than surprise she felt fear.

Changing tack she appealed to him in a calm, low voice. 'Frank . . .'

She stepped back but he still had a tight hold of her wrist and so he came forward, nearer to her, forcing her to retreat until her heels met the edge of the pool and she could go no further. Still he came closer until she felt the heat of his body and his breath. She was trapped. The physical fact of him was unarguable and when she understood that she was really in trouble her anger gave way to a cold flush of terror. When Frank saw her fear he was pleased – she could see it in his eyes: the gleam of power. Now he could do with her what he wanted.

'You see? *I* decide. Not you.'

He twisted her arm behind her back and jerked her wrist up towards her shoulder blade until she gasped. Now he was so close to her it was like being gripped by a bear on his hind legs, a bear who was going bite into her aching skull and then rip her to pieces.

'Frank – please – don't – please . . .'

She was whispering and begging and cringing, all the time cringing, away from his touch. He pushed one knee between her thighs, forcing her off balance, and bent her backwards over the water, holding her tightly. Then he put his other hand up her nightie and between her legs.

Kathleen jumped as if she had been branded with a hot iron. *This is not happening.* She started struggling and twisted and fought in his grip. *This is not going to happen.* She was caught in a vice – he could snap her in half, bent back like this – but the insistent push of his fingers made her recoil with such violence that she tipped backwards and pulled him with her into the pool.

There was a moment in the air – confusion and thrashing limbs – and then a colossal splash as they hit the water. Frank's elbow caught her hard in the jaw, whether by accident or on purpose she did not know, but she discovered that he had released her and so she kicked and kicked away from him until he caught her, first by the hair and then by the shoulders and had pushed her down, under the water. Was he trying to kill her? She kicked him as hard as she could

– anywhere; everywhere – but it was like kicking a tree and made no difference until suddenly, inexplicably, he let go.

She struggled to the surface and saw that Vincent was in the water with them, up to his waist and still wearing his suit. He had got Frank by the collar and was dragging him towards the steps at the shallow end of the pool as Frank, taken by surprise, flailed and thrashed, trying to get his balance.

Vincent was saying, 'Who the fuck are you?' But he was a pale reed in his pale suit and no match for Frank who wrenched himself free, got back on his feet and grew out of the water like a monster from the deep. Turning, maddened, he fell on Vincent with all his weight.

Kathleen struggled towards them through the water, her nightie making it impossible to walk. 'Stop it! Get off him!' Her voice was pathetic and feeble in all this turbulence and splashing. Her teeth chattered with terror.

Now Vincent was trying to get away from Frank and out of the water, back to safety and dry land. He was almost there – he had reached the steps and was on them, or up them, or nearly, but Frank caught him by one leg and yanked it back, tripping him up. Vincent spun around, lost his balance and fell slowly backwards, his hands clutching at nothing as he tried to save himself, until the back of his head struck the stone kerb at the water's edge, once and then again, a hard bounce. Then he was down; now he lay still.

From tumult to nothing in a split second. Everything was motionless but for the surface of the water, rocking to stillness. Then Kathleen said, 'Oh my God . . .' and ploughed her way through the water to the steps. 'Vincent? Vincent?' She crouched behind him, wedged her knees underneath his shoulders and lifted his head but it lolled in her hands.

There was no blood. She tried to drag his whole body upwards out of the water but he was too heavy; she had to shift and twist and pull by degrees until his head and chest were above the waterline. Into his face she said, 'Wake up! Vincent!' Her hands trembled over his hair, pushing it off his pale forehead, ghostly in the lifting dawn.

Frank had not moved except for his chest which went in and out, breathing hard. He watched them.

'Oh, God, Frank! What have you done?' Kathleen climbed out of the water. 'I have to get help. I have to get help.'

She pulled her sodden nightie up to her knees and ran back to the house. She shook Rocky awake and stuttered, 'Vincent – unconscious – in the water . . .'

He jumped out of bed and ran with her back to the pool.

Here she stopped. She stared down in confusion. There was Vincent, as she had left him, but he had slipped a little down the steps so that his nose and mouth were under the water.

'But . . . ?'

She looked around wildly. There was no sign of Frank.

Rocky meanwhile had run forward, got hold of Vincent under the armpits and now hauled him out in one movement as if he weighed nothing at all. He laid him on the stone and turned him first on his side – a trickle of water came out of his mouth – and then on his back.

Glancing briefly up at Kathleen, Rocky said, 'Go call an ambulance. Do it now.' Then he turned back to Vincent, pinched his nose, breathed into his mouth and pressed his chest: *one thousand two thousand three thousand*.

Kathleen found her feet and ran for the house.

X

He did not drown, they said. It was the fall that killed him. They quickly guessed what Kathleen already knew: that he had fallen backwards, clipping his head on the stone kerb at the edge of the pool. That soft, vulnerable place at the base of his skull had caved in like the shell of a soft-boiled egg.

Trying to reassure Kathleen they said, 'By the time you reached him it was too late. There was nothing you could have done. No one could have brought him round.' They said the same to Rocky who put his face in his hands and wept.

Kathleen did not weep, and nor did she speak. She shook from head to toe and stared unseeing at the ground. Holding a glass of brandy she sat outside at the stone table, hunched, her nightie drying out in the bright morning sun and her hand trembling enough to spill the drink over her wrist when she tried to sip it. People came up and asked her questions and then retreated. There was whispering; silence; birdsong. Bob lit a cigarette for her – this was the day to start smoking again. She looked down at her bare feet, filthy and cut to pieces. Vincent was dead. The sun burned, hotter and higher. Vincent was dead.

When the time came she did not make a decision to lie but simply went along with the acceptable story: yes, he was in the water when I found him and yes, he was alone. These assumptions were more likely and more convenient than the truth which was becoming, every moment, less like a memory and more like something dreamed; something imagined; something that had vanished in the dawn along with Frank. *To be credible*, Vincent had said at the beginning, *you must believe*.

And so she told them she had been woken by voices under her window. Men's voices? Yes. Shouting? No, not shouting, but raised. In French? Yes. Monsieur Wexler spoke French? Yes, fluently. That was surprising for an American, the two detectives said, and she explained about his Jewish mother. How many voices had there been? She wasn't certain, but she thought two. Two? Was she sure? She could not be certain, she said again, but she thought there were two: Monsieur Wexler and another. Somebody else. Somebody French? Of course, somebody French.

Yes, she told them, she had hurried downstairs and outside in her nightie to find out what was the matter. She followed the sound of these voices into the garden and then heard a mighty splash, down at the pool. When she got there she found Vincent already in the water; already alone. She plunged in – soaking herself – and dragged him to the steps. She tried to pull him out, but she was not strong enough. She ran back to the house to fetch Rocky. Yes, that was all.

No one else had heard anything? No one else had been woken by the noise? Rocky, Bob and Ava shook their heads. Rocky had stopped crying and instead rubbed his shaved head with the palm of one hand, a circular motion, around and around, making a scratching noise which no one could bear and yet no one could tell him to stop. Ava, translating for Kathleen, wept huge, perfect tears that rolled down her cheeks in obedient pairs. Bob sat beside her, helpless and worried, thinking of his wife in California and how little she needed to know of any of this.

'It was our last night,' he told their inquisitors. 'We'd been drinking.'

Drinking? All of you? Monsieur Wexler also? No, not Vincent: Vincent had been the only one sober and the only one outdoors.

'My room looks over the drive,' Bob protested, 'like Rocky's. Only Kathleen overlooks the garden. How could we have heard anything? Why would we?'

Not even a car, pulling up or leaving on the gravel below their window? No. Nothing. There might not even have been a car – no one knew. Could someone have come in on foot? Another way? Yes, of course. There are no fences or walls around the garden, just vineyards and olive groves – and all of those available to the network of dusty little roads and tracks that connect each farm, each house and each village. It would be possible to walk or drive for miles before meeting a boundary. Is there any evidence of a car coming or going after everyone else went home or went to bed? No. None at all.

And so it was decided, by unspoken consensus, that a curious stranger had wandered in on foot and had encountered Vincent, not yet asleep in bed but out on the lounger under the stars. One man had disturbed the other and there had been a confrontation; an argument; the stranger had tried to get away and Vincent had chased him down to the

249

pool. There they had fought, or perhaps merely scuffled, until Vincent had slipped, or perhaps been pushed, into the water. He had banged his head as he fell and the intruder, frightened of repercussions, had fled.

It was a story that made sense because there seemed to be no other. Even to Kathleen, who knew the facts, this alternative truth was the better story: more attractive, more persuasive and more credible. To paint over her memory with this version was the right and sensible thing to do. She did not want anything else – *caught in his grip; those fingers pushing* – to be true.

Two days passed when nothing new occurred. No one was allowed to go home. Everyone sat about, talking in anxious whispers. Bob and Ava began to argue. Sunbathing, swimming and eating seemed inappropriate, while smoking and drinking felt compulsory. Without Vincent they were un-shepherded and helpless – there were no meals or bedtimes. Kathleen did not want to be in her bedroom – Frank had come to find her here, after all – and so she locked herself in the bedroom Lauren had used, her bags packed, waiting to go home.

And then Mitchell Peters arrived, fetched from the airport by Rocky. His appearance was a relief: he would take charge, he would know what to do and he would make it happen. They gathered gratefully round him.

'Vincent's death was a tragic accident,' he declared. 'Fact.' He looked fiercely around as if waiting to hear an objection. 'Second fact: I'm shutting this production down. End of story. Third fact? You're all going home.'

By 'production' he plainly meant not just the film but the police investigation.

'He can't tell the police what to do,' Ava sniffed on behalf of the French nation. 'This isn't Italy.'

But when Mitchell Peters described what would happen it usually did – he was not the best producer for nothing. True to his word he called off the police, retrieved the actors' passports, bought a sheaf of new air tickets and sent each of them away: Bob to his wife in California, Ava to her mother in Paris and Kathleen to Walter in London.

'What happened?' Walter asked when she got home. 'He was drunk? On drugs? He drowned?'

Kathleen shook her head, no, and then told him the story she had come to believe herself.

XI

For Jem, the delicate beauty of winter in Provence was a revelation. She had either forgotten its magic or, as a child, had never noticed – why would she have noticed something that happened every day? But after winters in London every dawn here was a gift: bright sun in a cold, glass sky; sparkling days following nights as clear and cold as lake water; tracings of frost drawn over the car like white lace; dead leaves crisp underfoot. She thought she would never grow tired of it.

She woke early and Sonny late. While he slept on she would drift about the house, waiting for sunrise. She made coffee, lit the fires and stared at black windows waiting for first light. She liked to be outside when the sun rose.

Sonny slept in the spare room, next to Frank's. He slept like a teenager, long and deep, untroubled by spirits. To Jem the few weeks between their ages seemed a gulf of years. Loss, grief, solitude and mourning were unknown to Sonny, 'Except on stage. Mum died in front of me every night in *Hamlet*, but I know that doesn't count. It's all been easy for me.'

He was ashamed of himself and sorry for her but he did not know the truth: that Frank had killed her mother and gone to prison. She could not tell him that story. It was the very worst of all the untold stories she kept inside her, fermenting into a toxic liquor. When Sonny asked, 'What was he like?' she was choosy with her answer:

'He was an artist. He was very good-looking. He could imitate birds. He used to tell me stories about boarding school in England, and about his parents who lived in a big house and had a butler called Beaker.' She ransacked her memory for the sanitised history. 'He could draw – beautiful illustrations in pen and ink. He drew cards for my birthdays with pictures of me and my schoolfriends. He won a prize in France for his drawings in a children's book and the three of us went to Paris to collect it. He could make things – he made the mobile in my bedroom.'

Other questions from Sonny were more problematic:

'Why did you go and live with Marian? Why didn't you stay here with your dad? Why did you move to London? Why did you never see Frank again?'

'He had a breakdown after my mother died. He couldn't cope. He was too sad. He wanted to forget.' It should have been true but it wasn't. The words came out in lumps as if they had curdled. Why didn't he notice? She wished he would. She wished he would challenge her or catch her out – hiding the truth was making her sick inside. Last of all she said, 'I don't blame him,' and the sentence burned like acid in her mouth.

Here in France she found all the proof she needed for her fairy tales. She began almost to question her sanity, or at least her memory, when she discovered the photographs Frank had kept. She had been worried that Sonny would find something in the house to contradict her stories – the rotting portrait in the attic – but soon she realised that nothing of that kind had been allowed to exist. These remaining pictures, expertly curated, described a marriage of perfect contentment; a childhood of perfect bliss. Evidence to condemn him lived only in her mind. If she stopped believing her memory then perhaps the truth, without air or light, would wither and die. It was a tempting idea.

Here was Romy in a summer dress and espadrilles, holding the front door key for their new house – this house – the ravishing mess that it had been when they bought it. Summer sun beamed down from on high, right upon the top of her head, and showed her smiling, happy, young and unshadowed.

The next photograph had been taken two years later. This time Romy, heavily pregnant, was blurred as if she had been caught in the act of disappearing. A setting winter sun shone straight into her eyes and she had shaded them with one hand which left her face a dark, anonymous oval. Bathed in the falling light the beloved house, finished at last, looked golden and glorious. Frank was behind the camera – Jem recognised his shape in the shadow he cast in front of him, the shadow that reached over the foreground into the picture until it touched Romy's feet, as if he dabbed her with one of his inky fingers: *mine*. Looking, Jem felt chilled.

These few photographs, the grey coat Jem never took off, a mug in the kitchen reading 'Cherie' and Mimi's empty hutch in the garden. These traces remained of Romy's existence, but no more. It felt as if Frank had not only killed her but swallowed her whole. Even the cupboard where Jem

255

had found that coat had lost its trace of scent – freed like a butterfly only to perish. The coat smelled now as if it had always been her own. Jem tried to explain to Sonny, 'I wanted to find something here. Something of her.'

'It was so long ago,' Sonny said. He was trying to comfort her. 'What could be left?'

Her ghost. Jem could not say it. *I want to be haunted.*

She did dream of her mother once: she dreamed that she got out of bed and went downstairs just as she might any morning and found her mother in the kitchen cutting a round, ripe melon into four quarters. In the dream, Jem was amazed. 'I thought you were dead.' Romy shook her head, smiling, and Jem felt pure happiness rush through her in a beautiful cascade. The death had been a dream; this was the reality.

And then the penalty of waking: like swimming up from a deep place, far beneath light, with a dead creature heavy in her arms. She was struggling upwards under the burden of a terrible, piercing sadness which, dreadful as it was to carry, she could not bear to be without. As she approached from underneath the tilting, bright surface of the water she began to cry desperately, as if sorrow had cracked her open: the tears were a thousand coins spilling out from a broken jar.

Then she woke up. She lay shocked, her eyes wide open, her face dry. The wooden seagulls turned lightly above her head as if disturbed by a breath. Her mother felt so close that between them could only be the thinnest of skins, almost translucent. Until she heard Sonny's cough, from his bedroom along the passage, she could not have sworn she was still in the land of the living.

*

When he saw Frank's studio Sonny decided that he too could have been an artist. He wanted to connect with Frank and this was the way.

'I always liked drawing,' he declared hopefully. 'Maybe I got it from him.'

In front of the studio window stood a long desk. Sonny sat on Frank's stool and listened to the radio on Frank's laptop. He drew pictures with Frank's inkpens on paper torn from Frank's sketchbooks. On the desk, surrounding the space cleared for drawing, there stood a varied and comprehensive collection of objects: postcards, ink pots, jam jars containing brushes or dead flowers, old rags for wiping or drying, pictures snipped from newspapers, wine glasses still holding a crust of red in their base and several pairs of identical spectacles. These objects created such a vivid portrait of the man who had lived in this room that it seemed he had just got up to answer the telephone. He could not be dead.

Jem did not encourage him, Sonny noticed, and nor did she encourage any discussion of Frank. She would answer his questions, but with inhibiting care. He could not explain it. Was she possessive? Did she want to keep her father to herself? Or was it grief? Was she too sad to speak of him? But Jem's attitude did not seem honest, or helpless, or overcome, as Sonny might expect from one grieving. She was guarded. It felt as if something was hidden, something cloaked, treading softly through the house when his back was turned.

The closer he felt to Frank, the further Jem slipped away. When he was sitting in the studio it seemed more likely that Frank would walk in than Jem. If there had been a battle to inhabit the house, Frank had won: he had left an indelible mark behind while Jem's presence was no more permanent than a breath – when she left the room she seemed to vanish and her every reappearance was a surprise. He might have said, when she appeared, *but I thought you were dead*.

One evening in the kitchen Jem produced a sheaf of photographs, carefully collated.

'I found these,' she said casually. 'Some of them are of Frank.' She had tried to refer to him as 'Dad' but the word stuck in her throat.

'Let me see.' Sonny pulled his chair next to hers and picked up a picture. 'Is that your mother? She's so young.'

'Younger than me. Pregnant with me. And in this one,' she pointed out, 'Frank looks like you.'

'And you.'

'No.' Jem shook her head. 'Not like me.' She hesitated and then said, 'Your mother must have been pregnant then too. With you.'

'I suppose so. She and Dad – Walter – had been trying for ages.' He smiled bitterly. 'At least that's what she always told me.' He reflected. 'And she said I was a miracle. That was another lie.'

He peered at another photograph that Jem had carefully picked: her parents smiling, wrapped around each other.

'Look how happy they are. How did my mother get between them? She must have done a number on your dad. She's to blame for all this.'

'Blame? But you wouldn't be here without her.'

'I wish everyone would stop saying that! It's not the point.'

'Isn't it?'

'Aren't you angry?'

Jem smiled a grim smile. 'Yes, I'm angry.'

There was something about her voice that made Sonny look at her.

Aware that she had aroused his curiosity Jem was compelled to subside and say it again, but this time as if she were defeated: 'Yes, I'm angry.' She must not go on. To continue would be to reveal, and to reveal would be to lose him. The history proposed by these photographs was the better history – the good history. She imagined the alternative family album: pictures of Frank shouting with his mouth wide open and his fists clenched; pictures of Romy's bruises; pictures of Milou broken on the ground or of herself hiding under the bed with her hands over her ears. What was the point of the truth? Sonny believed what he was told and she had almost begun to believe it herself: that her father had loved her mother, that her parents had been happy and that her childhood had been bathed in a golden sunlight. In this way, could she kill that man under the light bulb? The monster with the moths around his head? In front of them lay a photograph of a handsome, dark-haired, smiling man with his baby daughter in his arms. It was the only story.

Then Sonny said, 'I wish I'd met him. Am I like him?'

'No.' Jem felt something like panic claw at her chest. 'You're not like him. You're like you.'

'I used to wish I was more like Walter. Now I wish I was more like Frank.'

'No, you don't. You can't.' Jem stood up and the stack of photographs slipped to the floor. 'I'm sorry. I—'

'Are you all right?' Sonny looked up at her, puzzled. 'What is it? Jem?'

'It's not you.' *It's him.*

'Then what? Or who? Please tell me. How can we be close' – he put out a hand and caught her arm as she turned away from him – 'if you don't tell me?'

'No!' Jem pulled her arm from his grasp. She looked at him, her expression shocked, as if she barely knew him or even recognised him. 'Don't do that.'

'I'm sorry. I . . .'

She felt breathless. 'Forget it.' Blindly she backed away from him and retreated to Frank's study. She shut the door behind her. Her heart was beating wildly, making her whole body shake, and strong arms were wrapped around her chest although there was no one here. Was this panic? Was it memory? It felt like suffocation. Her knees gave way and she sat at Frank's desk. She switched on the lamp. At once the room seemed to shrink around her until the pool of yellow light in front of her on the desktop was the size of a gold coin. The air was thick and tight; she was locked in a cupboard. She could not get her breath. The room began to tilt and spin and she clutched at the arms of the chair to save herself from falling out but here she was on the ground, despite her efforts, gasping for breath on hands and knees. The rug felt rough under her palms. *I am not ill*, she told herself, *I am only haunted.* What she knew but could not tell was choking her from the inside out; she would be found with her own lies stuck like vomit in her throat. She lay on her side and waited for death, paralysed like Milou. She heard someone at the door and hoped it was her mother, come to fetch her.

But it was Kathleen: very much alive and the last person Jem thought she might ever be pleased to see.

'Jem? Jem?'

She was shaken by the shoulder.

'Wake up. Wake up.'

And then Sonny's voice from far away, as if she were underwater and he on the surface.

'I don't know what's wrong. I don't know what happened.'

Kathleen knelt beside Jem and pulled her into a sitting position. 'Tell me where it hurts. Tell me. Jem?'

'My heart.' The only two words in her brain and so hard to get out. 'My heart.'

Kathleen drove Jem to hospital, very fast.

'I'm not having a heart attack on my conscience.' She could have added *on top of everything else*.

In the car, Sonny sat in the back and Jem sat in the front beside Kathleen. No one spoke. Jem leant on the window and looked out at the dark night passing – the starlit sky and the flick of black branches.

When Jem turned eighteen Marian said, 'I've done my duty', and moved to Texel House in Norfolk. It turned out that a long career in penny-pinching had left her rich enough to pick an apartment from a brochure and buy it with cash from her savings account.

'There's catering if I want it and a nurse if I need it,' she told Jem. 'It's called "Retirement Living Advantage Gold". I can stay there until they carry me out feet first.'

'What about London?'

'That's your home, silly. I'm giving it to you.'

'You can't do that. I couldn't take it. It's too much.'

'I can't take it with me. And who am I going to give it to besides you?'

Living alone after Marian had gone, Jem got a job. She had a few months of school left to run – including exams – but she liked working and especially at night. She liked to slink out at twilight and come home in the dawn like a tomcat. She slept after school and got up again at nine in the evening. In the summer it was still light and therefore easy.

The job was in a hotel in Wimbledon. She wore a nasty uniform with a too-short skirt and a shirt men could see through until she started wearing a vest underneath it. The work was dull but she liked the other employees, none of whom were English. In the depths of night she learned Spanish from one man, Diego, and taught him French in return. No one stayed working there for long and Jem liked that too.

One morning in June she was waiting at Wimbledon station for a train to take her home: Wimbledon to Waterloo by rail and then the Underground to Westbourne Park with a change at Baker Street. Home in time for a shower and a bit of toast and then off to school on her bike.

It was before the rush hour and the platform was almost empty. Jem's feet hurt but she had been tipped £200 by a drunk American guest and the lump of cash, tucked into the front of her tights for safekeeping, was offsetting the pain in her feet. She was not supposed to keep tips but she had kept this one because today was her final A-level exam and afterwards she would be free.

She limped right to the end of the platform so as to wait in the sun. There was nobody all the way up here but one middle-aged woman, also alone, who was looking down at the tarmac with a slight frown as if she were concentrating hard on some difficult task in the forthcoming day. Perhaps an interview or a presentation or a meeting with her boss.

It was a beautiful morning already: swallows were scribbling messages on the roof of a blue sky. An announcement said, 'The next train will not stop at this station. Please stand back from the platform edge.' Jem and the other lady were already standing well back from the platform edge and so neither moved – but when she thought of that moment afterwards Jem wondered whether in fact there was some small movement of resolution: perhaps the other woman had clenched her fists minutely or steeled herself in some way. Jem did not see it but that did not mean it never happened. It seemed impossible, afterwards, that the other woman, standing there so still, could have been enduring in silence the last few moments of an unendurable life.

The railway lines began to click and buzz as the through train approached at speed and just before it reached them – in the very last second – there was a sudden movement in the corner of Jem's eye. She turned her head in time to see that thoughtful, solitary woman take three quick strides forward and jump off the platform in front of the train. She passed so close that Jem felt the little puff of air that she displaced before her. Then the train was upon her or through her or over her and she had disappeared underneath and now its brakes began to scream.

It was almost impossible to believe even though Jem had seen it happen: *woman – train – woman under train*. Jem could not move. She stood stock still, staring down at the place where the woman had gone. The train had passed over, too fast to stop right away, and now it was gone she was looking at the steel rails, shining like blades in gravel that was both dirty brown and hot red.

The train shrieked to a stop a little way up the tracks. The driver ran all the way back to where Jem stood. He had left his train with its doors locked and no one could get in or out. There seemed to be no one here but Jem, the driver and the swallows overhead.

When the train driver looked down at the tracks he put his hands on his head. He had a curly bounce of hair like Dennis the Menace.

'No! No!'

He turned to Jem. He did not know if it was a man or a woman who had jumped – just a blur.

'A woman,' Jem said. When she turned to face him she saw that his eyes were round with shock. Two circles. She felt sorry for him. She did not feel startled, only curious.

He asked, 'Did you see her jump?'

'Yes.'

They turned back to look at the tracks again. The woman was cut into three: beheaded and also cut in half below the waist. It was odd to see that her body was still wearing some of its clothes and to think of her choosing the outfit when she got dressed, which might only have been an hour ago, or even less. Clothes to be killed in. Around her there lay scattered a muddle of pinkish chunks. Her head faced them, looking up. Her eyes and mouth were open.

The train driver looked away – 'Fucking hell!' – but Jem stared. Then an official-looking person arrived and beetled up to them with a 'seen it all before' air about him, which seemed a contrast to the driver who was trembling like a cold whippet.

'You all right, mate? This your first one under?'

'I couldn't do anything. I couldn't have done anything. She jumped before I saw her.'

The train driver was trying to light a cigarette, fumbling and fumbling, and so Jem took the lighter and held it for him.

'There. All right?'

'Cheers.'

The official man was blaring into a telephone. 'Yes, mate. No, mate. Quick as you like.' When he finished his call he said, 'They're on their way. Fire brigade. They know the drill. It won't take long.' He peered closely at the train driver and put a hand on his shoulder. 'Nothing you could have done. Happens all the time. D'you want to sit down?' Now he had got the ball rolling he was a kindly man after all.

Jem echoed, 'All the time?'

'Yes, love. This is my third.' He seemed only to notice now that Jem was a civilian. He narrowed his eyes. 'Pardon me, miss, but you shouldn't be here. Go down the end there please, with the others.' He indicated towards the centre of the platform.

Jem left them both, and the pieces of that shattered person on the line, and sat down on a red metal bench. She looked up at the sky where the swallows were still drawing landscapes in the warm air. Parents sketching Africa for their children. She wondered as she watched the swallows why she did not care about the woman under the train. Did not caring make her a rabbit, eating grass? Did she not understand about death or did she have no one to care for?

Then she realised, and it was a relief: *I do understand about death. That's why I don't care.*

In the car, Jem changed her mind: *I want to live.* She blinked and stirred, puzzled as a sleepwalker when woken. 'Sonny?'

'Yes?'

'Frank killed my mother. He was driving the car. I couldn't tell you. I didn't want to lose you. But keeping it inside' – she put her hand on her heart – 'has broken me in half.'

Sonny reached forward and took her hand in his.

'You're not broken,' he told her, 'you're not your father and you're not going to die.'

XII

The first person Sonny telephoned after Jem's operation was Lauren.

'I'm hoping Mum's with you,' she said when she heard his voice, 'because she's not with us.'

'She's here.' He described Kathleen's arrival, '. . . In the nick of time as it turned out. They found an aneurysm in Jem's heart. They replaced her aorta.'

'Replaced it? With what?'

'Fuck knows. All I know is, if the aneurysm had burst she'd be dead.'

'Mum saved her life.' It seemed almost impossible that Kathleen could have done something so useful, but the facts were unarguable.

'Not only that,' Sonny went on, 'but right now Mum's sitting in a chair next to Jem's hospital bed. She even slept there.'

'Atonement, I suppose. For past sins.'

'Yes, but why Jem? It's me and Dad she should be atoning to.'

It was a question neither could answer.

Sonny went on, 'How is Dad anyway?'

'He's cheered up a bit. Went to the barber and got his beard shaved off.'

'Beard?'

It had only been a month but there was much to tell and much that should never be told. Lauren restricted herself to saying only, 'He misses you. He wants you to come back.'

'And you? Are you OK?'

Ignoring him Lauren went on, 'Dad and Lester are planning a holiday. They want to go to Iceland and lie around in those nice hot springs which all have unpronounceable names.' She paused. 'D'you want to talk to him?'

Sonny was fidgety. 'Not now. Soon.'

Lauren, understanding, said, 'When you see him it will be all right.' Then she asked, 'What about Mum? Is she coming back?'

'I don't know. Shit, I've got to go. Mum's making signals – I think Jem's awake.'

And he was gone.

At first, when asked, Kathleen credited herself with the decision to drive to France.

'It was your birthday,' she told Sonny. 'I'd never missed it before.'

Then, pressed more closely, she admitted that Becka had come round to the bedsit and given her a bollocking.

'She told me that Walter had grown a beard and Lauren was crying in the street. She said they needed me.'

This was true, but it was not the whole truth. Becka had gone on to say, 'Are you going to live on your own in a bedsit for the rest of your life? Because no one else will look after you. You're too spoilt and too selfish. You have to go to France, fetch Sonny and bring him back. Then Walter might forgive you.' But Kathleen did not think Sonny needed to hear all that.

'I can't believe you listened to Becka. I thought you didn't like her.'

'She's very persuasive for one so tiny,' Kathleen patted Sonny's hand approvingly, 'and I like that.'

With this encouragement, Sonny telephoned Becka. 'What have you done to my mother?'

'I gave her a piece of my mind.'

'But that's what *I* want. When do I get a piece of your mind?'

'You will. When are you coming back?'

He could hear the smile in her voice and now he was smiling too.

'Saturday night – but I'm going to New York on Monday.'

'Oh.' The smile turned to disappointment.

'It's for an audition.'

'Don't they have actors in America?'

But Sonny was not in the mood to be teased – he wanted to get to the difficult bit.

'I want you to come with me. Will you?'

'Come with you?' She did not sound displeased, only astonished. 'Come with you as what? Driver? Assistant? Make-up artist?'

'Girlfriend if you want,' he said firmly, 'best friend if you don't.'

'Oh,' said Becka. 'Can't I be both?'

After speaking to Sonny Lauren hung up with a pang. Everyone seemed to have a plan. And what of her? Of course she wanted her brother to be happy and of course she wanted her father to have a holiday but at the same time she wondered what she was supposed to do. Back to her studio, now referred to by Kathleen as a 'cosy little home', and back to work, she supposed, but just now that plan seemed not so much a future as a retreat.

She looked down at Mike.

'Just you and me,' she said. 'Would that be so bad?'

Mike, who looked as if he thought it might, gave her an unimpressed look and then closed his eyes and scratched behind one ear with a hind paw.

Lauren related all this new information to Walter over their evening chess game.

'Sonny didn't want to speak to me?'

'He's nervous.'

'Nervous? Of what? I've never loved him as much as I do right now.' The sound of the words seemed to startle Walter, but then he looked as if he was pleased to have said them. 'What about Kathleen?'

'I don't know. We didn't get that far. I suppose when Jem is well enough they'll come back.'

'I might not want her back.'

'But you do.'

'You know nothing of how I feel.' He squinted down at the chessboard and pushed his knight forward and left with one crabby forefinger. 'Why doesn't she stay there if she loves it so much?'

'None of them can stay there. The house has to be sold to pay the tax bill.'

'I don't care about death or taxes. Certainly not French ones. The only thing I care about is that Kathleen thinks she can swan back in and take up where she left off. She can't.'

'Well, you can tell her yourself when she gets back.' Lauren moved her bishop. 'Check.'

Walter was resolutely in bed when Sonny arrived home, and resolutely out swimming the next morning when Sonny woke up. Like Sonny he was nervous; unlike Sonny he was inhibited by pride. Why should he have to make a representation of himself? Could they not just carry on as before? In his mind he held one trump card: something he could tell Sonny which would settle the matter. *But for me*, he could say, *you would not exist. Your mother would have got rid of you. You may not be my child but you owe me your life.* He could say that. It would be wrong, but he could. He felt the wrongness of it, he *knew* the wrongness of it, and yet it was as tempting as winning a war with a nuclear bomb.

Every morning after their swim Lester and Walter stopped at the same cafe. The woman who worked there called the swimmers 'pet' and exclaimed with amazement at their courage and fortitude whether it was summer or winter. On this particular February morning the achievement did seem rather remarkable: a thick frost was spread over the grass and as traffic descended the hill it vanished into a cold, muting fog.

In the cafe the windows steamed up and Mike nibbled his frosted paws. Walter and Lester held hot cups of coffee.

'Sonny's back, I see,' Lester said.

'Is he?'

'Yes, he is. You know he is.'

'I've no idea. I've not seen him. I was asleep when he got back.'

271

Ignoring the discrepancy Lester said, 'He came over last night. In fact I think he stayed the night in Becka's room.'

'Ah.' Walter passed a hand over his chin, feigning indifference.

'Aren't you interested?'

'No.'

Lester chuckled, disbelieving. 'Come on, old man, cheer up. When you see him it will be all right.'

'I don't know what to do.' Walter looked frightened. 'I don't know what to say.'

'Here you are, pet.' The waitress put a plate in front of Lester bearing a fried egg on white toast and three strips of bacon. 'And that's you.' Walter was having the same breakfast but between two slices of white bread for ease of consumption. 'All right? Anything else? Are you warm enough? I can move the table nearer the heater if you like—'

'Perfectly warm, thank you.' Lester pointed his ginger beard up at her and smiled. 'You *are* kind. This looks delicious. And might we have some French mustard?'

When the waitress had gone Walter grumbled, 'Anyone would think you were flirting.'

'Jealous?'

'Disgusted, more like.'

'We might be dead tomorrow.' Joyfully, Lester stabbed the yolk of his fried egg with his fork.

When Sonny walked into the cafe a minute later Walter did not see him but Mike did, getting up and almost knocking the table over with excitement. Lester looked up.

'Sonny! Gracious me – how are you? Come and join us. Pull up a chair.'

Sonny unwound the scarf from around his neck and

stood beside their table. 'Hello, Dad,' he said. 'Lauren told me you'd be here.'

Walter had put down his sandwich. He seemed to take an awfully long time to clear his throat and get to his feet. It would have been the moment to shed a tear if he had been that sort of person, but instead he blinked several times as if there were something caught in his eye.

'Sonny,' he said. He clasped Sonny with one hand and then two. 'Sonny.' Unsteadily, as if he might all of a sudden need something to lean on, he pulled the young man into an embrace. 'Oh I am glad to see you,' he said. 'Oh I am glad to have you.' He put a hand behind Sonny's head and pulled it closer to kiss him on the ear. 'Here we are,' he said then. 'Here we are.'

They clung together, both half-laughing, and when at last Walter had finished patting and squeezing he let Sonny go. Lester pulled up another chair and they all three sat down.

Sonny blew his nose and rubbed his eyes with a napkin. 'D'you want one of these, Dad? A hanky?'

'What? No. Whatever for?' Walter was determinedly preoccupied by his bacon sandwich. 'Now, Sonny, will you have some breakfast?'

'Yes, why not.' Sonny petted Mike, who was trying to wriggle onto his lap. 'I'll have the same as my father,' he said to the waitress.

'Aw,' the waitress cooed, putting her head on one side and looking from Walter to Sonny. 'I can tell you're family. You're peas in a pod.'

Having been cured of her conscience Kathleen could make up with Walter.

'I want to meet him in Paris,' she said to Lauren on the telephone. 'On neutral ground.'

'By "neutral ground" I expect you mean a really nice hotel?'

'Yes. Don't be so *pinched*, Lauren, you sound like an old woman. Don't you want me to make things right with your father?'

'Of course I do,' Lauren said automatically. Then she wondered if she did.

'Well then. All you have to do is bring him to me on the Eurostar . . .'

As Kathleen spoke Lauren felt again the pressure of that invisible thumb.

'. . . and I'll meet you at the Gare du Nord. Then I'll give you the car key and you can drive back to London. You must be longing to get on with your life.'

'Longing,' echoed Lauren. 'And what about Jem? Are you bored of her already?'

'Actually Jem's going to come and live with us for a while, once she's got rid of the house.'

'Us?'

'Yes, us: me and Sonny and your father. In Beech Road.'

'Right.' Lauren discovered she was frowning. 'In my bedroom?'

'Well, you don't use it. Why should it go to waste?'

'Quite.'

'And I've got *Mrs Peabody*, and Sonny's got this audition, and Walter's got that retrospective coming up at the Imperial War Museum—'

'And everything goes on just as before,' murmured Lauren.

Last week it had seemed impossible that anything could be resolved. Now everything had been resolved without her. Instead of relief Lauren felt she was sinking into the floor. If she sank any further her arms and legs would be pinned.

'I certainly hope so,' Kathleen was saying.

'Hope what?'

'That everything goes on just as before. That's what I want.'

She gave Lauren details of which train on what day she could meet at the Gare du Nord and then rang off, saying, 'I must go and help Jem. It's wonderful to feel useful.'

On the appointed day Lauren and Walter left Mike with Lester, the former looking at the latter in surprise, and caught a train from London to Paris. Walter was nervous. Lauren did not know how nervous until he had bitten her head off three times before even finding their seats on the train.

'Dad, please relax.'

'There's nothing wrong with *me*. I'm just working out in my mind what I'm going to say to *her*.' Then he put on his cushiony headphones – a present from Lauren the day before – and fell asleep listening to *Under Milk Wood*.

The smoothness of the journey made Lauren drowsy. One minute she was staring out at the Kent landscape and then she woke up to see northern France and its tidy fields, fences and roads flicking past in silence. England was cosied up with hedges and trees but France, she reflected, seemed not to be dressed for the weather.

Walter slept on beside her. He was used to sleeping on trains, planes and buses. This morning he had shaved with his new electric razor – ''Straordinary feeling' – and then dressed in clean clothes. Lauren had brushed his hair into its customary halo and then brushed his coat with a clothes brush. They had packed his suitcase: socks, underpants, shirts, corduroy trousers and a V-neck sweater.

'Pyjamas?' Lauren held out a pair.

Walter peered. 'Not those. Where are the ones your mother gave me for Christmas? Those will do.'

It was an admission, or near enough, that he would forgive Kathleen.

Lauren thought all of this over on the train, looking from the rushing landscape to her father's sleeping face. This was how husbands and wives forgave each other, she supposed. They just carried on. There was no need to forgive; forgetting was enough. She wondered what it would take to break a forty-year bond. Perhaps this one could not be broken.

Kathleen was waiting for them at the end of the platform. She was wearing a huge red scarf and looked nervous and wide-eyed, her hair mussed up with all the tweaking and fluffing she had done to it while she was waiting. When she saw them she waved extravagantly and rushed forward, fingers fluttering at her scarf, pulling it away from her face and her lipstick and saying, 'Walter!' She held his hands. 'I missed you! I love you!'

Walter laughed and perhaps even cried a little, unless it was the cold.

Then Kathleen turned to Lauren. 'Darling Lauren.' She hugged her tightly to her chest and then, breaking apart, said, 'I've been such a fool—'

'Yes, you have.'

'No, not that!' Kathleen laughed. 'I've been a fool because I've left the car key at Rex's apartment. He put me up last night. You'll have to go and get it. You don't mind, do you? He's in the Marais.'

'I know where he is, Mum, but I'm not going there. I can't.'

'Of course you can! You must.'

'No.' Lauren shook her head. 'No. I won't.'

'Oh, please, don't be difficult. It's not as if you've got anything better to do.'

Lauren opened her mouth to argue and then it struck her that in fact her mother was right: she had nothing to do and no reason not to do as she was told. In fact she had no reason to do or not do anything ever again. She had been pressed into the ground like a tent peg, right up to her chin.

Lest her gloom spread over them like fog she said good-bye to her parents and set off for the Marais. She knew the way. She had walked with Rex from his apartment back to the Gare du Nord at the end of that weekend together. They had held hands all the way and at the station he had hugged her as if he would never let her go and said, 'I don't want you to leave. Come back. Come and live with me.' It was the last she heard from him. When she thought of that now, four years later, she could manage a dry inward laugh which, she decided, meant she must have got over it.

When she reached the apartment building she walked up to the first floor, her footsteps echoing on the wide stone steps, her hand on the wooden banister. *I feel nothing*, she thought. *I am cured*. She did not even hesitate before knocking. After a short silence she heard muffled sounds from within as if a badger were stirring in its sett. Then Rex pulled opened the door. He was wearing a grey sweatshirt and shorts, his feet were bare and his hair was flattened on one side and sticking out on the other like an overgrown brown hedge. He must have been asleep. When she saw him Lauren felt covered by a great and wonderful warmth as if she were lying on a grassy hillside and the sun had suddenly come out and bathed her. She hoped such a foolish idea did not show on her face. All at once she was flushed with nerves and she clutched the strap of her bag tightly in both fists so she did not forget herself and topple into his arms.

Rex seemed not to notice this great changeable tumult occurring in front of him. He seemed in fact not at all surprised to see her, only pleased.

'Oh good,' he said. 'You're here. Your mother told me you were coming to stay.'

Lauren opened her mouth to disagree and then closed it. She thought of her mother, who had planned this moment. *It's not as if you've got anything better to do.*

'Yes, that's right,' she said. 'I've come to stay.'